ELLE GRAY
BLAKE WILDER

THE SECRET SHE KEPT

Copyright © 2021 by Elle Gray

All rights reserved.

No part of this book may be reproduced in any form or by any electronic or mechanical means, including information storage and retrieval systems, without written permission from the author, except for the use of brief quotations in a book review.

❦ Created with Vellum

PROLOGUE

I slip my hands into the pockets of my sweater as I stroll casually down the row of the flea market, ostensibly looking at the goods for sale in the various stalls. Given the number of people in shorts and flip-flops, you'd think it was a hot summer day. And although it's sunny and clear, it's far from what I'd consider warm. But I guess mid-sixties weather is what passes for a heat wave in the Pacific Northwest.

My fingers curl around the small pistol in my pocket. The weight of the .25 caliber Beretta in my hand is familiar. Reassuring. In all my years doing this job, I've never had to use it, but it's comforting to know it's there just in case. If there's one thing all my training has taught me, it's the value of being prepared.

On the opposite side of this row, Blake Wilder is standing with her boyfriend at a stall selling handcrafted afghans. I keep a surreptitious eye on them in my peripheral vision. My mark is dressed casually in jeans and a white t-shirt. She's tall and beautiful, and it's easy to see she's athletic and fit. My memories of her as a child are sparse, but even with the fragments in my head, I don't remember ever thinking she'd grow into such a beauty.

But she's more than just her looks. She's intelligent. Accomplished. She's held in high esteem by her peers and the higher-ups at the Bureau. Blake is a rising star, with accolades raining down on her from every direction. I have to say, she's living quite the life. And while part of me is happy for her, I'd be lying if I said there isn't another part of me that hates her for it, too.

As I watch Blake laughing and talking with Mark, casually laying her hand on him, giving him gentle pecks on the cheek and lips, I quietly seethe. It's so domestic, so *ordinary*—I can't stop the jealousy that washes through me.

I never got a chance at that kind of life. Normal. Domestic. Ordinary. Those are things I've never known. Things I'm never going to know. I don't get to have normal. I don't get to have ordinary. I don't get to have all the things Blake takes for granted.

Across the aisle, Blake and her boyfriend walk away, hand-in-hand and laughing together. No doubt sharing some inside joke with each other the way couples do. I know she's not, but it's as if she's rubbing in my face that I'll never have those things. My life just isn't built in a way that allows for anything like that. Most days it doesn't bother me, but once in a while, it really does.

I weave my way through the crowd, never losing sight of them. I grip the Beretta even tighter as my anger flows through my veins. As I do so often, I think about what my life could have been like had things not happened the way they did. I think about what my life could have been like had I gotten the chance to experience a normal, ordinary life. What could I have become? What could I have done with my life? Would Blake and I have been close? Would we have had nieces and nephews who grew up being the best of friends? Those are questions I've asked myself a million times, and I'm no closer to an answer now than I was when I first asked them.

Intellectually, I know it's not Blake's fault. Everything I've gone through, everything I've done—I know she had nothing to do with it. But seeing her out enjoying a day of normalcy with her man....it stings, I'm not going to lie. Seeing her living this amazing life and doing all the things she's done is like salt in my wounds.

But I have a purpose. A reason for my sacrifice. I'm making a difference in this world and it doesn't leave much room for anything normal. My relationships with people are transactional. Surface-level. I can't afford to let people get too close; I have no choice but to keep them at an arm's distance. It's just the way of things in my world. It sometimes feels empty—and I can't deny I feel lonely now and then—but I take solace in the fact that my life has meaning. That I'm having an impact on this world. The work I'm doing will leave behind a legacy.

But I'm human, too. Sometimes I want to give it all up and get what she has. Normalcy. Meaningful and non-transactional human contact. It's a life I can only dream of.

I follow them through the flea market, keeping enough of a distance that I can melt into the crowd if need be, but close enough that I can live vicariously through her—if only for a little while.

They stop at a cart selling churros and when Blake's eyes meet mine, I realize that I've allowed myself to lose my cover. I'm standing here totally exposed. The blood in my veins turns to ice when she pauses, and I see a flicker of recognition in her eyes. I don't know how she could possibly recognize me after all this time, but I see a hint of recollection, making my stomach tighten nervously.

After a long, painstaking moment, it passes, and she turns

back to her doctor boyfriend. She takes a bite of his churro and laughs, seeming to forget all about me. Heaving a sigh of relief, I melt back into the crowd, silently chastising myself for being so careless. In the month and a half I've been shadowing her, Blake has never gotten a glimpse of me—until now. Because I was so caught up in my head and in my memories that I was reckless.

I walk on, losing myself among the throng of people. I don't look back.

"I'll see you soon, Sis," I mutter. "Soon."

ONE

SPD Interrogation Room Four, Twenty-First Precinct; Downtown Seattle

"Did you kill Gina Aoki?" he seethes.

"That's a really dumb question," I reply. "If I had killed her—which I didn't—do you really think I'd just admit it?"

"Did you kill Gina Aoki?" he repeats.

I chuckle to myself. "You must think really highly of yourself and your presence, Deputy Chief," I reply. "I told you that day you threatened me on the side of the road that I'm not intimidated by you. I'm not afraid of you."

Torres' eyes flick to the camera in the corner of the room. No doubt he'll have his AV techs edit that bit out. Still, it was worth the attempt to get it on the record—if for no other reason than to irritate him. Which, judging by the look on his face, I managed to accomplish well enough.

"Your smart mouth and wild imagination aren't helping you, Wilder."

"That's Supervisory Special Agent Wilder, Deputy Chief,"

I snap back. "I'm here as a courtesy to you because I know you have some questions concerning my involvement with Ms. Aoki's murder because I saw her that day. The very least you can do is show some respect."

"Respect is earned," he fires back. "And right now, you're running in the red with me."

I smirk and take a look around the small, cramped interrogation room. Acoustic soundproofing tiles that used to be white but are now gray and cracked line the walls, and a two-way mirror is set into the wall to my right. The chair I'm sitting in is a metal folding job that's about as comfortable as sitting on a bed of nails. The rest of the precinct has been updated. It's sleek and modern. It's almost as though they intentionally made the interrogation rooms as uncomfortable as possible. I turn back to Torres but say nothing, waiting for him to go on.

He glares at me. "Also, you're here because you're a person of interest in a homicide."

"Because she had my business card?"

"Because according to her calendar, you were the last person to see her alive," he growls.

"No, I was the last person she had written down on her calendar," I clarify. "That doesn't mean I was the last person to see her alive. That's a sloppy assumption. I'm sure even a rookie would be able to make the distinction. What was her TOD?"

Torres glances at the folder sitting on his side of the table, but I can tell he doesn't want to give me the satisfaction of referring to his notes. I reach for the file, but he snaps it up before I can get my hand on it. His face is stony, and he does nothing but hold the file for a moment, satisfied that he beat me to it. I sit back and fold my hands in my lap, content to wait for him to stop acting like a child. Then, with a dramatic sigh as he opens it, Torres scans the pages inside for a moment then snaps the file shut again, his expression sour.

"The ME estimates her time of death is around six or seven that evening," he finally admits.

"Uh-huh. Well, I met with her several hours before that, as I'm sure her calendar confirms. It was a brief meeting," I tell him. "So, you've got a pretty wide gap in your timeline."

He scoffs as he paces the room on the other side of the table. His expression is dark, and a frown pulls the corners of his mouth down. Torres turns and glares at me.

"And where were you during the time she was killed?" he asks.

"I was working at home," I offer. "Where I stayed until I arrived at the field office the following morning."

"Can anybody verify that?"

I laugh softly. "You can track my phone. It'll show you I was at home all night."

He gives me a condescending look as if he thinks I'm an idiot. "You aren't really trying to pin your alibi to your phone, are you? It's easy enough to leave it at your home and slip out."

"Then track my car's GPS."

"Could have taken an Uber for all I know."

"You sure are making a lot of suppositions, but do you have any actual evidence, Deputy Chief?" I ask. "I mean, I know it's been a while since you came down from your ivory tower to run an actual investigation, but having physical evidence is still a thing."

I sit back in the seat, doing my best to ignore just how hard it is on my backside. I fold my arms over my chest, returning his contemptuous glare with a blank stare of my own. The air in the interrogation crackles with tension as we study each other from opposite sides of the table.

"Tell me something," I start. "Why exactly have you come out from behind your desk to run point on this investigation?"

"I need a reason to investigate a murder in my city? I'm the

Deputy Chief," he scoffs. "I take all murders seriously. I do everything I can to solve them and bring the offenders to justice. I take the safety of every single Seattleite very seriously."

"I'd heard rumors that you were toying with the idea of a run for mayor," I reply. "Your stump speech needs some work, though. It lacks warmth—and the feeling of competence."

His face darkens and he glares at me as if he'd enjoy nothing more than turning off the camera and having a go at me. I know I shouldn't antagonize him, but I can't seem to help myself. Everything about this man irritates me. It's not just his annoying arrogance that gets to me, though that's bad enough. It's his lack of compassion. His incompetence as an investigator. It's the fact that he's risen so high through the ranks of the SPD on the backs of the men and women who are actually doing the hard work to keep the city safe. As I said, it's everything about him.

Torres is where he is because he's a good-looking man who's connected. He knows the right things to say and the right people to say them to. He's the Deputy Chief and has an eye on either becoming Chief or the city's next mayor, because he knows which rings to kiss and is politically deft enough to know just how hard to kiss them. He's a political animal, not a cop. He hasn't been a cop for a long time—if he ever was.

Guys like Torres make the city less safe. And I think that's what I hate the most about him. He's in a position of power and influence. He's in a position to do some terrific things and actually make Seattle safe. But he's too busy accruing and consolidating power. The only thing he cares about is doing what's in his own best interest. He never sees a situation and fails to ask, "What's in it for me?" I hate people like that. Hence, my problem with Torres.

On top of that, of course, he has not-so-subtly harbored a

grudge against me personally for a long, long time. Even to the point of issuing extremely thinly veiled threats. But if he doesn't want me to show him up case after case, maybe he could actually get his own behind in gear and actually do something to make this city safe instead of just resting on his own laurels.

"I'm here as a courtesy," I tell him. "You know I didn't kill her."

"Do I? At this point, I don't know anything. I'm just trying to conduct a thorough investigation," he says. "You know, something you always accuse us of not doing?"

I give him a wry grin but say nothing. My opinion of the SPD's performance is pretty well known. I believe the department has a lot of dedicated, talented, and passionate officers and detectives. They're unfortunately handicapped by a command structure that's best epitomized by the man standing in front of me.

"What did you meet with Ms. Aoki about?" he asks.

"It was personal and irrelevant to your investigation," I say.

What I don't say is that it's perhaps because we met that he's investigating her murder, to begin with. If not for my poking around and looking into something it appears others would prefer I walk away and forget, Gina Aoki might well be alive right now. Although I'm drowning in guilt, I keep my face carefully neutral. Torres is a lot of things, but he's not stupid, nor is he completely unobservant. I have no doubt if he sees the culpability I feel written upon my face, he'll pounce on it.

"I'll decide what's relevant to my case, *Agent* Wilder," he spits. "Now, I'll ask again—what was your meeting with Ms. Aoki about?"

"It was personal and none of your business. It has no bearing on your case," I repeat. "All you need to know is I was at home during the time she was killed."

"That's actually not all I need to know—"

"It is. Ms. Aoki worked with my parents and I can assure you that my childhood has no bearing on your investigation."

Not exactly true, but true enough for him. The last thing I want is for Torres to go poking around into my childhood and the murder of my parents. He doesn't have the authority—not to mention the security clearances—required to delve too deeply, so I'm not too concerned about his gathering sensitive information. But I don't like taking chances. The less he knows about me and my life, the better.

"I've tried to be helpful. I've given you my whereabouts during the time Ms. Aoki was killed. I'll leave it up to you to do your due diligence," I shrug. "So, unless you have any other questions, I think we're done here."

He leans forward, planting his hands on the table. His expression is dark, and his face is a twisted mask of rage.

"I'll tell you when we're done," he snarls.

I flash him a grin. "Who do you think you're talking to? Some small-time crook you think you can bully into saying what you want?" I say as I get to my feet. "So, unless you're going to charge me with something and throw me in a cell, then yeah, we're done here."

Torres stands up again and folds his arms over his chest, glaring at me balefully. He and I both know he's got nothing to charge me with. He and I both know I didn't do this. And I know it's burning his ass that he can't arrest me for anything. But I'm sure it's burning his ass even more that he can't rattle me. He's made a point of trying to do just that for a long time now. I don't know what touched off this feud between us.

It could be that he doesn't like Feds. Or it could be my close friendship with Paxton Arrington—Torres' arch-nemesis. It's probably likely that each of those things plays a factor in his dislike of me. It probably hasn't helped matters that he thinks I take every opportunity to show him up and make the SPD look bad. Although I think the fact that he can look at what I'm doing and believe competent investigative work makes him and the SPD look bad, says a lot about him and his way of doing business.

"No?" I ask. "I thought not."

"Stay reachable, Agent Wilder," he sneers.

"I'm always around," I call over my shoulder as I walk out of the interrogation room, leaving Torres standing there with nothing but his impotent rage.

TWO

Office of SAC Rosalinda Espinoza; Seattle Field Office

"Did you lose your mind?" Rosie asks.

"Not that I'm aware of," I reply.

"Did you suffer a head injury recently?"

I grin at her. "No. I did not suffer a head injury," I tell her. "As far as I know, I've suffered no recent brain trauma."

SAC Rosalinda Espinoza—Rosie to most of us—leans back in her chair and looks at me closely, her eyes squinted in that way she gets when she's really irritated. I didn't expect that she'd have already heard about my talking to Torres. Good news apparently travels a lot faster than I anticipated.

"So, if you're not suffering from CTE or some other form of traumatic brain injury, can you explain to me why you'd go in and sit down with Deputy Chief Torres without a lawyer or your union rep?" she demands.

"Because I have nothing to hide?" I reply. "Because I didn't kill Gina Aoki?"

"You know that, and I know that. But Torres is apparently

looking to pin it on you anyway," she says. "Given what's gone down between you two lately, playing his game is only going to cause you problems you don't want or need."

I cross my legs and fold my hands in my lap, giving myself a five-count. I understand Rosie's frustration—and her fears. Guys like Torres don't like to lose, and they're not above putting their thumbs on the scale to ensure they get the outcomes they want. It wouldn't surprise me to learn that Torres is in the habit of ginning up evidence against suspects just to close cases. I can't prove that, of course, but it wouldn't surprise me if he had.

"I thought it best if I got out ahead of it and was transparent with him," I offer.

"Well, according to him, you were anything but transparent."

"So, he did call you."

A wry grin curls her lips. "About two seconds after you walked out of the interview room. As a courtesy, he said," she tells me. "Wanted me to know you'd been less than forthcoming with him—which he intimated puts you on his radar."

"Let him look into me. He's not going to find anything connecting me to Gina's murder."

Rosie sighs and shakes her head as she drops her pen onto the folders sitting on top of her desk. She takes a sip of her coffee then looks up at me.

"What did you meet with her about?" Rosie asks.

"It's not relevant to anything. It was personal."

"Blake, I need to know what I'm dealing with. I don't need the specifics. Just give me a broad-stroke overview."

I frown and look away for a moment as I think it over. Rosie is somebody I'd trust with my life. But I'm not willing to gamble with hers.

"Rosie, what I'm looking into—it's personal," I tell her.

"And it's already gotten two people killed. I don't want anything happening to you."

Rosie cocks her head at me. "What are you talking about?"

I give her a brief rundown of the situation with Mr. Corden and now with Gina. Nothing specific—just an overview. I don't want to get too deeply into it with her, just to be safe.

"Trust me when I say the less you know about this, the better," I tell her.

Rosie sits back again, a thoughtful expression on her face, and seems to be processing everything I told her. I can see she wants to press me for more details—likely trying to calculate any potential blowback on the Bureau. But she also wants to respect my privacy. Which I appreciate a great deal. She leans forward again and cups her hands around her coffee mug, gnawing on her bottom lip.

"Walk me through what you told Torres," she says.

So I do. I tell her everything I said from the moment I walked in to the moment I left. I even give her a timeline of my meeting with Gina Aoki, but decline to go into details about the substance of our conversation. Thankfully, she doesn't press.

"I really wish you hadn't gone in to see Torres," she sighs.

"As I told you, I've got nothing to hide. Detective Lee called and warned me that Torres would be coming after me hard, so I thought it best to get out in front of it," I reply. "Also, TJ warned me in confidence, so I'd appreciate it if that bit didn't leave the room. I'd rather not drag him into my mess if I can help it."

"Fair enough. But you know how Torres can twist this to look, right?"

I nod. "Yeah, but he was going to do that whether I sat down with him or not," I point out. "He's got an agenda—and a vendetta against me in particular—and is going to do everything in his power to tarnish my reputation."

"Just be sure you don't give him the ammunition to do it."

"There's no ammunition to give him. I didn't do it."

"I know that, Blake. But you're about as good at playing politics as I am," she counters. "And that's what this is—politics. It's a game to him. He knows you didn't do it, but he's going to do his best to create the appearance of impropriety. So, just keep your head down and don't play his game. And before you talk to him again, make sure you have a lawyer or your union rep present. Am I clear?"

I blow out a long, frustrated breath. She's right, of course. The appearance of impropriety is often even more damning than any real impropriety itself. If you're perceived to have gotten away with something—like murder—that stink will linger, and you'll never fully get out from under. And in an organization like the Bureau, where everything can get political very quickly, that could be the death knell for any career. The thought sends a cold chill down my spine, simply because I don't want to be marginalized or sidelined over something I had absolutely nothing to do with.

"Blake? Tell me you understand," Rosie presses.

"I hear you. I understand."

"Good," she nods. "Now, chewing your butt isn't the only thing I called you in here for."

"That's good to know."

Rosie slides a slip of paper across her desk to me. "A friend of mine is a commander down in Tukwila. They've got an active crime scene right now and asked for our help."

I grab the paper and see the address listed, as well as the name of the woman who I assume is her friend.

"What are we walking into?" I ask.

"Body in a barrel," she explains. "Fished out of the Green River this morning."

"Lovely."

Rosie shrugs. "Could be worse."

"Yeah, it could always be worse," I comment as I get to my feet. "Let me just check in with my team, grab Astra, and we'll roll out."

"I'll let Sandy know you're on your way."

THREE

Criminal Data Analysis Unit; Seattle Field Office

"Okay, people, what do we have today?" I ask as I come through the doors. "Mo, where are you at with your analysis on Bremerton?"

I step to the front of the bullpen, pacing in front of the bank of monitors mounted to the wall. Mo looks up from the files spread out on her workstation, then checks something on the computer screen in front of her. Maureen Weissman—otherwise known as Mo—is a bit rough around the edges but is sharp as a tack and is starting to find her groove here in the CDAU.

Early on, I'd started to think I made a mistake with her—especially given what a liability she was in the field. But she's really rounded into form. She came over to us from White Collar, which didn't really prepare her for the grisly things we often see, but she's doing better. At least she hasn't thrown up on a crime scene again. That's got to count for something.

"I've got a sharp uptick in opioid deaths that exceeds the

annual statistical average," she replies. "They seem to be on pace for a record year, I'd say."

"Got any leads on where the drugs are coming from?" I ask.

"I'm going through prescription records now. I've found a couple of clinics that seem to be handing out scripts like candy," she replies.

"You got the names of the doctors or the owners of these clinics?"

"Not yet. I haven't dug too deep yet, but it looks as if they're owned by shell companies," she tells me. "I have Rick looking into the companies to see if they tie to the clinic doctors or if they're third parties. I'll know more after we audit all of these files."

"Good. Good stuff. Keep me in the loop," I say, then turn to Astra.

"There seems to be something going on in Spokane," she announces without my even having to ask. "They're on pace for significantly more sexual assaults this year than they had last year."

"Serial rapist?"

"Possibly. Could account for the uptick," she says. "It's at least worth looking into."

"Agreed."

"And in addition to what I'm doing for Mo, I'm just working on being my normal, fabulous self," Rick calls from his workstation in the back of the bullpen. "In case you were wondering."

"You should work harder on that," Astra quips.

Rick is our tech analyst and a wizard with all things cyber. He's nearly on par with Paxton's best friend-slash-personal hacker Brody. If there are digital breadcrumbs to follow, Rick is going to find them. He's here to assist us with records searches and deep dives on suspects. He really is invaluable to this unit, and I'm glad I thought to request a tech analyst when I was given the green light to put it together.

As a whole, I think the unit has come together well. We're a team, but we're also tight. We're like a family. Yeah, we're sometimes a bit dysfunctional, but what family isn't? I'm extremely proud of this team and what we've been able to accomplish so far. We've taken a host of criminals and violent offenders off the streets, quite respectable for a unit some people didn't think would amount to much.

"Alright, well, you two keep doing what you're doing. Astra and I are heading down to Tukwila," I tell them.

"We are?" she raises an eyebrow.

I nod. "Rosie passed a case to us."

"Good thing I love field trips."

I give her a grin. "You might not be saying that about this one. Body in a barrel," I tell her. "They apparently fished it out of the Green River this morning."

Astra frowns, her expression one of disgust—bodies in barrels are never the most pleasant things to deal with. But then she looks at me and shrugs.

"Well, I suppose it beats sitting here listening to Rick talk to himself," she says.

"You do know they say geniuses often talk to themselves. It's usually the only intelligent conversation they can get," he shoots back.

Mo tries to stifle a snort-laugh, and even Astra cracks a smile at that. She likes to rough him up about things from time to time, but I know Astra. She thinks of him like a little brother. An annoying little brother, but a little brother, nonetheless. Astra groans and gets to her feet and looks at me.

"Can we go? I'm sure our floater's going to make for better company than this nerd," she tosses a thumb back to Rick, the smile still on her face.

I see Rick open his mouth, ready to deliver another zinger, but I hold a finger up and he lets the words die on his lips.

"Don't make me send you to your rooms, children," I say. "Rick, do me a favor and start getting the incident reports from the sexual assaults in Spokane. I want to start going through those when we get back and see if we can find anything to support the idea of a serial out there."

"Aye, aye, Captain," Rick salutes. "Have fun in Tukwila."

"Yeah, it's going to be a real blast," I mutter.

FOUR

Southeastern Command Zone; Tukwila, WA

"I think Torres may have a crush on you," she says.

"Don't make me smack you."

We made the thirty-minute drive in about twenty and I pull to a stop in a parking lot beside an abandoned motel. The building is dilapidated, surrounded by chain link fencing—an effort to keep out the transients and kids looking for a place to get high. But the holes in the fence show that effort hasn't been entirely successful. The brick walls are chipped and cracking, and the boards that once covered the windows have all been busted out or ripped down entirely.

"It seems to be the only explanation for his obsession with you," Astra offers.

My expression sours. "Yeah, I'm sure it's not that. Between my friendship with Pax and the fact that we keep showing him up, he's desperate to take me down a few pegs."

"Yeah, it could be that too," she chirps. "But seriously,

watch your back, Blake. That dude is bad news. Real bad news."

"Tell me about it."

I shut the car off and we climb out, heading for the tapeline. The sky is the color of slate, and there's a lot of moisture in the air that seems to be promising rain in our not-too-distant future. The parking lot is filled with emergency vehicles and clusters of Tukwila cops, firefighters, and paramedics. The scene is organized chaos, with people dashing about on various errands.

"SSA Blake Wilder, this is Special Agent Astra Russo." We badge the large, bored-looking cop on the tape as I make the introduction. "We're looking for Commander Erskine."

He looks vaguely interested by the badges, but that soon fades as he holds the tape up for us. We dip beneath it and turn to him. He jerks his thumb over his shoulder.

"She's down at the riverbank with everybody else," he says.

"Thank you," I reply.

We walk down the pathway toward the river that runs behind the derelict motel. In the distance, I hear the faint rumble of thunder.

"Nothing like a spring storm to add a layer of the ominous to a crime scene," Astra notes.

We follow the path to a pop-up tent that's been set up near the bank of the river. To the side of the tent, I see crime scene techs clustered around the barrel, taking photos and collecting samples. A blue tarp has been laid out on the ground underneath the tent, and I spot the unmistakable lumps of body parts being spread out, photographed, and cataloged.

"Disarticulated," I note.

"That's pleasant."

"Hey, at least you're out of the office."

Astra shrugs. "Touché."

There's a tall, lean woman standing over the blue tarp, her

arms folded over her chest, staring intently down at the body parts. She looks over as we approach and gives us an expression that's trapped somewhere between a grimace and a smile. The woman is dressed in a smart charcoal gray suit—it's not designer, but still a little better quality than you'd find on the rack at a department store. It tells me she wants to look good but doesn't want to be seen as ostentatious in her dress. She wants to look sharp but utilitarian, and as somebody to be taken seriously—a byproduct of being a woman in a male-dominated profession.

She strides over, intercepting us before we can get to the tent. Her dark hair is pulled back into a tight ponytail and she's wearing minimal makeup—just a bit of color around eyes that are a piercing shade of blue. I'd put her in her mid-forties, though she looks younger than that. There are soft lines around her eyes and mouth, and up close, I can see flecks of silver in her hair, but anyone who wasn't paying attention would miss those details.

"Commander Erskine," I say, extending my hand.

She nods and gives my hand a shake, then turns and shakes hands with Astra. She takes a beat to look us over, then offers a grateful smile.

"Thanks for getting here so quickly," she says. "And please, call me Nora."

"I'm Blake and this is Astra," I reply. "Rosie tells us you've got a nasty one."

She glances over her shoulder and frowns, then turns back to us. "Yeah. This one's bad. I've honestly never seen anything like it in the twenty-six years I've been with the department."

I nod. Tukwila is a small town that houses somewhere around twenty thousand souls or so. It's a sleepy little suburban community that's neither rich nor poor. It's not as nice as some other communities, but not as bad as others. They kind of walk a middle path here. Almost as though they're caught somewhere between quaint and nondescript.

"Anyway," she goes on. "I figured since something like this is outside our usual scope of crime, we could use a little help."

"Your techs seem to be handling it pretty well," Astra notes.

"They usually do a pretty good job with sample collection and whatnot," she replies, looking back at the techs. "But I'm talking more about the body itself. I mean, taking somebody apart like that—it can only be a serial killer, right? I mean, the level of sadistic—"

"I'd pump the brakes on that," I interrupt. "I think it's way too early to be making any assumptions just yet. That could come back to bite us in the backside later," I explain. "But I would like to take a look at the body now if that's alright."

"Oh, right. Of course," she replies. "Please, just follow me down. I will warn you, though, it's nasty and definitely not for the faint of heart."

"No worries," Astra replies with a grin. "That's kind of our thing."

We follow her the rest of the way and are soon gathered around the blue tarp, looking down at the ravaged remains of what was an African American male. Other than that, though, it's hard to tell anything more about him, because he's been savaged. Torn apart. The crime scene technician is laying the pieces out, roughly reassembling the body and cataloging it all.

"As you can see, he's been dismembered," Commander Erskine says.

"Disarticulated," I say, pointing to the pieces of the legs that are sitting on the tarp. "All of the limbs were cleanly severed at the joints rather than just hacked off."

Astra looks at me. "You thinking our perp has some surgical skill?"

"Can't say yet. You can learn to disarticulate a body on

freaking YouTube these days," I reply. "But it's interesting that our guy didn't just take a chainsaw and cut the vic into pieces. He took the time to sever the limbs at all the joints."

Astra nods then squats down, studying the body closely. "Cuts look clean, that's for sure," she says. "Guy didn't use an ax or anything."

Erskine shakes her head. "Why would somebody do something like this?"

"Lots of reasons," I say. "Could have been trying to send a message. Could have been a matter of practicality—he needed to make sure the body would fit in the barrel."

"Hands and head are missing," Astra notes.

"Obvious forensic countermeasures," I say and turn to Erskine. "Don't suppose there are any pieces left in the barrel?"

"Nope. That's it, I'm afraid," she replies. "Whoever did this apparently doesn't want you to ID the vic anytime soon."

I sigh and stand back up to look around the scene, noticing for the first time that we've got eyes on us. Some of the Tukwila cops are watching us as if we're aliens who just beamed down from the mothership. Some of them have expressions of open hostility on their faces and others look indifferent. Just once, it would be nice to be welcomed onto a crime scene.

I look down at Astra. "We're going to need to run his DNA through CODIS. See if we can make an ID," I say, then turn to Erskine. "Can your techs get us samples we can take back to the field office for testing?"

"Absolutely," Erskine nods.

She walks over to one of the men standing near the barrel and quietly confers with him. Astra stands up and we linger there, staring down at the mutilated corpse.

"This is a bad one," Astra says.

I nod. "I think Erskine was right to call us in. This one is going to be hell to crack. I just have a feeling."

As I stand there staring at the body, I feel something tickling the back of my mind. There's a certain familiarity I'm feeling right now, though I can't say specifically what it is. But until I can figure it out, I don't want to say anything, so I keep it to myself. Something about this just feels….familiar. As though I've seen it somewhere before.

"What are you thinking?" Astra asks.

I shake my head. "Not sure yet. Just trying to absorb it all."

The way the Green River flows, it would have eventually carried the barrel to where it becomes the Duwamish, then out to the Puget Sound—and from there, who knows? Maybe all the way to Russia, depending on the currents. Which means it was dropped into the river somewhere upriver from Tukwila to make its journey. But there's a lot of rural land that way, and not a lot of gang activity. Which makes me wonder how the barrel got up there—and why.

I squat down and look at the body parts arrayed on the tarp, frowning. Reaching into my pocket, I pull out a pair of black nitrile gloves and pull them on. The crime scene tech—a young, squirrely-looking guy with a shock of curly brown hair and brown eyes behind his round frameless glasses—stops his cataloging and looks up at me with a raised eyebrow.

"You always walk around with nitrile gloves in your pocket?" he asks.

I glance at the name patch on his coveralls. "Don't you—Calvin?"

He chuckles. "No, I do not. I carry a box in my bag," he replies. "I'd kind of feel a bit obsessed with my job if I carried them in my pocket twenty-four/seven."

"Oh, she's definitely obsessed with her job," Astra chimes in. "A dog with a bone when she gets on a scent, this one."

He laughs and all I can do is shake my head and not point out the fact that Astra is pulling a pair of nitrile gloves out of her own pocket as we speak. I reach out and take hold of the left lower leg and look closely at it, turning it over in my hands. Astra looks thoroughly disgusted, which makes me grin. Not seeing anything, I set the piece back down and pick up the other one.

I shrug. "Yeah, well, call me obsessed with my job, then. There are worse things to be," I say. "Especially when it leads me to find things like this. I'd say this makes me good at my job. Wouldn't you?"

It's grisly and morbid as hell, but I hold the section of leg up and show Astra what I found. Along the side of the knee is a long surgical scar—which makes me think he was an athlete who blew his knee out. But on the back of the right calf is a distinctive tattoo. The dark ink against his dark skin makes it difficult to see, but turning it into the light makes it stand out a bit more. Astra and Calvin lean closer to inspect what I'm showing them.

My eyes are drawn back to the surgical scar, though. I have to wonder if it's that scar that led him to where he ended up. I wonder if the injury dashed his sports dreams, leaving him no choice in his mind but to join a gang.

"What is that?" he asks, pointing to the ink.

"It's a gang tat. That's the symbol for the Eighth Street Kings," I say. "If I recall, they're one of the bigger street gangs in Seattle."

I point to the distinctive design. It's a stylized figure eight with a crown around the top loop and a pair of bullets crisscrossed behind it. I've seen it spray-painted on walls and doors in Seattle more times than I can count. Astra looks at it and nods.

"Didn't know you were so well versed in street gang iconography," she says.

I grin. "I know a little about a lot of things. One of these days you're going to remember that," I say, then look to Calvin. "You guys have a gang problem down here? Got a chapter of the Kings running around Tukwila?"

He shakes his head. "No. We don't have a gang problem here. So far as I know, we don't have any street gangs at all."

"Which then begs the question—what is a Seattle gangster doing in pieces in a barrel floating in the river down here in Tukwila?" Astra ponders.

"That's a good question. A very good question," I reply. "But before we answer the why, let's figure out the who. Let's see about identifying this guy."

"Copy that, boss."

FIVE

Organized Crime Bureau; Seattle Field Office

"Jonas Hobbs."

He looks up from the papers on his desk, a wide smile on his face. Jonas gets to his feet and comes around his desk, pulling me into a tight embrace. He steps back but leaves his hands on my shoulders, looking at me with the pride of a father in his eyes.

"Blake Wilder. As I live and breathe," he says. "I didn't think royalty hobnobbed with mere mortals like me anymore."

"Well, I like to remain humble by walking among the peasants," I reply with a grin.

"Consider me honored."

Hobbs is a fireplug of a man. Five-ten, stocky build, and stronger than an ox. He's got dark eyes, and hair that's more gray than black now. He's wearing a dark suit that's a good five years old but is still fashionable, and a tie that's full of bright colors and geometric patterns. It looks like something straight out of the '80s. He's always thought his ties were playful and showed off his personality. I've always said they were abominations. Today's selection is covered in red, blue, yellow, and green triangles.

"I see your taste in ties hasn't improved much over the years," I note.

"You still know how to hurt me, Wilder. My ties are a window into my soul. You know that," he says, tipping me a wink.

Hobbs was my mentor when I was first assigned to the Seattle Field Office and spent some time in the OCB. In truth, he was more like a father figure to me. He took me under his wing and looked out for me. Hobbs is a good man. Clever, intelligent, and determined. Astra likes to say I'm a dog with a bone, but it's Hobbs' unit where I learned to be as doggedly determined as I am. So, in most every way, who I am as an investigator is his fault.

"Have a seat," he offers.

Hobbs walks around and drops down into his chair as I take the seat in front of his desk. His gaze remains fixed on mine for a long moment, and he can't seem to keep the smile off his face.

"You're doing some good work, Blake. I'm really proud of you," he says.

"Thanks, Hobbs. That means a lot," I reply. "I'm only doing what you taught me to do."

"Rubbish," he brushes me off. "Learn to take a compliment. You're doing great stuff."

"Thanks, Hobbs."

His office is tidy but cluttered, which is how it was when I worked in the OCB. It hasn't changed one iota. He's got stacks of files on his desk and the credenza behind him, as well as boxes of evidence stacked in the corners. He calls it a working man's office. It's one of his habits I'm glad never wore off on me. I can't stand the clutter. Honestly, I have no idea how he finds things in this chaos. But he somehow manages to do it.

"How are things going here?" I ask.

"Sisyphean. You know how it is," he replies. "But no matter what, we have to keep trying to push that rock up the hill."

"Well, if not for the bad guys, we'd be out of jobs."

He chuffs. "I think that's a tradeoff I'd be willing to make."

"And what would you do with yourself without the job?"

He shrugs. "I don't know. Yoga instructor, maybe?"

He draws a laugh out of me. "Yeah, I can't see you teaching the downward dog to a group of twenty-somethings."

"Maybe not. But I certainly enjoy watching those twenty-somethings do the downward dog in those leave-very-little-to-the-imagination yoga pants."

"You are awful," I squeal. "Absolutely awful."

"You say that like it's news."

We share a laugh and I shake my head at him. Same old Hobbs. He's always had an eye for the ladies—which is probably why he's not married. Anymore, at least.

"So, what brings you by?" he asks.

"I needed to pick your brain about something."

"Yeah, well, this old brain isn't what it used to be. Can't promise you'll find what you're looking for. But pick away."

The reason the man in the barrel in Tukwila twanged the chords of familiarity occurred to me when we were driving back. It reminded me of a case I worked shortly after I started with the OCB. It was actually one of my very first cases. I haven't thought about it in years, but once the thought crossed my mind, all the grisly details came pouring back. And even though I know our vic was a gang member, the way he was disposed of reminded me of that old case.

"Do you remember that case we worked when I first joined your team? The body in the barrel?"

"The Russian mob. Yeah, I remember that," he nods. "Nasty bit of business that was."

"Yeah, that one. Anyway, do you remember the victim? Paul Summers, I think his name was?"

"Oh, yeah. That's one of those things I'll never get out of my head no matter how hard I try," he replies.

Paul Summers had been a confidential informant of ours. He was a twenty-year-old kid and we'd busted him on a drug charge that had him looking at fifteen to twenty years in prison. But he'd agreed to work with us to bring down the Bologev crime family if we helped him with his pending case. So we'd sent him in wired. A few days after that, he went missing and we didn't find him for a couple of weeks until he....turned up.

Summers had been cut into pieces—disarticulated, actually, just like our mystery man. His remains had been stuffed in a barrel and left in a public park. A pair of homeless guys who thought they'd hit the jackpot opened up that barrel and got the surprise of a lifetime. We knew it was the Bologev family—their cleaner, Alexei Polskovet, specifically—but we could never conclusively tie it to them. So as of today, the murder of Paul Summers officially remains open-unsolved.

"So, is there a reason for this little trip down memory lane? Or did you just want an excuse to come down here and lord your celebrity status over us peons?" he asks with a grin.

"Celebrity status? You're really taking this a bit far, aren't you?"

"I don't see you all that often, so I have to give you crap when I can. It's a moral imperative for me."

"Fair enough," I reply with a grin. "I'm actually here because we caught a body today that made me think of the Russians."

"Yeah? Somebody turn your vic into a jigsaw puzzle?"

I nod. "Yeah. Completely disarticulated," I tell him. "Head and hands were missing."

"Trying to prevent an ID," he furrows his brow, already snapping into investigative mode. "That doesn't sound like our Russian friends. They like to advertise when they've killed somebody. Sends a message."

"Yeah, that was my thought, too. I've just never seen any other cases when the bodies were completely—"

"Taken apart?"

"Exactly."

Hobbs leans back in his seat and considers me. "Unfortunately, deconstructing a human body isn't quite as unique as it used to be," he says. "Seems to be the latest fashion among all the groups out there looking to send a message these days. Mob. Cartels. Street gangs. Hell, psychopaths looking to get rid of a wife are doing it."

"Yeah, I was afraid of that," I say. "But the way this was done—it was professional. It wasn't some cartel chopping up a rival. It was meticulous. Perfectly disarticulated. To me, that screams organized crime."

"It's possible. We still have some old-school mobsters in the city. Italians. Russians. Others," he shrugs. "They're a dying breed, but they will not go gently into the night."

"You ever hear of the Italian or Russian mobsters doing business with street gangs?"

Hobbs frowns and thinks about it for a moment. "I wouldn't rule it out completely, just because I try to never say never. But in general, the mobs are usually pretty insular. They don't usually do business with the gangs or outsource work to them," he says. "Let me put it this way, if any of the various ethnic mobs are working with street-level gangsters, it'd be the first time I've heard of it. They usually keep things pretty in-house. It's a lack of trust with a dash of racism thrown in for flavor."

"I guess good help is hard to find. At least, help of the right skin tone."

He chuckles. "Yes, it is. And for the different families, it's all about trust. They'd never trust somebody out runnin' and gunnin' on the streets. They'd flip way too easily if they got pinched, and the families know it," he says. "I take it your jigsaw puzzle guy was a gangster."

"Possibly. He had Eighth Street Kings ink."

"Huh. Very well could be a rival gang sending a message."

"Could be," I say. "But why take the head and hands? Why not let him be IDed if they were looking to send a message? I thought the gangs were all about signing their work?"

"They learned it from the families. What's old is new again, apparently. I swear to God, these creeps have no original thoughts of their own," Hobbs mutters with a chuckle. "Anyway, you might want to talk to Edgar Morello over in gangs. He's a good friend of mine. Good investigator. Guy knows these streets inside and out. He might know who got run through the woodchipper and why."

"That's a good idea. Thanks for the tip."

"Of course. I'm sure your dizzying intellect would have gotten you around to Morello sooner or later," he says. "Surprised it didn't help you bypass little ol' me completely actually."

I smile. "Yeah, I know, I'm a terrible human being. And I'm sorry I haven't been around very much—"

Hobbs raises his hand to stop me. "There's no need for you to apologize, kid. You are the job, which means you're working twenty-four/seven. Trust me, I get it. Took me two marriages to figure it out, but when I did, I stopped fighting it," he says. "And when you are the job, you don't have time or space for anything else, really. So don't apologize. Fact is, the phone works both ways. I'm usually so busy, I don't make a lot of calls either."

"Thanks, Hobbs. I appreciate your graciousness."

"You caught me on an off day."

We share a soft laugh. "We'll have to carve out the time to have a drink. I miss you, old man. We need to catch up."

"I'd like that. I've missed you too, kid."

I get to my feet. "Thanks for the tip on Morello."

"Hey, it's what I'm here for—to catch bad guys and be your concierge."

"And don't you forget it," I flash him a grin.

SIX

Wilder Residence; The Emerald Pines Luxury Apartments, Downtown Seattle

I CLOSE the door behind me, dropping my keys onto the small table beside it and dumping my bag next to the table. It's been a long day and I'm beat. I want nothing more than to shower and collapse into bed. But I know sleep won't be coming for a few hours yet. I've still got work to do. Besides, my mind is too keyed up to sleep right now. I've been down this road often enough to know that the minute I lay my head down, the thoughts in my brain will all start competing for attention, like an Internet browser with too many tabs open.

After getting a bottle of water out of the refrigerator, I head down to what's become my war room and stop at the doorway when I notice light coming from under the door. My mind reels with a thousand possibilities. Has someone broken in? Is an operative of The Thirteen in my apartment right now, stealing my information?

Adrenaline burns like liquid fire in my veins. I quickly pull my weapon. Clicking the safety off, I grip it tightly as I reach out with my other hand and grab the knob. I turn it quickly, push the door inward, and rush over the threshold. My weapon is at the ready and every nerve is taut.

"Jesus, Mark!" I gasp and lower my weapon. "What are you doing in here?"

He swivels in the chair he's sitting in so that he's facing me. If he's even remotely disturbed that I had my gun on him, a hair's breadth from firing, he gives no indication of it. If anything, he looks slightly annoyed as he gestures to the wall behind him. The surface of the wall is covered in photos and pages of text, each thing on my "board" a link in the chain that connects me to the murder of my parents.

"You've been busy. Added a lot since I last saw this wall of crazy," he starts.

"Wall of crazy?" I snarl.

He frowns. "Sorry, maybe 'wall of obsession' is the better descriptor."

I let out a frustrated breath and ignore his jabs. We've been over this before—multiple times—and I don't feel like hashing it all out again.

"How did you get in here?" I ask.

"It was open."

I silently chastise myself for apparently not locking the door. When I left this morning, I was in such a rush—and half out of my mind from sleep deprivation—that I didn't think to double-check the door to my war room. It's a stupid oversight after going through all the trouble of putting a new lock on the door. But I'll deal with that later. Right now, my focus is on the man who shouldn't be sitting in my chair.

"So, is that what we're doing now?" I ask. "You're just snooping around where you have no right, then criticizing me for what I'm doing?"

He shakes his head and mutters softly to himself. "You're playing a game with powerful people, Blake. They could kill you—"

"And yet, they haven't."

"Not for lack of trying," he snaps. "This is a dangerous game you're playing."

I lean against the doorway and take a couple of beats to tamp down the anger that's rising perilously high inside of me right now. I don't feel like going over this again, but apparently, I don't have any say in the matter.

"Blake, this is getting to be an obsession with you—"

"Damn right, it's an obsession!" I roar. "My parents were murdered, and I want to find out who did it. Why are you having such a difficult time understanding that?"

"I'm having trouble with the toll it's taking on you—and on our relationship."

"Oh, so your objection is based on you and what you want," I snap. "Good to know. And here I've been thinking that my happiness, or maybe just my peace of mind, mattered to you."

He opens his mouth to reply but lets the words die on his lips—which is probably wise. I'm quickly approaching a point when I'm going to say something I might regret. But then, maybe I won't. In my current mood, it's hard to know for sure.

"Blake, I'm having trouble with the fact that doing all of this," he waves to the wall behind him, "could get you killed. Will probably get you killed, eventually."

"Thanks for having such confidence in my abilities," I growl. "You seem to forget that I'm a trained federal agent."

"I haven't forgotten, and it has nothing to do with my confidence in your ability," he says softly. "But if you're right about this—conspiracy—then these people can get to Supreme Court Justices, Blake—they can murder Supreme Court Justices. And if they can do that, what makes you think they can't get to you, too?"

The scathing reply that's sitting on the tip of my tongue withers and I look away. I know what he's saying isn't entirely wrong. It's a thought I've had before. The road I'm on could ultimately end in my death. If what I think is going on is really happening, I'm up against some powerful people. People who have no compunction about killing innocents to preserve and consolidate their power.

I run a hand through my hair and frown, already knowing where all of this is heading. There was a time I would have fought like hell to put us onto a different path—something I've done several times already. But I just don't have the energy for it anymore. And although I care about Mark, sometimes that's just not enough. Not when there are bigger things in play.

"I can't do this anymore, Mark. I won't," I finally say.

A look of exasperation crosses his face. "What are you talking about?"

"This. Us," I tell him. "I can't keep circling back to this same conversation and fighting about it every few weeks."

"I've supported you every step of the way—"

"Until you don't," I cut him off. "And that seems to happen every few weeks. Our fights about it happen like clockwork. I can practically set a watch by it."

"That's not fair. I only talk to you about it because I care about you. Because I'm worried for you," he says, his features etched with concern.

"And while I appreciate that, it gets exhausting, Mark. I don't need you to hold my hand. I'm a big girl and I know the risks I'm taking," I reply.

"But these risks you're taking—"

"Are mine to take. Nobody else's. They're mine," I tell him. "And I don't need you hovering over me like Mother Hen, clucking your tongue at me. I know what I'm doing is dangerous and I'm willing to accept the risks to find out who murdered my family."

"Blake—"

"No. I'm done talking about this. And I think we need to take some time—apart."

He recoils as if I just slapped him across the face, and his expression is indescribable. There's a hardness in his face I've never seen before. A tension in his jaw and tautness in his body that's unfamiliar to me. But there's also a sadness in his eyes that sends a lance of pain through my heart.

"Are you serious? You're breaking things off with me?" he asks. "Because I expressed concern for you?"

"No, because you…" I sigh and let my words trail off.

I take a couple of moments to gather my thoughts. The air between us crackles with a nervous energy that sends a flutter through my heart. I lick my lips nervously and swallow hard, fighting the emotions that are churning wildly inside of me. Clearing my throat, I square my shoulders and straighten my spine.

"We need a break, Mark… I need a break," I finally say. "I just need some time and space."

"Space."

I nod. "Yes. I need to be able to focus on my case without having somebody questioning my every move or trying to discourage me from pursuing this."

Mark's face darkens and he looks down at the floor for a moment. He shakes his head then gets to his feet. And when he looks at me again, his expression is carefully neutral, but that sadness that wrenches my heart lingers in his eyes.

"I'm sorry about your folks, Blake. But this isn't healthy," he says. "And you're only going to get yourself killed if you keep chasing these people."

"As I said. I appreciate your concern, but until you've found your parents murdered and your sister abducted, your opinion on the matter doesn't much matter to me," I snap. "This is my family and I'm going to do what I feel is right by them—no matter the consequences or what anybody thinks about it."

"Blake—"

"Please," I interrupt him. "Just—leave your key on the table on your way out."

Without waiting for him to reply, I turn and walk to my bedroom, closing the door softly behind me. I sit on the edge of the bed and wait, listening until I hear the front door close. Once it does and I know he's gone, I get up and head out to the main room, picking up the key Mark left behind. I stare at it for a long moment, letting the weight of what I've just done press down on me. Waiting for the wave of sadness to wash over me.

But strangely enough, it doesn't. The grief doesn't come, and the burden of pain is a lot lighter than I expected it to be. I'd honestly expected to be something of a wreck after Mark left. But the truth is, I don't feel nearly as bad as I'd anticipated. If I'm being totally honest with myself, I'm not sad at all.

Which tells me all I need to know. Or maybe he was right—maybe I am unhealthily obsessed after all.

SEVEN

SSA Wilder's Office, Criminal Data Analysis Unit; Seattle Field Office

"I'm proud of you, girl," Astra says, a wide smile on her face.

"Proud of me?"

She nods. "It's been a long time coming."

A rueful grin touches my lips, and I look down at the cup of Starbucks coffee in my hand. I sigh, set the cup down on top of my desk, and lean forward. I peer through the wall of glass and out into the bullpen, watching Rick conferring with Mo at her workstation. My thoughts are scattered this morning, and I'm almost trying to make myself feel guilty about breaking things off with Mark last night. The surprise is that I just don't.

"I didn't expect such jubilation over my breakup," I note. "I thought you liked him."

"I did like him. And he made you happy for a while. But what I didn't like was that he wouldn't give you the space to be you and do what you need to do. It seemed as though he was trying to be more of a father figure instead of your boyfriend," she tells me.

"Yeah. That's kind of what I've told him several times before. And I just ran out of patience with it all last night. But still, I keep thinking I should feel guilty. He was hurt and upset last night, and I know I should feel bad," I say.

"How he reacts is neither your fault nor responsibility. You were open and sincere with him, and I know you weren't a jerk about it."

"No, I really tried not to be. I was just honest," I say. "But it's weird. I feel guilty about not feeling worse that I ended things with him."

"Tell me something," she says. "On a scale of one to ten, how sad are you that it's over?"

I shrug. "Two, maybe? Maybe less."

"That should tell you all you need to know."

"I know. And it does," I reply. "Honestly, it just surprises me that I don't feel much one way or the other about it. I mean, it's not as if I didn't care for him or anything."

"I know you did. But I suspect that deep down, you knew he wasn't right for you," she says. "Hell, I knew it ages ago."

"And you couldn't have given me a heads-up?" I gesture wildly, with a grin that betrays my faux-frustrated tone of voice.

"One thing I don't do is force my relationship opinions on anybody. Unless I'm asked directly, I've always found it's the best policy to let people discover these things on their own. Less drama and resentment that way. And let's face it, you wouldn't have heard me until you were ready to hear me, anyway," she says.

"You're a wise woman, Astra Russo."

"Yeah, I know," she replies with a smile.

I gnaw on my bottom lip and study her for a moment. "To

be honest, I think I probably should have done this a while ago."

She nods. "Yeah, you should have. The minute he started getting on you about this investigation you're running. If he can't support you in trying to find out who murdered your parents, I don't know that you can count on him to support you in anything else that's important," she says. "I mean, I get that he's worried for you. Hell, I'm worried for you. But I support you and am going to do whatever I can to help you."

"I appreciate that, Astra."

She gives me a gentle smile. "Of course. That's what friends do," she says, then adds pointedly, "and it's what boyfriends are supposed to do."

"You're not wrong," I reply. "And I appreciate your having my back."

"Always, babe," she tells me. "I'm always here for you."

I give her a smile, and a companionable silence descends over us. Astra gets me. She may be one of the only people in the world who does. I can count on her to always give me her real opinion, even when she knows I won't like it. Maybe especially when she knows I won't like it but need to hear it anyway. But I know that for better or worse, she'll always back my play. It's something I appreciate about her more than I can say.

"Anyway," she says, breaking the silence between us. "Now that you're single, Benjamin has a friend who is gorgeous and—"

I hold up my hand and shake my head, but smile. "Hard pass. I think I'm going to stay single for a while. The last thing I need is somebody else trying to smother me when I need to put all my focus on the case."

"Fair enough," she chuckles. "But when you solve this—because you are going to solve it—you're going to meet Benjamin's friend."

"If you say so," I say with a smile.

I appreciate that she isn't lecturing me on the dangers inherent in what I'm doing right now. She knows better than most just how dangerous it is. After all, she was shot at, too, the night we went out to see Corden. So if there's somebody who's earned the right to lecture me about the danger, it's Astra. But I'm grateful to her that she isn't trying to dissuade me from this path or harp on me about all the bad things that could potentially happen. She's simply there for me. It's something I wish Mark could have done. I need support, not condescension.

"So anyway, where are we with the case?" she asks brightly.

"Right. The case," I say. "I stopped in and had a chat with Hobbs over in OC yesterday—"

"And how is the old man doing?"

"As snarky and sarcastic as ever."

She grins. "Two of his better qualities. And what did he have to say?"

"Not too much. But he pointed me toward Edgar Morello over in street gangs," I reply and look at my watch. "And speaking of which, I should head on over there. What do you have going on right now?"

"I'm going to start sifting through the incident reports from Spokane," she tells me.

"Good. Do me a favor, if you would, and put a call in to the ME's office. See if they've got anything on the guy in the barrel yet."

She laughs. "It's only been a day. You don't seriously think they're going to have anything yet, do you?"

"Probably not. But if they know we're watching this closely, maybe it'll light a fire under their butts. Help keep them motivated."

"That's a good point."

"Yeah, I have them every once in a while."

She laughs. "No sweat. I'll give them a call and put a soft squeeze on them."

"Thanks, Astra."

"You got it, boss," she says, getting to her feet. "I'm off. I've got a hot date with a stack of paperwork ten feet high."

I walk with her out to the bullpen and go over to check on Mo and see how she's doing with the opioid issue in Bremerton. After that, I head out of the CDAU and to the elevators, taking one up to the cushy upper floors to see how the other half lives.

EIGHT

Anti-Street Gang Unit; Seattle Field Office

I GET off at the fourth floor and head through the warren of corridors until I find the unit offices. The door slides open as I approach, and I walk into the bustling bullpen and stand there for a moment. Nobody approaches me, so I take it upon myself to look around. I walk through the bullpen, then up a small staircase and along a row of offices, coming to a door at the end of the hallway. The frosted glass window is engraved with Morello's name. It's open a crack and I can hear a man's deep, rumbling voice. It sounds as if he's on the phone, so I knock softly.

"Yeah, hang on a second," he says to whoever he's talking to, then calls out. "Yeah, door's open. Come on in."

When I push the door open and step in, he gives me a nod and gestures to the chairs in front of his desk. He finishes up with his call as I take a seat and wait. I look around and see that Morello is about the same age as Hobbs and seems to have the same affection for a cluttered office and ties that are an absolute aberration—Morello's is a pastel blue with pink stripes on it. It makes me wonder if it's a generational thing or something.

Morello's hair is dark, but it's flecked with gray, his eyes are the color of caramel, and his skin has an umber tone to it. His face is smooth and unlined, and he's got a youthful appearance about him. If not for the splash of silver in his dark locks, you'd never be able to pin him down to a specific age. Unless you looked into his eyes. His eyes are old. Wise. He's a man who's obviously seen some things. It's a hazard of the job, I suppose.

"SSA Wilder, good to know you," he greets me, his voice deep and gravely.

"Likewise. But please, just call me Blake."

"Alright. Fair enough. Then call me Edgar," he replies. "Jonas has told me a lot about you. That boy's proud of you the way a daddy's proud of his daughter. I've known the man for almost thirty years now and I ain't never heard him gush over somebody the way he does with you."

"He's a good man. I was lucky to have him as a mentor."

"I'm pretty sure it was the other way around. Way I hear it, you made the old man look good more often than not," Morello counters. "To which I say, God bless you. Lord knows that man needs all the help he can get."

A grin curls the corners of my mouth, which makes Morello laugh. I've never been comfortable with compliments, so to hear that Hobbs has been that effusive with his praise to a man I've never met before makes me feel awkward.

"Yeah, that's what I thought," he says.

"I didn't say that."

"Didn't have to," he says. "So, what can I do for you today, Blake?"

"Well, we caught a body yesterday all the way down in Tukwila. It was floating down the Green River. Vic had some Eighth Street Kings ink on him," I explain. "But he was completely disarticulated. Whoever did our guy was thorough. And clean. He wasn't hacked apart with a machete or an ax. Looked surgical to me."

"Huh. Got a name?"

I shake my head. "Head and hands were missing. We've got no way to ID the guy yet. I'm hoping for a hit through CODIS, but I don't want to wait for the testing to get done to get a jump on this case."

"Good thinking," he replies. "But with no name, I'm not sure what I can do for you."

"I was wondering if maybe you'd heard any chatter about a King who went missing," I say.

He shakes his head. "Nothing yet. But I'll keep my ear to the ground and let you know if I hear anything."

"I appreciate that," I reply and sit back in my chair. "Can you tell me who the Kings' biggest rival on the streets is? Maybe a gang who has a penchant for cutting a person into pieces? It's possible they were trying to send them a message."

He scoffs. "I think it'd be easier if I listed off the gangs who didn't take a person's body apart to send a message these days," he sighs. "Don't get me wrong—it was never exactly safe, but the level of brutality these days..." He lets his words trail off with a shake of his head. "I've never seen anything like it."

I offer him my file of crime scene photos to review, but he holds out his hand to stop me. "I'll pass, thanks. Seen plenty of this stuff to get the picture. What I don't get, though, is the head and hands. The M.O. of most gangsters is to make ID as simple as possible to get that message out. They'd want everybody on the streets to know who killed the vic and why they did it. Preventing an ID doesn't make sense to me, not in these streets. They're all about the showmanship and drama."

"I had the same thought. But I was hoping for a little background information. Just something to start connecting some dots and eliminating others," I say. "My first thought was the disarticulation was done by the Russian mob. I had a case like that once years ago. But can you think of any reason the Kings would be involved with one of the Russians or any of the other ethnic mobs who seem to favor that sort of method of execution?"

"I ain't heard anything to suggest the Kings were involved with the Russians," he replies. "Way I hear it, the families would never do business with street gangs. Too unreliable and untrustworthy."

"Yeah, that's what Hobbs said."

"He'd know," Morello replies.

"Which brings me back to the idea that this was street violence," I say. "Maybe a drug deal gone wrong?"

"It's possible. But I still don't get why they'd take the head and hands," Morello says. "If your vic got caught stealing, skimming, or something else like that, whoever did it—be it the Kings or somebody else—would want to put everybody on notice. They'd display the body, not hide it in a barrel and dump it upriver somewhere with the hope it's never found. That's just how these cats roll."

I purse my lips and let everything he's said rattle around in my mind for a moment. None of this is making the least bit of sense, and yet, I can feel the presence of a bigger picture in the background. It's like staring at a freaking stereogram though—there's so much noise, it's making it impossible for me to see through to the image underneath.

"So, if somebody had a beef with the Kings, who do you think it would be?" I ask.

His chuckle rumbles like thunder rolling in off the Sound. It's so deep and reverberating, I can practically feel it on my skin.

"There ain't a gang out there on the streets that don't have beef with the Kings. They ain't the biggest gang out there, but they're the most brutal. Hands down," he tells me. "They've offed dudes from every other pack of thugs out there, and believe you me, they made it hurt. Dudes they killed died hard deaths. So, there ain't a crew on the streets right now that doesn't want their pound of flesh from the Kings."

"Charming," I reply.

He nods. "These cats don't screw around. They're territorial and they're nasty. All of them," he says. "But to answer your question, the crews who seem to have the most beef with the Kings are the Twenty-Third Street Killaz, which is a Mexican gang, and the Iron Dragonz, an Asian gang that's supposedly tied into the Yakuza. I've never seen evidence of that, though. But those three crews are always trading blows and dropping bodies all over the city."

I commit the names to memory and will ask Rick do a deep dive on them when I get back to the shop. I want to know everything there is to know about them before I go and question them.

"I can tell by that look on your face that you're planning on talking to these cats."

"I'm not thrilled with the idea, but I don't see any way around it," I tell him. "They might have the answers I need to figure out who killed the man in the barrel."

He nods. "I wouldn't have expected anything less. Jonas always said you had bigger stones than ninety percent of the field office."

"Yeah, well, he used to tell me I took stupid risks and did foolish things."

Morello shrugs. "Both things can simultaneously be true."

"Fair enough."

"Can I offer you a piece of advice?"

"Of course," I reply.

"If you're going into their world, tread lightly. Just because you're a woman doesn't mean they're going to cut you any slack," he tells me. "These cats are dangerous, and they'll kill anybody for any reason. Just watch yourself—and have somebody watching your back."

"I will," I nod. "And thank you. I appreciate your help."

He chuckles. "I'm not sure what help I actually offered, but you're welcome. And if I hear anything I think can help you, I'll let you know ASAP."

"Thank you, Edgar."

"Anytime."

I leave the anti-gang unit and head back to the shop with no clearer picture of what's going on. But at least I have a direction to run now. Unfortunately for me, that means heading into a damn viper's nest.

NINE

Wilder Residence; The Emerald Pines Luxury Apartments, Downtown Seattle

The sounds of Wynton Marsalis' trumpet float through my apartment, providing me with the soundtrack to drive myself crazy. I stare at the pages sitting on the desk in front of me, then look up at the wall—specifically at the photo I found among my mother's things. I look at the faces of Gina Aoki and Mr. Corden, feeling that familiar stab of guilt all over again.

I get up and walk out of my war room, needing to take a breather. I let the music wash over me as I head into the kitchen and grab a bottle of water. I twist off the cap and drop it on the counter, then take a long swallow, relishing the feeling of the cold water slipping down my throat. There's a dull ache in the back of my head that seems to be growing. It's probably my body's way of telling me it's time for bed. Not that I usually listen to my body or anything.

My phone chimes softly from its spot on the counter: incoming message. It's well after eleven, so I assume it's either

Astra checking up on me, or somebody letting me know we've got another body. I don't feel like going out to a crime scene tonight. I'm tired and need to get a little sleep, at least, but if somebody dropped a body, I know I won't get any.

I call up my text messages and frown when I see it's from Mark. A fresh wave of annoyance flashes through me. I know it's not a very charitable response to have, but things between us are over and I don't see the need to drag this out any longer. I know I should delete it, but I call up the message anyway—then can't stop myself from rolling my eyes when I read it.

"*I don't like how we left things. We need to talk. Call me. Please.*"

After I read the message, I delete it and set my phone back down on the counter. Maybe radio silence will convince him that I was serious when I said it's over. As far as I'm concerned, there's nothing left for us to talk about. I certainly can't tell him the biggest reason I broke things off with him. It's something I haven't even talked over with Astra—and probably won't now. There's no point in it, anyway. It's not going to change anything. I've made my decision and I'm going to stick with it because it's the right thing to do.

I broke things off with him because, yes, I was tired of having the same fight over and over again. And yes, I was exhausted by his constant nagging and picking at me over me trying to find my parents' killer. As if I need to justify it to anybody. But more than all that, I needed to get Mark away from me simply because it's not safe to be around me. I've become toxic, and the target on my back is automatically transferred to whoever is closest to me. I think Gina Aoki and Mr. Corden could both attest to that. I care about Mark, and the last thing I want to see happen is for him to be hurt because I'm doing what I feel I have to do.

I carry my bottle of water across the room and open the

window. Cool air surges in, making me shiver. I love it, though. I've always loved the rain and cold weather. I know a lot of people hate Seattle because it's so cool and damp most of the time—although they tend to exaggerate about how much rain we actually get. Some people say they get depressed about how perpetually gray Seattle—and by extension, the entire state of Washington—is, but I've always thrived here. The cool air is invigorating; the rain and thunderstorms that roll through are inspiring. Yeah, I'm aware that people think I'm odd. I don't care, though. Not really.

I draw a deep breath and let it out slowly as I stare out at the city beyond the window. The twinkle of the lights in the dark is mesmerizing to me. With the window open, the buzz of city life floats up and seems to combine with Marsalis' music, somehow making it even more beautiful and soothing to listen to. I stand there for a little while and absorb the atmosphere, letting the cool air and the music sluice away my tension.

Eventually, I feel relaxed enough to go back to my war room, but rather than sit down, I lean against the doorjamb and stare at everything I've got pinned to the wall across from me. If I thought the man in the barrel case was bad, this is even worse. This is like the most intense stereogram I've ever seen. I can see everything in the foreground, but the actual picture remains buried in all the colorful noise and I can't focus hard enough to see it.

My eyes stray to the three Supreme Court Justices, all of them having died over the span of three years. Justice Amelia Sharp died a few months ago of a heart attack while she was in her rose garden at home. Justice Edmund Boone had a stroke while he was playing racquetball a couple of years ago. And a year before that, Justice Arnold Kettering died in a single-car accident when he lost control of his car and hit a freeway abutment on a rainy night.

On the surface, their deaths are reasonable; nothing has come up that's raised any red flags. Yet Mr. Corden was under the distinct impression all three were assassinated. There's nothing in his notes about how or why, but he was sure of it. I'm not naïve enough to think that things in Washington aren't shady as hell and political assassinations aren't a thing. They are. People have been killing others for profit and position since the dawn of civilization. It's not a new story.

But with no proof of anything to go on, it's a case I can't make. It's a case I can't even attempt to make. I don't have enough for a warrant, nor do I have anything I can use to haul somebody in. And I won't try to make the case until I have evidence. If there is a conspiracy afoot—a conspiracy that got my folks killed—the last thing I want to do is stick my head out of my hole until I'm ready. If I tip my hand that I'm looking at someone, but don't have enough to bring him or her in, I might as well just strap a target to my own back.

No, if I'm going to get to the bottom of this and find out who murdered my folks and stole my little sister away from me, I need to move cautiously. I need to be more careful with this than anything I've ever dealt with before. I need to treat anything and everything with kid gloves and move slowly and deliberately. I need to build a rock-solid case before I do anything—otherwise, I'm going to find myself neck-deep in a river of crap.

Moving foolishly, or as if I've got a giant pair of stones, as Hobbs says, is only going to put me in mortal danger. It's going to get me killed. And I can't die just yet. Not until I see this through and get justice for my family. Not until I have justice for Mr. Corden and Gina Aoki. I can't bring them back, but maybe I can ease this burden of guilt on my shoulders. If not for me, if not for my pursuit of the truth, both of them might still be alive. I've tried to rationalize it away in a thousand different ways, b u t t h e g u i lt i s s o m ething I can't seem to shake.

Folding my arms over my chest, I wander over to the wall and look closely at the pictures of the three Justices. I'm convinced they're the key to all of this. I think Mr. Corden was trying to tell me as much by including the partial dossiers on each of them in the file I found in his camper. But whatever it was he was trying to tell me about them, about why they're the key to this whole thing, died with him.

I finally drop down into the chair and stare at the wall, my vision trained on the photos of the Justices. As I let my mind unspool, letting my thoughts drift away on the currents of music floating through my apartment. Wynton Marsalis has given way to the piano of Count Basie, and I let myself float along with those beautiful notes, letting myself go completely blank.

I've found that I often do my best thinking when I'm not thinking at all. When I'm not trying to actively unravel some Gordian knot and just try to relax, the answers seem to come to me a lot more easily. The problem is getting my mind to shut off and go blank. It's often a real struggle to turn the volume in my brain down. I'll eventually get to that point when I'm thinking without thinking, but it's difficult. It takes a little effort.

And that's when I see what I should have been seeing all along. It's not the dead Justices that are important. It's their replacements. I want to slap myself stupid for not thinking of that until now. There's something about the replacements for Justices Boone, Kettering, and Sharp that I need to be looking at.

I glance at my watch and see how late it's getting. Now that I have an idea where to be focusing my energy, I feel slightly better. I just hate that it took until now for me to see it. But I'm not going to see much more if I'm half-drunk with sleep deprivation. For now, I think it's best if I go to bed, get some rest, and let my subconscious keep picking at that Gordian knot inside my brain.

Maybe when I wake up, I'll feel refreshed and have a few more answers. Or at least, have a few more relevant questions I should be asking.

TEN

Criminal Data Analysis Unit; Seattle Field Office

"So, I talked to the ME's office and put a little pressure on them," Astra says. "They say they're backlogged, so we're going to have to wait a while for information. We did get the murder book and preliminary observations, but that's about it."

"Wonderful," I reply as I pace at the front of the bullpen. "Did we get the samples from Commander Erskine yet? I want to get them to Quantico. I think we'll get the results faster if we run this through the in-house lab."

"Got them this morning and turned them around," Mo reports. "They should hit the labs in Quantico later today."

"Excellent," I nod. "But that's still going to take a couple of days. I want to get an ID on our vic before then if we can."

"Yeah, about that....knowing we were in a holding pattern, I took the liberty of pulling missing persons reports for Seattle going back for the last month," Mo pipes up. "I know we don't have a fixed TOD just yet, and I'm no medical examiner, but judging by the condition of the body in the crime scene photos,

I can't see its being much longer than that. Even preserved in a barrel. It may be a dry well, but at least it's a starting point."

Astra gives Mo a mischievous grin. "Well, gold star for you," she crows. "Look who's going for the teacher's pet award."

Mo flashes her a devious smile in return. "Don't be jealous. I mean, you can't win it every single day, Russo."

"She shoots, she scores," Rick calls from his workstation as he thrusts his arms victoriously into the air.

The room erupts in laughter and more hurled insults back and forth. I enjoy seeing my unit coming together this way. When Mo first came in from White Collar, she was a little—stiff. She was rigid and a by-the-book, never-color-outside-the-lines kind of woman. I kind of worried about how she would fit in a room full of big personalities like Astra and Rick. I figured there was going to be some tension, but there's been remarkably little of that.

Day by day, she's been loosening up a little bit more. She and Rick, in particular, have formed a pretty strong bond. And now, maybe with his influence, or just the general atmosphere in the shop, she's getting to be just as snarky and sarcastic as the rest of us. She's got a dry, scathing wit that I like. And every now and then, she'll bust out with some one-liner that leaves us all gasping for air because we're laughing so hard.

"Great idea, Mo. Good work," I say. "What have you found?"

"So far, we've got twenty missing. Of those, we have six black males," she says.

Pictures of six black males, ranging in age from twelve to twenty-four, pop up on the screens mounted to the wall at the front of the bullpen. I step back and take a look at them for a moment as I ponder ways to filter this down.

"Okay, eliminate the twelve and fourteen-year-old," I start. "The body is an adult."

Two pictures come down, leaving us with the four black men who went missing in the last month. All of them are within the potential age range of the body pulled out of the barrel and are of a similar body type—tall, lean, and athletic. Our vic could be among these four. It's also possible that he's not. Without a way to make a solid ID yet, it's impossible to know for sure. But as Mo said, at least this is a starting point.

I turn to Rick. "Rick, can you tell me if any of these men have been in trouble with the law before?" I ask, and he nods. "Also, Mo, can you check to see if they've got any known gang affiliations."

"On it," she says.

"What about me?" Astra asks.

I grin. "You just sit there and be pretty."

She laughs and gives me the finger. "You're such a jerk."

"Sometimes," I reply with a chuckle. "Until we have something definitive to run with, there's not much for you to do. Sorry. No gold star for you today."

"Oh, my God, I hate you so much right now," she laughs even harder.

"Boss, of the four, three have records," Rick calls from his workstation.

The screens at the front go blank for a moment then a picture of one of the missing men comes up. At twenty-four, he's the oldest of the group, even though he's got a baby face that makes him look a lot younger.

"This is Anthony James. He's been busted for possession, stealing a car, and assault," Rick reads from his monitor. "His last arrest came when he was nineteen. Been clean ever since. Went missing a month ago, first reported by his sister."

"No known gang affiliation," Mo adds.

The next picture comes up on the next screen. "Antoine Booker, age nineteen," Rick says. "His jacket starts when he was twelve and includes car theft, attempted rape, aggravated assault, and possession with intent to distribute. Reported missing two weeks ago by his aunt."

"He's pretty accomplished for somebody that young," Astra comments.

"It says here that he managed to skate on some of his more serious charges," Mo notes. "He's also known to be a member of the Savage Playboys. They're a small, little-thought-of street gang here in Seattle."

I don't think this is our guy, but it definitely piques my interest. You don't see guys change gang affiliations often. Usually never, to be honest. But it does make me wonder if Antoine tried to jump from the Playboys to the Kings, and maybe that's what got him killed. I don't think it's likely, but it's an interesting bread crumb that I'll store away for later use.

"And contestant number three is Eric Gathers. Twenty-two," Rick says. "Jacket includes assault, theft, and vandalism. Reported missing by his father three weeks ago."

"Gathers is a member of the Forty-Five Boyz," Mo tells us. "Apparently named for their weapon of choice."

"Charming," Astra says.

I look at his picture for a moment. He's got high cheekbones and a strong jawline. But it's his eyes that capture my attention. They're a hazel, almost golden color, and have an intensity in them that can't be denied—not even in a photograph. Even through a computer-enhanced image, he has a presence about him.

"What about the one without a police record?" I ask.

"Terrence Meadows. Age twenty, a student at U-Dub. Reported missing by his brother a week ago," Rick reports.

"Any of these four turn up at the morgue?" I ask.

Mo's fingers fly over the keys on her computer, and she

looks at the screen as it processes the information. A moment later, she turns to me and shakes her head.

"None of them has been reported dead by the ME," she announces.

"I've got no death certificates on file for any of them, either," Rick offers.

"If the ME's office is as backlogged as they say, it could be that they haven't been processed and no death certificates have been issued yet?" Astra attempts.

"That's possible," I say, then turn and look at Astra. "Up for a field trip?"

She smiles. "You know how much I love spending my day down at the meat locker."

"Have to do our due diligence," I reply.

"Yeah, so you keep saying," she says and gets to her feet. "Well, let's go cross our t's and dot our i's, then."

"That's my girl."

ELEVEN

King County Medical Examiner's Office; Seattle, WA

"I LOVE the smell of bleach and antiseptics in the morning," Astra muses.

The doors slide open and a rush of cool, acrid air washes over us as we step into the ME's office. We walk across the tile floor and to the reception booth. The woman behind the thick plexiglass gives us a wooden smile, with boredom or perhaps irritation in her eyes. She presses the button on her side of the intercom.

"What can I do for you?" she asks, her voice sounding tinny coming through the speaker.

Astra and I badge her. "We need to speak with Dr. Rebekah Shafer."

"Do you have an appointment?"

"No, we don't," I reply. "But we just need a little information. If you could page her to the front, I'd appreciate it. Tell her it's SSA Blake Wilder and Special Agent Astra Russo."

The woman looks thoroughly unimpressed with our creds, but she taps in a few commands on her computer, then turns back to us.

"Go have a seat. She'll be out when she has a chance," the woman says.

There's an audible click when she cuts off the intercom—which seems like the equivalent of slamming the phone down on us.

"She's a charmer," Astra mutters as we walk over to the waiting area.

"I'm guessing personality isn't a factor in their hiring process," I add.

We stand together at the far end of the waiting area for about twenty minutes before Rebekah comes out. She gives us a small, nervous smile and motions us forward. I know Rebekah is nervous about helping us with Deputy Chief Torres breathing down the back of her neck. The last time we talked, she made mention of some of his veiled threats to her job if he continued helping us—helping me.

She shepherds us quickly down the corridors to her office, closing the door behind us as if she's shutting out an approaching zombie horde. Only then, with the door closed and us safely out of sight, does she give me a genuine smile and a nervous laugh.

"Sorry," Rebekah says. "Things around here have been tense and...well..."

"And being seen with me is detrimental to the health and well-being of your career," I finish for her.

"Honestly, yeah," she replies. "He's got eyes and ears everywhere. I'm sure he's going to hear that I tried to smuggle you guys in here. The man is like an octopus—he's got his fingers in pies everywhere."

"I'm sorry to bring this kind of heat down on you," I tell her.

She shakes her head. "I know it's not you. I know it's him," she says softly. "But this little war you two have going on is making everybody jumpy. But it's as you said, Blake, I can choose to do my job or play politics. I choose to do my job."

"Well, the good news is, we're here on business that has nothing to do with the SPD, so Torres shouldn't have room to give you any grief," Astra chimes in brightly.

"No?"

I shake my head. "We got this case passed onto us directly from Tukwila PD."

"Excellent. That is good news," Rebekah says. "So, how can I help?"

"We're looking to see if the ME's office has processed any of these four men who've been reported missing within the last month," I say and slide the slip of paper with the names across her desk.

Rebekah picks up the paper and reads off the names, then sets it down and starts keying them into her computer. She works in silence for a minute, her face screwed up in concentration. When she's done, she turns back to us.

"Okay, Eric Gathers was just IDed last night," she says. "But the other three aren't in the database."

So that's one down, but three still to go. Astra and I exchange a look, and I can see her wheels spinning, too. I turn back to Rebekah.

"Do you have any John Does in the refrigerator?" I ask.

"Of course. We always have at least a few of them."

"Great. Can we go down and take a look?" Astra asks.

"Yeah, I don't see why not."

Rebekah leads us through the warren of corridors until we reach a large, stainless steel door that's wide enough to admit a gurney and has a white sign with black letters that reads, "Open Unidentified Room," though it's colloquially known around the ME's office as the "Doe Room." Rebekah punches in a code, and when there's a soft beep and hard thunk of a lock disengaging, she opens the door and ushers us inside. On all three walls around us are rows of doors that open into the refrigerator trays housing the unidentified dead.

"Okay, so what are we looking for?" Rebekah asks. "Or more precisely, who?"

"Black male," I tell her. "In the age range of nineteen to twenty-four."

Rebekah consults her tablet and keys a few things in before looking back up. "We've got five John Does meeting that criteria."

I pull the photos of the three missing men who remain outstanding and hand them to Rebekah. She consults her tablet again, then starts moving along the rows of doors. She stops before one drawer and pulls it open. She seems to be comparing the face in the photo with the face on the slab in front of her. She drops the photo on top of the sheet and moves on to check the others. Not wanting to get underfoot, Astra and I stand back and just watch her work until she's done. And when she is, Rebekah is still holding two of the photos—no matches.

"At least we can take one more name off the list," I mutter.

"Two down, two to go," Astra reminds me.

We walk over to the tray where Rebekah is standing and look down at the body of twenty-four-year-old Anthony James. And judging by the five puncture wounds in his chest, I can see he didn't die a particularly pain-free death.

"Anthony James," I say. "Twenty-four, resident of Seattle his entire life."

"I'm not sure what kind of a life you can put together in just twenty-four years," Astra mutters.

I shrug. "It's what you make of those years, I guess."

Anthony James looks as if he lived a hard life. His body is crisscrossed with a lattice of scars and he has some gang ink he apparently tried to remove himself. The things you have to resort to when you can't afford the expensive laser surgery, I guess.

"He died of massive blood loss," Rebekah reads off her pad. "One of those stab wounds nicked his aorta. He was dead long before the EMTs arrived on the scene. According to reports, the fight broke out over a gambling debt."

"I guess Anthony didn't make very good use of his years," Astra says.

"I guess not," I say.

Rebekah looks at me. "What is it you guys are working on? I can keep my eyes peeled and let you know if I see anything."

"Body was pulled out of a barrel they found floating in the Green River," I explain. "He was completely disarticulated, head and hands missing."

She nods. "I heard something about that. I wrote it off, though," she says. "I had enough on my plate, so I didn't really pay attention."

"That's our guy. We're looking for an ID," I tell her. "After that, we can start piecing things together and figure out who killed him."

"Piecing things together. Because he was cut into pieces, right?" Astra says with a grin. "I see what you did there."

I chuckle. "You are a sick woman."

"I see why you two get along so well," Rebekah adds.

"This is all her," I say. "She's twisted."

"Pot? This is kettle," Astra says.

We all share a laugh that soon fades away. It's kind of hard to keep up the good spirits in a room where you're literally surrounded by death. But we got what we came for. We can cross two names off the list, which is leading me to think that although Mo's idea was good, it's ultimately going to be a dry hole. And that will land us back at square one. But still, making sure we're doing our due diligence is part of the job.

"Thanks, Rebekah," I say. "I appreciate this. And don't worry, we'll be more discreet the next time we need to talk."

"I hate that it's like this—I hate that politics is taking precedence over the work. But I appreciate you understanding," she replies.

"Have to play the game if you're going to win," I say.

"Sadly, yeah."

"Don't worry, we'll see ourselves out, so you're not seen with us any more than you already have been," I tell her.

She gives us a grateful smile, then Astra and I make our way out of the Doe Room and back through the twisting labyrinth of corridors that leads us back out to the front. On our way through, we run a gauntlet of SPD detectives. It's clear some of them are Torres loyalists by the way they're eyeballing us.

"Well, that was fun," Astra mutters once we're back out of the building.

I pull out my phone and start keying in a quick text as we walk back to the car.

"What are you doing?" she asks.

"Giving Rebekah a heads up that some of Torres' guys are in the building and spotted us," I explain. "I'm really worried she's going to be collateral damage in this stupid little war."

"Well, if she is, I'd be willing to bet you could pull some strings and get her a gig at the labs in Quantico."

I give her a smile. "You really do have the best ideas every now and then."

Though it's a possible solution if Rebekah gets caught up in this fight brewing with Torres, I really hope it doesn't come down to that. I'd hate for her to have to uproot her entire life because of me. Or actually, because of one man's issues with me.

TWELVE

Boogie's Billiards Parlor; Downtown Seattle

THE SIGN out front says Boogie's has been operating continuously in Seattle since 1985, and judging by the state of things inside, it hasn't been cleaned since then, either. The odor of cigarette smoke is thick in the air; the establishment clearly defying state smoking bans. The stench of stale beer and body odor also saturate the air around us.

"I'm going to need a scalding hot shower after this," Astra comments as we walk through the billiards hall.

"With bleach and scrub brushes," I add.

We've just come from Terrence Meadows' house only to find that his brother's report turned out to be erroneous. Turns out, Terrence wasn't missing at all. He'd simply skipped town to go on a spontaneous weekend trip with his girlfriend. They apparently drove up to Vancouver to play in the casinos and get away from the pressures of school for a little while. They were all very apologetic about the mix-up and frankly, I'm glad to have gotten at least one sliver of good news out of this day.

But after that, we hit Antoine Booker's place and spoke to his aunt Florence—and got nowhere. She wasn't quite altogether there. According to Antoine's sister, May—who cares for the older woman—Florence suffers from dementia and put in the call to the police to report Antoine missing during one of her episodes. May said it had been some time since they'd seen him, but that it was nothing new. She said he was often gone for weeks at a time and that he didn't really have much to do with their family—that his gang was his family.

It was obvious that being there was a waste of time, and that Antoine may or may not even be missing. Heading back to our car though, we were approached by a kid who couldn't have been more than thirteen or fourteen. He told us that Antoine came around often, bringing groceries and whatnot for Florence, but May would chase him off. She didn't approve of Antoine's being in a gang and didn't want the trouble it brought anywhere near their aunt. I can't say I really blame May for that. But I'm not too crazy about her not telling us that Antoine does come around to help with Florence.

But their family dynamics are neither my business nor concern. All that matters is running down Antoine to see if he's the man in the barrel or not. And to that end, the kid who approached us said that the Playboys like to hang out at Boogie's. Though for the life of me, I can't figure out why anybody would willingly spend time here. The place is a dump. It's filthy, my feet are sticking to the floor, and there's garbage everywhere. The only clean things in this place are the pool tables. Those are somehow pristine.

We approach a small group of men seated at the bar in the back. They've all got drinks in their hands and are speaking in low tones, then laughing in louder ones as they watch us. There are six of them seated at or behind the bar, and I'd peg all of them to be in their twenties. They all have hostile expressions on their faces and stare at us with open disdain.

"You lost, cop?" starts the man seated closest to me.

Even though he's sitting down, I can tell he's well over six feet tall. He's got broad, sloping shoulders, a thick neck, and a body that's taut with corded muscle. He's got braids in his hair that fall to his shoulders, a neatly trimmed goatee, and hands that are so large, they should probably be called paws. He's a good-looking man who can no doubt appear downright terrifying if he wants to. Right now, he just looks amused.

Astra and I badge him and the rest of the group. "SSA Wilder, Special Agent Russo," I introduce us. "We're looking for Antoine Booker. Seen him?"

"Yeah, I seen him. About five-nine, five-ten. Long dreads, dark eyes. Squirrely little cat," he cracks with a grin.

The others chuckle and make comments under their breath to each other, clearly amused by his attempt to mock us. I give him a smile and a nod.

"That's great. Seen him lately?" I ask.

He shrugs. "Hard to say. People come and people go all the time," he tells me. "It ain't my job to be their keeper."

"No, of course not," I reply. "But we got a report that he was missing. We needed to follow up just to make sure he's alright."

The man scoffs. "Man, when you ever been worried about a black man who goes missin'? Get outta here with that crap. We know you're just lookin' to jam him up. We look stupid to you or somethin'? We know how this game is played."

"I'd never say you looked stupid," Astra chimes in, taking a step forward. "But right now, you're not looking all that bright. We're trying to help here."

"Man, cops ain't never helped us with anythin' before. I

don't buy that you'd start now," he fires back, his voice deep and gruff. "SPD ain't never done sh—"

"We're not SPD," I reply and hold my creds closer for him to see. "We're FBI."

"Even worse," one of the other guys mutters.

"Look, honestly—I get that you're not fans of SPD. We aren't either," Astra says. "But we really are trying to help. We just need to eliminate Antoine as a possible victim of the crime we're investigating."

"Victim?" asks the large man, a sudden light of curiosity in his eyes.

I nod. "Yes, victim."

"What the crime y'all investigatin'?"

"Homicide," Astra says.

The big man chuckles again and I swear it reminds me of the sound that passes Morello's lips when he laughs.

"So, wait. Y'all are investigatin' a murder, and y'all don't know who got theyselves killed?" he asks. "What kinda half-assed Feds are y'all?"

"If I had to guess," starts a man who stepped through the door behind the bar, "I'm thinkin' they've got no way to ID the body. Which means the head and at least the tips of the fingers were taken. How'd I do, Agents?"

All his friends turn and look at him, an expression caught somewhere between disgust and respect on their faces. A slow smile curls the corners of his mouth as he stares right at us. I can see in his eyes that Antoine isn't your typical mindlessly violent gangster. Not this guy. He's smart. Very smart. What's more, he knows it. And given that he's got intel that hasn't been released to the media, I'd say that he's a pretty well-connected man. Which makes him a dangerous man.

I give him a smile. "Antoine Booker."

"Alive and well," he replies. "So, I'm obviously not the dude all chopped up and stuffed into that barrel."

Antoine is about five-ten and lean. He's got a rich ochre skin tone and dark eyes that are direct and piercing. He's athletic, and as the big man said, has dreads that fall to the middle of his back, though they're all tied back with a dark-colored ribbon right now. He's wearing a black and white tracksuit and some brilliantly white sneakers. I see a flash of gold in his ear and my eyes are drawn to the diamond stud embedded in the lobe.

Judging by his demeanor and the way everybody is looking at him, with a respect that borders on awe, I'd guess that he isn't just a member of the Playboys—he runs the group. Which makes my earlier thought that he might have been trying to switch gang allegiances entirely moot. And it makes him all the more imposing, given that he's only nineteen. I don't care if your gang has ten or a hundred members, it takes somebody with some serious smarts and spine to run one. I shudder to think what he's done to earn the awe I see in the eyes of the other men.

"And where'd you hear all that, Antoine?" I ask.

He shrugs. "Word gets around."

"I bet it does," I reply. "Can we talk for a minute? Privately?"

He gives me a casual smile, his eyes moving up and down as he takes my measure. In most guys, I think the elevator eyes are creepy simply because I can see the thoughts going through their heads—and more often than not, it involves seeing me naked. With Antoine, though, it's almost clinical. It's not a sexual thing, it's a trying-to-see-through-me thing. Trying to determine whether I pose a threat to him or not. His gaze is that of a predator sizing up his rival, to figure out who's going to come out on top in a scrap.

Antoine must not think Astra and I pose much of a threat, because he gives me a wide, bright smile.

"Yeah, sure. Why not?" he asks. "I'm always happy to help law enforcement."

His boys chuckle as he walks out from behind the bar and I guide the three of us toward the front door. Personally, I'd like a little fresh air and I'm sure Astra will appreciate it as well. None of us speaks until the doors close behind us and we're sucking deep breaths of the crisp air on the street. When I've got the stench of the pool hall out of my nose, I turn to face Antoine.

"Nineteen years old and you're running your own crew. I've never heard of anything like that before," I say. "You must be something special."

"Or something more violent and brutal than everybody else," Astra notes.

"Do those things have to be mutually exclusive?" he asks with a smile.

"What happened to the man who used to run your....club?" I ask.

"He retired."

"Retired?" I ask.

"Sure did," he nods. "Wanted to spend more time with his family."

"You seem like a man with big plans," Astra offers. "Got big plans for the Playboys, do you, Antoine?"

He shrugs. "What kind of man would I be if I didn't have plans? What kind of man would I be if I didn't strive for more or try to better my lot in life?"

"So, you're just going to knock off everybody who gets in the way of your getting what you want?" Astra asks.

He chuckles to himself. "Getting what I want doesn't entail violence, Agent Russo," he says and taps his head with his finger. "This is my most dangerous weapon. I don't have to shoot somebody when I beat him by outthinking him. When you can outwit somebody, you take away his power and control. And when you take his power and control, it's even more effective than killing him. Credibility is king, Agents. When you have all the credibility, you're going to find yourself on top."

"Yeah, but on these streets, you can't attain that credibility without leaving a trail of bodies behind you no matter how smart you are. We both know that," Astra presses.

"As they say, you can't make an omelet without breaking a few eggs."

Antoine speaks with the quiet confidence of a man who knows exactly what he wants and intends to get it. He's intelligent and articulate. He's not like most of these mindless mobsters and gangsters. He's not like the common criminals we run down. If anything, his calm, cool demeanor strikes me as similar to that of some of the sociopaths and serial killers we've gone after. They've all had this self-possession and ironclad determination about them. They've all seemed to make it inevitable that they'll get what they want.

"Fair enough," I acknowledge. "But tell me, since you somehow know about it, do you know who the man in the barrel is? Do you know who put him in the barrel in the first place?"

"I'm sorry, but I'm afraid I don't," he replies.

He's looking me dead in the eye, and as good as I am about reading people, I swear to God I can't tell if he's lying to me or not. There isn't a ripple of deception in his face that I can see. There's just—nothing. His face is totally expressionless and blank. For all I know, he could have killed our man in the barrel himself and I wouldn't know it.

But I don't think he did. As I study him, I get the feeling Antoine is telling me the truth. That he really doesn't know.

And unless it was him or one of his boys, I don't think he would have lied to me about it. It's entirely possible I'm wrong, but I like to think I've been doing this job long enough and have developed good instincts to get a bead on a person. And my instincts are telling me that Antoine is being honest with me.

I slip a card out of my pocket and hand it to him. "Alright. But if you hear anything that might be relevant, I hope you'll give me a call," I tell him. "I appreciate your time."

"Of course."

He gives Astra and me both a long look, a smirk tugging a corner of his mouth upward. He slips the card into his pocket then walks back into the pool hall, leaving us standing on the corner looking at each other.

"In twenty years, that kid is going to be running the Seattle underworld," I mutter.

"You think?" she scoffs. "The kid is creepy as hell. And he's smarter than any gangster I've ever met. Yeah, we're going to be seeing and hearing more about him."

"Yeah... I think you're right," I nod. "And I guarantee he's going to be even more dangerous as he gets older."

As we head back to the car, I wonder how long it's going to be before the Playboys make their move and take over the city. With a guy like Antoine running the show, already commanding the respect and loyalty he does, I can't imagine that it'll be long. And when they do, there are going to be a lot of bodies dropping around Seattle.

THIRTEEN

Creative Design Solutions; Downtown Seattle

After striking out all the way around with our potential victims, I found myself feeling restless and not wanting to go home. I just don't feel like sitting there staring at the wall as I wait for the answers to come to me—the answers to both my parents' case as well as the man in the barrel. Having a million more questions than I do answers is enough to drive me mad.

So instead, I've opted to do a little more digging on my own. I may not come up with any answers to the questions I have, but the act of doing something and being proactive is a lot better than sitting around waiting for something to happen. I always prefer being active and trying to take control of a situation. That's just how I'm wired. I've had enough of life happening to me—rather than trying to seize control and make something happen—to last me forever, thank you very much. I may not always be successful, but at least I try. And while I may not always be satisfied with the outcomes, I think it's a whole lot better than doing nothing.

"Can I help you?"

"Yeah," I say. "I'd like to look at the crime scene."

I stop before the cop standing in front of the door to Gina Aoki's office. Creative Design Solutions is—was— Gina's startup tech company. She did IT work, but she was also a software and app designer. And by all accounts, she was very well respected in the tech community and made a pile of money doing it.

CDS, as it says on the door, is a small office that's thoroughly modern in design. It sits on the edge of a campus of office buildings that look similar—lots of glass, steel, and strange angles in the architecture. From what I know, CDS was a one-person operation. Gina was it. The alpha and omega of the company. I can definitely see the appeal of working solo—zero layers of BS and bureaucracy to deal with. It's one reason I sometimes envy Paxton. But my creds get me into places he can't go—legally, anyway—which is why I'm in no rush to go into the private sector.

And speaking of my creds, I whip mine out and show them to the cop on the door. He looks at the badge, then at me, his expression telling me he's unimpressed. I suppress the grumble. Once upon a time, the sight of FBI creds would make people tremble and then comply. Nowadays, though, it seems that all they earn me is scorn and derision.

"Nobody in or out. It's still an active crime scene," he grunts.

"I understand that, but I need to take a look at it."

"Sorry, I have orders. Nobody in or out," he repeats robotically.

I have to tamp down the frustration that's growing inside of me. I know this guy has orders and that he's expected to follow them. This isn't his doing. But it's hard to keep my temper in check all the same.

"I get it, Officer....Doran," I say after a quick check of his name plate. "But I'm with the FBI—"

"I was told that the FBI especially was not allowed on the crime scene," he cuts me off. "So, if you have a problem with it, take it up with my supervisor."

I step forward and glare at him, clenching my jaw. "Officer Doran, I'm with the Federal Bureau of Investigation," I say, purposely putting emphasis on the word 'federal'. "I make one phone call and let my boss know you're interfering with a —*federal*—investigation, and you're going to be opening up a whole Pandora's Box of trouble that you, trust me, don't want to deal with. Now, I'm going onto that crime scene, and if you have a problem with it, have your supervisor call mine and we'll see what happens, huh?"

Officer Dolan hesitates for another moment but then steps aside, his eyes narrowed and his jaw clenched. And this is exactly why relations between local PDs and the FBI are usually a bit strained. I don't like bigfooting my way onto a scene. I don't like flexing my federal muscles. I'd prefer it if we all got along, because in the grand scheme of things, we're all on the same team. We all want the same thing—to make the world safer.

But the reality of the situation is that there are always competing agendas. There are always those who put their own schemes and plots ahead of the job. People like Deputy Chief Torres who see solving crimes and taking down criminals as headline makers and tickets to a promotion, rather than as a sacred duty to protect the public from these evil beings. Not all of us are doing this job for the right reasons. And that goes not just for the local PDs but for the Bureau as well. There are rotten apples on every tree.

I have a job to do, though. One I hold as a sacred obligation, so I'm going to do it my way and do whatever I need to in order to get the job done and protect the people. Even if that means I have to force my way onto a crime scene now and again. I'm not going to let punks like Torres keep me from doing my job. So, hard feelings among the rank and file be damned. It is what it is; I make no apologies.

I open the door and step into Gina's office space and am immediately hit with the smell. Death, especially when there's a lot of blood involved, carries a particular odor. It's like a metallic tang. Kind of like the taste of having a penny in your mouth. However you describe it, the smell is never very pleasant.

The office floor plan is open, and with windows all around; plenty of natural light filters in, leaving the room looking fresh. There's a conference table with six seats around it on one side of the large room. There's also a sitting area with two pairs of large wingback chairs sitting on either side of an oval-shaped coffee table. The whole ensemble is set up on a circular rug that's splashed with a riot of color. And it looks as if there's a small kitchenette near the back of the space, and next to that, Gina's office.

I pull a pair of nitrile gloves out of my pocket and snap them on to avoid contaminating the scene. Once I'm gloved up, I walk back to the office and push the door open. Everything's covered in fingerprint dust, and some of the yellow evidence markers were left behind. I stand there for a moment, looking at the papers and other items scattered around the floor. Things on her desk have been knocked over, picture frames and coffee cups are shattered—and of course, the blood. There is so much blood. It's dried and a brownish-red color now, but it's unmistakable.

My eyes track the thick spray of it that cuts across the top of her desk in a sharp line, covering everything in its path. That's the arterial spray that would have jetted out of her severed carotid. There's a larger pool at the edge of her desk and an even larger pool on the floor behind her desk where she had fallen and then bled out. I stand back and take it all in, trying to put it all together in my mind. Trying to "see" the crime in my mind's eye.

She was killed after normal business hours. Between that and the fact that she didn't have any meetings scheduled that evening, it appears that she possibly knew her attacker. Gina seemed to me to be the type who was meticulous about her calendar. So her killer either dropped by unannounced or she was comfortable enough with him to let him into her office after she'd closed for the day. My theory isn't definitive, of course. It is just a theory. But it's a scenario I've seen play out about a million times, so it's experience that's informing my opinion.

I spend a little time poking around her office. Not that there's much left. The SPD did a pretty thorough sweep and anything of value has already been taken. The truth is, I don't even know what I'm doing here. I know I'm not going to find anything. Any potential clues have already been bagged and tagged. But even knowing I wouldn't find anything important, I still felt compelled to come.

Maybe on some deep level, I feel the need to punish myself. I can feel the familiar tendrils of guilt wrapping themselves around my heart, squeezing me so tight I can barely breathe. The deaths of Gina and Mr. Corden are both on me, and I feel the weight of that guilt on my shoulders. I've carried that weight every day since Mr. Corden's death, and it only got heavier after I learned Gina had been killed.

I've tried to lift that burden off me. I've tried to rationalize the guilt away a thousand different ways, telling myself that it's not my fault. That I didn't kill them. But no matter what I tell myself, or how many times I say it, my feeling of culpability never lets up. I hide it well enough that most days I can ignore it—or at least pretend that I don't feel it.

But in the quiet of the night, when it's just me and my thoughts, the self-reproach I sometimes feel is relentless. It's soul-crushing. No matter what I say or do, I cannot escape the certainty of my thoughts that if it hadn't been for this quest I'm on, neither of them would have been killed. And that point is really driven home as I stand here, among the blood and wreckage that marked the last moments of Gina Aoki's life.

"I'm so sorry, Gina. I never meant for this to happen," I whisper. "I never wanted you to get hurt."

As my eyes fall on the dark stain on the carpet once more—Gina's blood—my guilt and my grief are joined by my anger bubbling up from deep inside me. I feel dark. But I feel more determined than ever.

"I'm going to get him, Gina. I'm going to get the man who killed you," I say. "I promise you that I'm going to get justice for you. I swear it."

It's a promise I don't know that I can keep, but I'm damn sure going to try. She deserves justice every bit as much as my parents do. And I'm going to do everything in my power to see that she has it.

FOURTEEN

Criminal Data Analysis Unit; Seattle Field Office

"Rough night?" Astra asks as I step to the front of the bullpen.

"What makes you say that?"

"Because you look like twice-warmed-over roadkill," she replies.

"Hey, thanks for that. At least I know my self-esteem will never get too out of control with you around," I crack.

She grins. "What are friends for?"

"I'm beginning to wonder that myself," I reply.

She gives me a wide grin and blows me a kiss. The truth is, I didn't sleep much last night—for the last week or so, honestly—so I probably do look like twice-warmed-over roadkill. I feel like the bags under my eyes have become suitcases. Ever since I went to Gina Aoki's office to look around a few days back, sleep hasn't come easily. I can almost feel her presence hovering over me. Judging me. Waiting for me to figure out who killed her.

I'm sure it's only my guilt over her death weighing down on

me as it has from the start. But that burden is getting heavier by the day. On those long, sleepless nights, I've had some time to think and reflect on why her death seems to be hitting me on a more personal level than Mr. Corden's. And what I've realized is that although, yeah, I feel guilty about Mr. Corden's being murdered, he was coming to me. He contacted me out of the blue, wanting to set up a meet. That was his choice, and given what he knew and was trying to tell me, Mr. Corden was well aware of the risks involved with what he was doing. He accepted those risks.

Gina, on the other hand, is on me. She had a good idea of the danger, and she did everything she could to avoid the risks. But I dragged her into this. She would have been content to live out her days without ever seeing my face or hearing my name. But I badgered and guilted her into talking to me and she finally relented. Now she's dead. And try to rationalize it in as many different ways as I have, I can't. It's my fault Gina's dead. She'd lived for twenty years in peace, but one hour of talking to me and she ended up on a slab in the morgue.

I push all those thoughts to the back of my mind. I'm sure I'll have more than enough time for further self-recrimination tonight when I'm not sleeping again. I'm sluggish and want nothing more than to go home, crawl into bed, pull the covers over my head, and sleep for the next decade or so. Maybe when I wake up, things will have magically sorted themselves out. Or at least they'll start to make sense. Barring that, though, I'm going to need to push through both the mental and physical fatigue. There's work to be done and killers to catch.

"Okay, so where are we?" I ask. "Have we gotten any of the reports back from—well—anybody yet?"

"We got some preliminary findings from the King County ME," Mo announces. "And by preliminary, I mean the basics."

"Well, what do we have?"

"His estimated height and weight. Which is six-three, one hundred and eighty-five pounds, if you're interested," she replies. "They can't pin down an exact TOD but they're estimating he was in the barrel for at least a day."

I look at her, waiting for her to continue, but she doesn't. "That's it? That's all there is?"

She shrugs. "Aside from the crime scene photos, evidence list, and preliminary chronology, that's all they sent along. They're still waiting for results from the tox screen."

I pinch the bridge of my nose, trying to fight off the wave of irritation washing over me. Maybe this whole thing with my parents has seeing conspiracies where they don't exist, but I'm about positive we're being slow-walked by the ME's office. And if that's true, then the hand behind the slowdown has to be Torres. Something's going to be done about him sooner, rather than later. I just don't know what that is yet.

I turn to Astra. "Anything from Quantico?"

She beams at me. "I thought you'd never ask," she chirps. "I got the results back this morning and they were able to run the tox screen. He's one hundred percent clean. No alcohol, no drugs. Nothing."

I nod as I absorb the information. That he had nothing in his system is surprising to me and it puts a crack in the lens through which I've been viewing the case. From the start, I've assumed that drugs were involved with this whole thing—that they were the root of this man's murder. I try to remind myself that not all dealers use their own product. There are plenty of dealers who don't use at all. They're totally fine with poisoning other people but would never deign to poison themselves. For them, it's all about the money.

But as the thought crosses my mind, I have to admit that it feels wrong. It feels like trying to force myself into jeans that are four sizes too small—they just don't fit no matter how hard I try to wriggle and jam myself into them. There is no rational basis for that feeling. No logical reason for it. There is certainly no evidence that contradicts the idea that this was a drug deal gone bad or had drugs at the root of it—yet the thought has persisted.

Although, as I let all the information bounce around in my mind, I also have to admit that there is no rational basis or actual evidence that supports the idea that this has anything to do with drugs in the first place. There was nothing found on the body. Nothing at the scene. Nothing to indicate that this was drug-related other than the gang ink and my own personal bias. The only thing making me think this is drug-related is the fact that the victim is in a gang and slinging dope is usually their biggest—and most times, only—revenue stream.

"Did Quantico run the DNA?" I ask.

Astra nods, her smile still wide and a light of excitement in her eyes. "They did and there was no match in CODIS."

"Then why in the hell are you grinning like a kid on Christmas morning?"

"Because I'm already looking forward to the moment when you tell me just how utterly brilliant I am," she chimes.

"And why would I do that?"

"Because your girl here, in a stroke of genius and foresight, had the lab rats in Quantico run the DNA through the genealogical database as well as CODIS."

My eyes widen as I look at her. The only reason she's practically bouncing in her seat is that we got a match. Which means we're going to be able to ID our victim.

"Tell me," I say.

"We have a mitochondrial match," she says.

"You're kidding me," I reply, feeling a spark of hope ignite inside of me.

The use of genealogical databases to hunt down criminals

has been a controversial subject. Many argue it violates the Fourth Amendment against illegal search and seizure. In a case like the one that caught Joseph DeAngelo—the Golden State Killer or the original Night Stalker, depending on your preference—opponents of genealogical searches fought his arrest, saying he never consented to have his DNA taken, thus it was a violation of the Fourth Amendment. Proponents argue that there is no expectation of privacy in a genealogical database, and it isn't sacrosanct, like doctor-patient or clergy-penitent privileges are.

I tend to stay out of such debates, because that sort of thing is well above my paygrade. At heart, I'm a cop and I welcome any and all tools that will help us put bad guys away forever. Genealogical profiling has helped us do that, and until the use of those databases is ruled illegal by the Supreme Court, I'll keep using them. They can often lead to massive breaks in a case. Such as this one. So now, instead of being back at square one, we're jumping ahead on the board.

"No, ma'am, I'm most certainly not kidding you," she says. "The mother of our victim is named Grace Davis."

"Wow. Talk about burying the lede," Mo says dryly.

"Uh oh. Sounds like somebody's a little salty that I'm taking that gold star back from her," Astra teases.

"Don't worry, I'll get it back again soon," Mo fires back.

"And the result is conclusive?" I ask, bracing myself for disappointment.

"One hundred percent," she tells me.

"Grace Davis, age forty-one, unmarried, is the mother to Ben Davis, age twenty-five—her only child. She's a lifelong resident of Seattle and has worked as a CPA at a small firm for fifteen years," Rick calls from his station. "Ben Davis is a pre-med student at Washington State. Has a juvie record for vandalism and simple assault—both charged as misdemeanors."

I feel that spark inside of me begin to grow, filling my belly with the warmth of excitement I get when a case starts to build some momentum. Now that we have the name of our vic, we have a solid direction to run in, and the sluggishness that had gripped me earlier is being quickly melted away.

"This is good. Good stuff," I say. "Guys, do me a favor and put your other case on hold for a minute. I need you guys to do a deep dive on Ben Davis for me. I need to know everything there is to know about him. Also, send the DNA profile Astra got from Quantico over to the King County ME's office. We at least need to appear to play ball with them. And Rick, send the address for Grace Davis to my phone, please."

"You got it, boss," they chime almost in unison.

I turn to Astra and grin. "Gold star for you today. Excellent work," I say. "Let's go meet Grace Davis and see if we can figure out what's going on."

FIFTEEN

Davis Residence, Highland Park Neighborhood; Seattle, WA

"It occurred to me that Grace never filed a missing persons report. She may not even know her son was murdered," Astra notes as we get out of the car.

"Yeah, I had the same thought."

"So, how should we play this?"

"Carefully," I tell her. "And gently."

We walk across the street as I take a look around the neighborhood. Tall trees line the street, filling the gutters with clots of leaves. It's working-class for sure—neither rich nor poor. The cars in the driveways all look nice, but not too nice. Not a Mercedes or a Tesla to be found anywhere. The cars reflect the houses—functional without being fancy. The homes and the yards are all fairly clean and well-squared-away for the most part, but they're all simple.

This is the kind of blue-collar neighborhood where people come out and hold community cookouts in the street on the Fourth of July. The sort of neighborhood where people know their neighbors and look out for one another. This isn't like some of the socially and financially elite neighborhoods where that sort of familiarity with your neighbors is considered gauche, and the only interaction you have with them is during "social season"—meaning gatherings at art galleries, fund raisers, and the like. You'd never catch a neighborhood in Laurelhurst or Denny-Blaine hosting a cookout in the street. They'd consider it beneath them.

Like every other house on the street, the Davis home is nice, but not fancy. It's made of white clapboard and red brick, with dark green shutters and trim. Up close, it's easy to see that the house hasn't been painted in a good long while. There are cracks in places and the paint is peeling in others. The yard is in good order, though, with everything tidy and neatly trimmed. I suspect every other home in this neighborhood is a lot like the Davis home—nicer from a distance than up close. Home repair and upkeep is expensive. I doubt most of the people in this neighborhood have the financial flexibility to sink money into something like painting the whole house or updating their roofs.

We mount the three steps and walk across a wooden porch that's painted the same shade of green as the shutters and trim, but is faded and dull. Scratches and scuff marks crisscross the wood, adding to the impression of a home slowly falling into decay. I glance at Astra, then raise my hand and knock on the door. From deeper in the house, I hear footsteps, and a moment later, the door opens a little bit, and we find ourselves looking at our victim's mother.

"Grace Davis?" I ask.

"That's right," she replies. "And you are?"

We both badge her. "I'm Special Agent Russo," Astra says. "This is SSA Wilder. May we come in and talk for a moment?"

"What is this about?" she frowns.

"Please, Ms. Davis, I think it would be better if we discussed this inside," I say.

An expression of fear crosses her face, and she looks from me to Astra and back again. I try to give her a reassuring smile, but it has no effect. I'm sure it doesn't help that my smile probably looks as wooden as it feels, given the news we're about to drop on her. Despite her reservations, she purses her lips and straightens her spine, then opens the door to us. Astra and I murmur our thanks and step inside.

Grace Davis is a small woman. She's thin, standing five-four at the most. And yet despite that, she's got a presence about her that makes her seem larger somehow. Her skin is a rich sepia tone, and her eyes are like warm coffee. She's got a smattering of white in dark hair that's cut short, almost buzzed really, and there are soft lines around the corners of her eyes and mouth. She's only forty-one, but you can see that she's lived some life. Yet despite whatever trials she's gone through, she's endured and has a strength that radiates from her, maybe because of them. Probably because of them.

The interior of the house is a reflection of the woman herself. It's neat and orderly. There's the usual clutter that comes with a house that's well lived in, but everything has a place and everything's in that place. The décor is tasteful but somewhat conservative, and everything is done in soft earth tones. She has a few pieces of religious iconography—there's a crucifix on the wall just above the door and a small figurine of the Virgin Mary on the mantel above the fireplace. There is no television in the living room, but classical music is playing from a stereo that's tucked into the corner. The furniture doesn't all match, but everything looks comfortable. You can see that this is a family home.

Ms. Davis leads us to the living room and offers us a seat on the sofa, then sits down on the loveseat just perpendicular to it.

She folds her hands in her lap, nervously wringing them together as she faces us. The wall behind the loveseat where Grace sits is covered in photographs—mostly of her son, Ben. Same with the wall behind the sofa. There are pictures of him in a basketball uniform. High school graduation. Pictures of him from when he was a child to some more recent ones. It's obvious she takes great pride in him. Which makes the news I have to deliver even more heart-wrenching.

"Wh-what is this about?" she asks again. "Why is the FBI at my door?"

"Ms. Davis, we're here about your son, Ben," I start.

"What about him?" she asks with a tremor in her voice. "He's up at school. I know he didn't get into any trouble down here."

If only that were true. "Ms. Davis—"

"Please, call me Grace."

"Very well... Grace," I say. "I'm Blake and this is Astra."

I realize I'm stalling right now, but I've never been very good about death notifications. It doesn't help that Grace is already looking at me with wide eyes that are filled with fear. It's as though she already knows what I'm about to tell her and is praying that she's wrong.

"Ms. Da—Grace," I tell her. "I'm truly sorry to say that your son's body was discovered near the Green—"

I don't even fully get the words out when a keening wail shatters the air around us. It's a sound filled with the sharpest note of pain I've ever heard. Grace buries her face in her hands and howls in her agony. I shift on my seat and glance at Astra, who looks every bit as uncomfortable as I do. We remain as we are, though, letting Grace feel her emotions without interruption. I know exactly what it's like to feel the bitter sting of loss, and it tears my heart to pieces to see and hear this woman going through it.

It takes a little time, but she manages to pull herself together. As she does, I get up and run into the bathroom, quickly returning with a box of tissues. She accepts them with a murmur of thanks and pulls one out, drying her eyes and nose. The look of grief on the woman's face is piercing. It's haunting and I know I'll never forget it.

"A—are you sure it's my baby? Are you sure it's my Ben?" she asks.

"Unfortunately so, Grace," Astra says delicately. "We were able to match him to you through mitochondrial DNA. It's— conclusive. I'm so sorry."

Grace shakes her head and dabs at the fresh tears that are flowing down her face. She takes a couple of beats and looks at us. I can see her battling her emotions, but I can also see that strength I sensed earlier asserting itself. Her jaw is clenched and she's fighting to keep more tears from falling. I admire her grit and the control she has over her emotions. That's an attribute I wish I had sometimes.

"Where was he found?" she asks.

"He was pulled out of the Green River near Tukwila," I explain. "Do you know what he might have been doing down that way?"

She shakes her head again. "He was in Pullman. At school," she says with a slight quaver in her voice. "I didn't know he'd come back this way. He shouldn't have been. Not with classes still in session."

I get to my feet and go to the mantel, looking at the photo of Ben set there. He's in a purple and white basketball uniform, down on one knee, one arm resting on his leg, the other hand on top of the ball. He looks so young. So innocent. He was a baby-faced kid who, as the later pictures show, grew into a handsome man. In the picture I'm looking at, I can see the hope and optimism in his eyes and in his smile.

It's not hard to see that this was a kid who loved the game and had big plans for his future. It's a thought that brings Antoine Booker to mind again. They're like two sides of the same coin.

"My boy—he loved the game. It was his biggest passion in life," she says quietly. "He was already being scouted. Was invited to join an AAU team, and the college scouts were already thicker than ants on honey when he was playing in high school. They said he had what it took to make it to the next level."

I recall the scar on the side of his knee we found and just know that surgery altered the trajectory of his life. And it's potentially what ultimately ended it.

"What happened?" I ask. "I saw the scar on his knee. It was surgical."

She sniffs loudly. "He tore the ligaments in his knee during one of his games. It was bad. Doctors said even if he did play again—which they doubted—he'd never be the same kind of player. The injury would rob him of his explosiveness, they said," she tells us. "After that, the scouts stopped coming around and the scholarship offers dried up. Ben was lost without basketball. Adrift. He had no focus and felt he had no purpose. I told him that God had bigger plans for him, but he couldn't hear me."

"Is that when—is that when he joined the Eighth Street Kings?" Astra asks, a bit more indelicately than I'd hoped she would.

Grace looks at Astra as if she'd been expecting the question, and nods. "Yes. That's when he joined the gang and started to get into some trouble. Nothing major. He got caught spray painting on a wall, then was charged in a fight with another boy," she sighs. "He was just so angry. So hateful. He felt as if his entire reason for being was taken away from him when he hurt his knee, and he hated the world for it."

I've known people like that. I can sympathize with how he must have felt. I know when my family was taken from me, I felt something similar to that as well. But what I learned is that what matters is what you do next. How you channel all that energy and emotion you're feeling into something productive and positive. It's up to you to decide what it is you're going to do with all of that frustration and anger roiling around inside of you. It's up to you to take charge.

You have to decide whether you're going to let it lead you down a dark and dangerous path, where you're going to make horrible, life-altering decisions. Or if you're going to rebound and overcome it, find some way to make good decisions that will lead you down a path that will make your life better.

I've only known her for a few minutes, really, but I can tell that Grace would have provided him every resource available, and every ounce of support she could, to help guide him down that better path. But it's as she said, he couldn't hear her.

"But my baby came back to me. He saw what he was doing and saw a better way," she continues. "He got out of that gang and decided to do something good and useful with his life. He took some night classes down at the community, college then transferred to Washington State. He was studying to be an orthopedic surgeon. Wanted to be a sports doctor."

The pride she has in Ben drips from her every word. She cherished her son and truly believed in him. Believed in his better angels. But as the words fall from her lips, it's as if Grace realized he would never be that sports doctor he'd dreamed of being, and her heart shatters all over again. It's painful to watch her unraveling the way she is. The fact that she is trying so hard to hold it together speaks volumes about her strength.

"Who did this to him?" she asks. "Who murdered my baby?"

"We're still investigating, Grace. We only made his ID today, so we're having to start from the beginning," I tell her. "Do you know of anybody who might want to hurt him? Anybody with a grudge or anything like that?"

Grace shakes her head. "No, he was well-liked by everyone. Ben always had a way with people. They just loved him."

I can see she honestly believes that, but what parent doesn't think everybody loves her kid? Even one running the streets with a gang. That thought is derailed by another thought of Antoine Booker. The guy is charismatic. He has a strange sort of charm about him that's undeniable. And then I think of Fish, aka Huan Zhao, one of the underworld's crime bosses. All of them have a certain something about their personalities that makes you want to like them. It's like some magical aura, and once you're inside it, you can't help but see their charm. Maybe that's the way it was with Ben, too.

"How did he die?" she asks.

I clear my throat. "The ME hasn't made that determination yet. But I know they'll be in touch with you now that his identity has been established."

Astra glances at me. I feel like a jerk for punting on that question, but I really don't know how to tell Grace that her son was cut into a hundred pieces. She seems like a good woman and a good mother, and I hate to break her heart any more than it already is.

"Grace, did Ben ever mention having trouble with any of his former gang members?" Astra asks. "Anybody threatening him or anything like that?"

She shakes her head. "No. I mean, he had some issues with a couple of those—people—when he first got out. But that went away over time. Or at least, he stopped mentioning it to me."

"Did he ever give you names of these people he was having trouble with?" Astra presses.

"No. He never did," she says. "He said he wanted to keep me as far out of that trouble as he could. Told me it was over, and it didn't matter anymore, anyway."

"I'm sorry to have to ask, but what about his father?" Astra asks.

"He died in a car accident when Ben was still in diapers."

"I'm very sorry to hear that," Astra says.

This poor woman has endured so much pain and heartache in her life that it absolutely breaks my heart for her. Nobody should have to go through that. Astra looks at me and my eyes drift over her head to the pictures on the wall behind her. I think about the arc of his life—from budding basketball star to street gangster to pre-med student. And that's when the question pops into my mind.

"Grace, what prompted the change in him?" I ask.

"What do you mean?"

"What was it that made him get out of the gang and go to school?" I ask. "I mean, that's a pretty big and positive life change, so I'm wondering what the impetus was."

The ghost of a smile touches her lips. "He said he just wanted something better for his life. And for me," she says. "But I always suspected there was a girl involved."

"But he never told you about her?"

"No, he was always very private about his girlfriends," she tells us. "Said he'd never bring one around unless he knew she was the one. But when he decided to go back to school, he was happier. He had that smile I only saw when he was with somebody he really cared about."

We spend another half an hour or so with Grace, just getting some basic background information about Ben, then urge her to call somebody—a friend, relative, or somebody who could be with her. I tell her I know what she's going through and having somebody there helps. Even if only a little.

After that, Astra and I head out. We gleaned a lot of information, and I'm anxious to start putting all these puzzle pieces together. It feels as though the picture hidden in the stereogram is beginning to take shape.

And I'm desperate to see it.

SIXTEEN

Office of SAC Rosalinda Espinoza; Seattle Field Office

"Will you sit down and relax?" Rosie asks.

I was ambushed on my way into the shop this morning. Rosie sent me a text telling me to get to her office before I head into the CDAU. What she didn't say was that she had this piece of human filth in her office waiting for me. She probably knew I'd make an excuse and bug out. She's smart like that.

"I'm fine standing, thank you," I snap.

With my arms folded over my chest, I lean against the wall on the other side of the room, staying as far away from Deputy Chief Torres as I possibly can. Rosie is sitting behind her desk and sighs heavily, giving me a look of pure exasperation. But whether she's exasperated with me or him, I haven't the first clue. For his part, Torres is sitting casually in the chair in front of Rosie's desk, one leg crossed over the other, his hands folded in his lap, and an expression of patience on his face. But then he raises an eyebrow at Rosie, as if to emphasize to her just how petulant and unreasonable I'm being.

"The Deputy Chief has a couple of questions," Rosie says.

"And you couldn't just call?" I ask.

"And give you the chance to duck that call?" Torres replies smoothly. "I know how your mind works, Blake."

"That's SSA Wilder to you, Deputy Chief," I spit. "And no, you could live a hundred lifetimes and still never have an inkling of how my mind works."

"Blake," Rosie cautions me.

"Fine. What do you want today, Deputy Chief." I don't even give him the satisfaction of a question mark at the end of my sentence.

"You do realize you can just call me Chief, don't you? You don't have to be quite that formal with titles."

"I'm sure you'd like to be called Chief, but you're not quite there yet, are you, Deputy Chief?" I respond, hitting the word 'deputy' a little harder than necessary.

"Let's all settle down," Rosie cuts in.

She gives me a pointed look, silently telling me to cool it. I can't help but notice the fact that she's trying to stifle a grin, however. Torres undoubtedly notices it, too, because his expression quickly darkens. He turns to me with a light of pure malevolence gleaming in his eyes.

"I'm told you visited my crime scene," he starts. "I'm further told that you bullied your way past the officer on duty with your badge and threats of a federal investigation."

"I wasn't aware your officers were so thin-skinned," I respond. "Or so well versed in dramatics. But then, I suppose I should have expected that of those under your command."

Torres looks to Rosie, obviously expecting her to rebuke me. And when she doesn't, his mask of patience slips, then melts away completely, and he scowls at me. But then he takes a beat and quickly gathers himself. That mask clicks back on his face in record time, and he gives me an expression to show he's the most reasonable man in the world.

I glance at Rosie, who subtly rolls her eyes. She doesn't like his being here any more than I do, but unlike me, she at least has to pretend she's got an open door with local LEOs. Which means, she also needs me to play pretend with her. And not wanting her to get hit with any blowback, I vow to do my best to be civil.

"What is it you'd like to know, Deputy Chief?" I ask.

He still bristles at my use of the word 'deputy' in his title, but apparently decides it's not a hill worth dying on as he sits back in his chair again and adopts the air of a man perfectly at ease and relaxed. It's amazing how quickly he can go from reasonable man, to fire breathing demon, and back to reasonable man again. It's a skill I'm sure will serve him well if he runs for mayor after all. He just needs to learn how to keep that mask from slipping in public and save his fire breathing for people behind closed doors.

"What were you doing on my crime scene?" he asks.

"I visited the crime scene because I wanted to get a sense of it. I want to know what happened to her," I offer.

"And why is that, SSA Wilder?" he asks, grudgingly including my proper title.

"My reasons are personal and that's all you need to know," I reply.

"I'm afraid I'm going to need to know more than that," he says.

"Actually, you don't," I tell him. "I'm here as a courtesy. I don't have to speak to you about any of this."

Torres looks at Rosie and she shrugs. "SSA Wilder is correct, Deputy Chief. Unless you're charging her with something, she doesn't have to speak to you. She doesn't have to stand here and listen to you at all if she doesn't want to," Rosie says. "But she's here and you're free to ask whatever questions you like. Just know that she's free to take a pass on them. She's also free to contact a lawyer or union rep if she wishes."

I see Torres' jaw clench and know he's really struggling to keep his temper in check. And in the expression on his face, I can see he realizes he overplayed his hand. By forcing me into Rosie's office to question me, he now has to comport himself properly. He can't act the way he would if he had me alone. Can't threaten me. He'd expected that, being a woman in a position of power, Rosie would be on his side and force me to answer his questions. And the fact that she's not doing any such thing is infuriating him.

"So, you're alright with the agents under your command strong-arming their way onto a crime scene?" Torres spits. "Especially when that agent is a person of interest in an ongoing murder investigation?"

Rosie arches an eyebrow, and her face grows tight. She gives Torres a look bordering on open disdain but manages to pull herself back. But judging by the set of her jaw and the narrowing of her eyes, I can see that Rosie is done playing around with him.

"Oh, she's a person of interest? And why is that, Deputy Chief?" she asks. "Do you have something—anything—connecting her to the murder?"

He clears his throat and sits back in his chair. "We're still processing all of the evidence we've collected as we speak."

"So, the answer to that is no," Rosie states. "Do you have any reason to suspect that she is involved with Ms. Aoki's murder in any way?"

"We know that, according to her calendar, Ms. Aoki met with SSA Wilder the day she was murdered."

"Uh-huh. And according to her calendar, how many other people did Ms. Aoki meet with that day?"

Torres clears his throat and shifts in his seat. He clearly wasn't expecting to be put in the spotlight like this and is wholly unprepared for it. He's obviously expects people to always defer to him and never question his moves or motives. That's what happens when you're surrounded by yes-men twenty-four/seven.

"Deputy Chief? How many others did Ms. Aoki—"

"I heard your question," he snaps. "And her calendar lists about a dozen other meetings that day."

"And of that dozen or so, how many others have you brought in for questioning?"

Torres glowers at her, the hatred in his eyes palpable. "I'm not able to comment on the specifics of an ongoing investigation."

"That's what I thought," Rosie replies with an exaggerated shrug. "Listen, Deputy Chief Torres, I helped set this meeting up out of professional courtesy. But that professional courtesy isn't without its limits. Especially when it seems as if all you're trying to do is either smear or railroad a highly decorated, veteran FBI agent."

"That's not what's going on here," he protests. "And you should know better. You talk to everybody a victim saw or spoke with—"

"And you've talked to Blake. Twice now. And you've yet to bring anything to the table that implicates her in any way whatsoever," Rosie fires back. "All you have is this vendetta you've got against her. And I will be damned if I let this witch hunt continue."

"Witch hunt? With all due respect, SAC Espinoza, this is hardly a witch hunt. Or a vendetta," Torres replies smoothly.

"From where I sit, that's exactly what it is. Don't think that

I didn't hear about your little roadside stop and chat a little while back," Rosie drills him, her voice colder than ice.

Torres' eyes flick from Rosie to me, then back again. He's careful to keep his expression cool and neutral, but it's enough to tell me that he's enraged I had the audacity to mention it to my boss. As if I wasn't going to. That's the first rule of politics—cover your butt. If I learn nothing else from Torres—and I likely won't—that lesson was pure gold. And judging by the look on Rosie's face, she didn't miss it, either.

"Moving forward, if you have any further questions for SSA Wilder, you can speak to our legal team here in the field office. We have dozens of lawyers who would be more than happy to answer them, Deputy Chief," Rosie continues. "Also, I would suggest you stop your targeted harassment of SSA Wilder. No more surprise roadside stops. And if you so much as run into her in a coffee house, I would suggest you turn around and get your caffeine someplace else. Because if you don't, and you continue to badger her, don't think I won't be on the phone with the Attorney General of the United States in the blink of an eye. Do we understand each other?"

Torres stares at her balefully for a long moment, then gets to his feet. He never breaks eye contact with her as he buttons his coat.

"Am I clear, Deputy Chief?" she presses.

"Crystal," he replies, then turns and walks out of the office, slamming the door behind him.

Rosie blows out a long, irritated breath and leans back in her chair. I feel the tension in my body start to melt away, but then Rosie rounds on me.

"Don't think I don't have a few choice words for you too, Wilder. Stop antagonizing him," she growls. "Stay off his crime scenes and stay off his radar completely. He's looking for a reason to pin this murder on you. Don't give him one."

As much as I want to speak up and defend myself, I know that silence is probably the smartest way to go. She doesn't want to hear my justifications and rationalizations. She wants me to shut up, listen, and heed her words. Which I intend to do.

"The same goes for you—if you see Torres anywhere, you are not to engage. I don't even want to hear that you commented on the weather to him. Do you understand?" she demands.

"Yes, ma'am. Perfectly."

"Also, you know how much I hate giving you orders, but the Aoki murder is his case. It belongs to the SPD and we're not taking it," she goes on. "You're to stay away from it. No looking into the files. No visiting the crime scenes. Nothing. You are not to go within a country mile of anything Gina Aoki-related. Am I clear?"

"Yes, ma'am."

She looks at me for a moment then nods. "Okay. Good. Now, go get to work. You have a killer to catch."

"On my way," I say.

I head for the door, but she stops me. I turn back to her and see concern etched into her features.

"Keep your head on a swivel out there," she says. "That man is on a crusade, and he's not going to stop until one of you is unemployed, in prison, or dead. Just….be careful."

"Yes, ma'am."

I walk out of her office, heading for the shop as her words continue echoing through my mind. He's not going to stop until one of us is unemployed, in prison, or dead. I'd love to be able to say that she's overreacting or being a little melodramatic about the whole thing. I'd love to be able to say that Torres is a jerk, but this will all just fade away and he'll lose interest in me when he finds his next crusade.

But the truth is, she's right. We're headed down a dark path, and if he doesn't think he can make the case and pin Gina Aoki's murder on me, then I wouldn't put it past him to try something different to take me down—or take me out completely.

Keep my head on a swivel, indeed.

SEVENTEEN

Criminal Data Analysis Unit; Seattle Field Office

"What was that all about?" Astra asks.

"What was what all about?"

She arches an eyebrow at me. "I saw you heading into Rosie's office," she replies. "What did you do?"

I laugh. "What makes you think I did anything?"

"Because Rosie doesn't call you into her office unless she's about to take a bite out of your backside," she cracks.

"Now, I'd pay to watch that," Rick calls over.

"Rick, do I need to send you to the sexual harassment seminars again?" I ask.

"No ma'am," he shakes his head. "I'm pretty confident in my abilities to properly sexually harass anybody. I don't need a seminar to teach me."

Astra and I burst into laughter. That was about the last thing I expected to hear come out of his mouth. But maybe it shouldn't have been. His ability to avoid taking anything seriously and instead come out with something snarky is about on par with Astra's.

"Funny," I say. "That's funny."

"So what was it Rosie wanted?" Astra asks again.

"Torres came in. He wanted a sit-down," I explain.

"Yeah? And how'd that go?"

"Let's just say Rosie might have taken a nibble of my backside, but she took a whole chunk out of Torres'. It was a thing of beauty to behold," I say.

"That's our girl," Astra crows. "But to be honest, I'm getting a little bit worried about Torres. The guy has a special kind of hate for you. I would've thought he'd have let this whole thing go by now."

"Yeah, that makes two of us," I tell her. "And yet, here we are."

"Well, just make sure to watch your back."

"Plan on it," I respond. "And thanks."

"Of course."

I clear my throat and look around, having been so preoccupied that I'm only just now realizing for the first time that we're a man down.

"Where's Mo?" I frown.

"Bremerton," Rick says. "Said she was going to follow up on some of the doctors she thought were overprescribing opioids in the city. Said you told her it was alright."

I nod. "That's right. I forgot," I tell him. "Thanks for that."

I like to see Mo taking a little more initiative like that. She identified a case and has been doing all the legwork on it. I can see her confidence building up a little more every day, and I think that's a good thing. She's smart and competent. Has solid instincts. She's an effective agent. But stuck behind a desk up in White Collar, she never got a chance to show what she could bring to the table. Nor did she get a chance to show her skills in the field. I like what I'm seeing from her now that she's getting a little more self-assured in her work.

"So what's on our agenda for the day, boss?" Astra asks.

"You and I are going to have some fun."

"Yeah?"

"Mmm-hmmm," I nod. "We're going to go talk to some of the Kings."

"As I've said a thousand times, you certainly know how to show a girl a good time."

"I thought you'd enjoy this."

Astra smirks at me. "Well, it could definitely be fun. I haven't beaten anybody senseless in a while. I'm a little rusty, but I think I can manage."

"Don't forget to limber up first," I reply. "You're not as young as you used to be."

"Hey now, Benjamin keeps me plenty young," she says. "And flexible."

"Oh, my God, I so didn't need to hear that," I gasp and then giggle.

"I'm not opposed to hearing a little more," Rick calls out. "Please continue."

"You're such a pig," Astra calls to him.

"Oink oink," he fires right back.

I shake my head. "Rick, can you tap into OC's database and pull up on what they have on the Eighth Street Kings? I want a leadership tree, known hangouts—the works."

"We going in with SWAT at our backs?" Astra asks.

"Not yet. I'd rather not call them in unless it becomes necessary," I tell her. "I'm planning to just go in, have a conversation. I think having a contingent of armed men behind us might put a damper on that chat. Get it started off on the wrong foot, you know?"

Astra scoffs. "Yeah, well, usually it turns out that what you plan on happening ends up bearing very little resemblance to what actually happens," she says. "Ever notice that?"

"I have, actually. Damnedest thing, isn't it?"

She grins at me and shakes her head. On the wall-mounted monitors at the front of the bullpen, pictures and charts start going up. I look at them, trying to memorize the gang members' faces.

"The guy running the Kings right now is Eric Demone. Otherwise just known as Demon," Rick reads from his screen. "Mr. Demone is forty-three years old and has done bids for aggravated assault, attempted murder, and rape. He was also suspected of a home invasion triple homicide, but the case fell apart when two key eyewitnesses turned up dead—also something they could never pin on him. Collectively, he's spent twenty of his forty-three years on this planet in prison."

"He seems nice," Astra comments.

The man on the screen looks hardened. Tough. His skin is a dark umber, his eyes are the color of coffee, but they're dull and lifeless, and he seems to have a permanent sneer on his face. A scar runs from his right temple down to the middle of his cheek, and he's got a full, James Harden-style beard.

"His right-hand man is Mack Robinson. He's either a Marvel or Wesley Snipes fan because he goes by the name of Blade. He's thirty-eight years old and did ten years for manslaughter. He was also suspected in that triple homicide, and according to reports, is almost assuredly the one who offed the two witnesses against Demone," Rick announces. "He's the Johnny Ringo to Demone's Curly Bill Brosius. And on paper, he appears to be a lot smarter than his boss. Probably won't be long before Ringo there is running the Kings."

Mack is smooth-skinned and clean-cut. His skin is a warm russet color and he's got milk chocolate-colored eyes. The smile on his face in his mugshot is disarming. It's confident and warm, yet still kind of boyish. You definitely wouldn't think a vicious killer is hiding behind it. Robinson looks far younger than thirty-eight and doesn't have that hardened look about him that Demone does. The ten years inside didn't seem to age him the way it does most people.

"Or it could be that if he's a lot smarter than Demone, he just enjoys being the power behind the throne," I note. "Some people prefer being Machiavelli, operating behind the scenes and in the shadows."

"If I were in Blade's shoes, I'd definitely prefer being Machiavelli. Demone is going to take all the slings and arrows. He'll be the first guy others shoot at," Astra adds. "Meanwhile, he's still reaping the rewards of leadership, I'm sure. If he's Johnny Ringo and is that much smarter, he's no doubt manipulating Demone and getting whatever he wants."

"Either way, be careful, guys," Rick says. "Something tells me that they won't exactly just broadcast whichever theory is true to a couple of FBI agents."

"So those are our dates for the day, huh?" Astra asks.

"Sure are. You ready for this?"

"I'm always ready," she says with a snort.

"Alright, then," I nod. "Rick, do me a favor and send their usual haunts and addresses to my phone, if you would, please."

"You got it, boss."

Astra and I head out for our date with a couple of killers. All the while, I feel an itch between my shoulder blades. The hair on the back of my neck is standing on end. And I can't escape the feeling that I'm being watched. My first thought is that Torres has somebody surveilling me. And the thought that follows that one is that Torres has hired somebody to murder me.

Clearly, I'm going to need to find a way to keep my head on a constant swivel.

EIGHTEEN

Splits & Strikes Bowling Alley, Beacon Hill District;
Seattle, WA

THE MOMENT we step through the door and walk into the bowling alley, I feel the eyes on us. And the deeper we go, the more intense that feeling gets. We obviously don't belong here and stand out like a pair of sore thumbs. All around us, I see people casting furtive glances our way, while others are just staring openly. We draw so much attention that even the sounds of balls rolling down the alleys and the crash of the pins is absent.

"I suddenly know how Custer must have felt," Astra whispers.

I stifle my laugh as we walk through the alley. It only takes us a minute to spot Demone and Blade. They're posted up at a table just outside the bowling alley bar, watching us as we approach. And as we get close to them, two men who look like they should be playing middle linebackers in the NFL step between us and our quarry.

I look up at the man in front of me—and as he's close to six-five or six-six, I do have to look up—and give him my best smile.

"How are we today, gentlemen?" I ask.

He grins, showing off a freshly jeweled grill over his teeth, but doesn't say a word. He's dressed in white tennis shoes, black pants, and a black t-shirt that's stretched to the limit over his muscles, one wrong flex away from bursting into atoms. The black skull cap on his head completes the outfit. The man standing next to him, dressed almost exactly the same way, could easily pass for his twin.

"I like the way your grill matches your chain," I say, pointing to the thick gold rope around his neck. "They really bring out your eyes."

The man in front of me turns to his partner and chuckles. "She got jokes."

His partner turns to me, completely stone-faced and unamused. There's a glint of malice in his eyes that sends a cold shiver down my spine, and for the first time, I wonder if coming here was the right thing to do. We're outnumbered—and I have no doubt, completely outgunned. I cast a glance over at Astra and see that she's got an amused twinkle in her eye, which I totally don't get. But she's got a smile curling the corners of her mouth upward.

The man in front of me turns his eyes back to mine. "You two don't belong here," he says. "You'd best get steppin'."

"Trey," comes a deep, raspy voice behind him. "Show these two officers some respect and get out the way."

The two men hesitate for a moment, then grudgingly step aside. They retake their positions on stools that flank the table with Demone and Blade—who I keep thinking of as Ringo. Demone is dressed in a black track suit with red stripes down the sides of his legs and arms and sneakers that are blindingly white—sneakers that no doubt cost a small fortune. Blade is in black jeans and a red and black checkered button-down, long-sleeved shirt. The shirt is buttoned up to his neck, the sleeves are all the way down, and he, too, has white sneakers I'm sure cost almost as much as the one pair of Louboutins I splurged on a few years back.

Demone snaps his fingers and points to us. Trey gets off his stool and fetches us a couple of chairs. When he sets them down, he returns to his stool and stares at us with about as much emotion in his face as the Sphinx.

"I've never seen a mountain move before," I start. "That was interesting."

Demone chuckles and looks over at Trey. "You're right. She got jokes."

Trey grunts, making a sound like two boulders rubbing together, but doesn't say a word. Demone turns back to us and smiles warmly.

"Can I offer you ladies a drink?" he asks, the tone of his voice just skirting the edge between respect and derision. "The bartender here can make you a mai tai? Or maybe a cranberry sour, if you prefer?"

"Shot of Bushmills. Neat, please," Astra replies.

I have to keep myself from turning to her or betraying any emotion on my face. I know she's trying to establish a little credibility with them. If we've got credibility, they're more likely to trust us. If they trust us, they're more likely to talk to us. And since we have nothing tying them to Ben's murder, we're going to need them to talk to us if we hope to make the case.

"Make it two," I add.

Demone gives us a small nod of respect. It's a little thing that's stupid, really. But showing that we're not the types who'd drink a mai tai—though I do love one every now and then—earns a mark of credibility. For some reason, these guys are more apt to trust somebody who can drink like they do, rather than drink something that comes with an umbrella in it. I don't know why. It's never made all that much sense to me. I imagine it's some macho, alpha-male bullcrap. But if you work the streets long enough, you get to know these little cheat codes.

Trey's clone disappears through the door and into the bar. While he's gone, none of us says a word. We just sit at the table staring at each other as if in some silent battle of wills. It's all part of the ritual—and I've learned that when you're in enemy territory, it's always best to observe the rituals if you want to make it out with your skin intact. I cast a glance over at Blade, who's said nothing this whole time. All he's doing is sitting back, arms folded over his chest, watching us. I can tell he's trying to visually dissect us, and I get the impression this is a man who does not miss much. He hasn't said a thing, but I already know he's sharper than a—well—blade.

The man comes back with a tray that's got fresh drinks for everybody. He sets the glasses of Bushmills down in front of Astra and me, then the other pair in front of Demone and Blade. We all reach for them at the same time and raise our shot glasses. No words are spoken, but we all quaff the Irish whiskey in one swallow and set our glasses back down. I grimace as the amber liquid burns its way down my throat, settling into my stomach and sending tendrils of heat through my entire body. Yeah, I'm not much of a drinker.

But the ritual is done. We've all now broken bread together—figuratively, of course—and have established some sort of rapport. Now, the real conversation can begin.

"I didn't figure that you'd be running your empire from a bowling alley," I start.

Demone shrugs. "I like bowling. It's a great American pastime."

"It was first developed in Egypt," Astra corrects him. "Like five thousand years ago."

"Well, like so many other things we value in this country, we appropriated it, repackaged it, made it our own, then took credit for it," Blade speaks up for the first time, drawing a forced laugh from Demone, who clearly had no idea of the history of the game.

Blade's eyes are sparkling with amusement and his voice is rich and buttery smooth. It's almost hypnotic. He could easily be a DJ on one of the jazz stations I listen to. Also, I can't really argue with his point, as it's pretty much spot-on.

"Well, it don't matter how it got here, anyway. It's here now," Demone shrugs. "But the question is, what can we do for you, Officers?"

"It's actually Agents," I say as we badge them. "SSA Wilder, Special Agent Russo from the Seattle Field Office."

"Oh, we must be movin' up into the big time if we got the feebs up in here now," Demone chuckles, nudging Blade with his elbow. "My bad. What can we do for y'all—*Agents*."

"We found one of your—associates—recently," I tell them. "Ben Davis. He was stuffed into a barrel and sent down the Green River. He was in pretty rough shape—"

"In pieces, actually," Astra jumps in. "Lots of little pieces. And I'm not being figurative."

"Right. And we were curious what you might know about that," I finish. "We saw his ink and know he was part of your organization. Or at least, he was at one time."

Demone looks over at Blade, and I can see some silent bit of communication pass between them. I don't know what it is precisely, but it looks to me as if both of them were taken aback. My gut tells me they have no idea what I'm talking about.

"What do you mean, 'in pieces'?" Demone frowns.

"Dismembered," Astra explains. "Literally taken apart piece by piece, then stuffed in a barrel and sent down the river."

"Are you both being serious right now?" Blade asks.

I nod. "We are."

"Damn," Demone mutters, then looks up at us, his eyes hard. "Who did it?"

Astra and I fall silent for a moment and exchange a look. Blade obviously doesn't miss it, because he stares at us. The frost coming off his glare could freeze the entire city solid.

"They think we did it," he announces.

Demone looks from Blade to us, his entire body tensing and his eyes narrowing. "That right? You think we killed Benny?"

"We're not making any assumptions about anything just yet," I say diplomatically. "Right now, we're gathering information. It's just part of the investigative process."

"But it wouldn't be the first time somebody was killed for leaving an—organization—such as yours," Astra adds, less than diplomatically.

And just like that, the air between us grows cold and crackles with tension. Demone and Blade stare at us hard, as if they find the mere suggestion they were involved in somebody's death offensive.

"We're just asking questions right now," I tell them, trying to cool the tempers before they get out of control. "We really aren't making assumptions. I prefer to make my cases based on facts. And the truth is, Agent Russo is right—people looking to get out of a gang haven't always made it out successfully."

Blade stares at me for another moment, but then his expression softens. "Nah. It wasn't like that. Benny was a good kid. We'd never do him like that," he says, then with a smirk adds, "I assume everything we say right here is off the record, since you're just fact findin'. Right?"

"We're completely off the record," I nod. "I give you my word. Nothing said here will come back on you."

Astra cuts a glance at me and I shake my head. It's probably dumb to make that sort of guarantee when you're dealing with career criminals, but I'm fairly certain that they aren't going to say anything too incriminating. I'm also fairly certain they had nothing to do with the death of Ben Davis. When they speak of him, I can see a genuine sense of affection in their eyes. It's as Grace said—he apparently just had a way with people to make them love him.

"I knew he wasn't gonna be a King for life when he first joined up," Demone tells us. "Always had one foot in, one foot out. And in this life, you can't straddle that line. You gotta commit one hundred percent."

"So why did you let him join the first place?" I ask.

"Some kids gotta see what this life is like to know it ain't for them," Demone goes on. "I wanted to give him a taste of the life to convince him he needed to go do somethin' with his life. Somethin' good to help provide for his mom."

"Family's all we got in this world. Some dudes join us because they need family," Blade adds. "Benny had a family. His mom is a good woman, and Benny needed to do right by her."

I stare at the two men before me, unable to keep the surprise from my face. Granted, my interaction with street gangs is limited, but this isn't what I was expecting. My understanding was always that once you're in a gang, you're in it for life. That they don't tolerate disloyalty, and trying to get out is a death sentence.

I'm not saying Demone and Blade are good guys. One look at their jackets says they're about the furthest thing from good guys that you can get. They're murderers. Rapists. They peddle drugs and push that poison onto children. These are not good men. And yet, they've got an unexpectedly soft side. They take care of their own. They look after them and try to steer them onto the right path.

It's not something I would have ever expected from these guys—that they'd try to protect Ben like that. But even more than that, I'm blown away by the fact that they put such a high value on family, given how little value they put on human life as a whole.

"You look surprised," Blade observes.

I shrug. "Honestly, I suppose I am."

"Like folks say, don't ever judge a book by its cover."

"So, this wasn't a drug deal gone wrong? This wasn't one of your boys looking for a little payback for something Ben did?" Astra asks.

I watch them closely, looking into their eyes, as they both shake their heads. Their reaction seems genuine, and they honestly seem upset about the fact that Ben is dead. I don't think these guys are good enough actors to fake that.

"No, it wasn't us," Demone says. "But I guarantee you if we find out who did it, they're gonna end up in a barrel."

"Yeah, not the smartest thing to say to a couple of Feds, Demone," I say.

Blade grins. "You said we're completely off the record here."

I laugh despite myself. If I'm being completely honest here, there's a small piece of me buried deep down inside that wouldn't mind if the Kings got to Ben's killers before we did. I'll never openly advocate street justice, but I can't say that once in a while it doesn't feel a little satisfying.

"Alright," I say as I get to my feet. "Thanks for the chat, fellas. I appreciate your candor."

"My what?" Demone asks.

Blade chuckles and shakes his head. "You coming in here....that took some real stones, ladies. Respect," he says. "And don't forget, when you deal straight with us, we'll deal straight with you. You have my word."

"I'll remember that," I nod.

Astra stands and together we head out. The glares I felt when we walked in here are still present, but they don't feel quite as hostile as they did before. I won't say they're friendly. I'm not getting warm fuzzies or anything. But I suppose with Blade's and Demone's tacit endorsement, they don't feel compelled to murder us on sight. Which is good.

"You buy it?" Astra asks. "That they had nothing to do with Ben's death?"

I nod. "Yeah. Actually, I do," I shrug. "I think they were telling us the truth."

"Strangest damn thing, but I do, too. Turns out people really do contain multitudes," she responds. "Of course, that puts us back at square one again."

"Not completely square one," I correct her. "Which reminds me, we're headed to Pullman in the morning. Pack an overnight bag."

"Pullman? Can't we go to Cabo?"

"Sure," I shrug. "If the killer leads us down there."

"You're no fun."

"No, I just don't want to have to deal with all the travel paperwork," I say and flash her a grin. "Our flight's at eight."

"You better bring coffee," she tells me. "Lots of coffee."

NINETEEN

Emmanuel's French Bistro; Downtown Seattle

"Sorry I'm late," I say as I slip into the booth.

"That's alright, dear. We're used to it," my Aunt Annie says.

Maisey elbows her mother and murmurs something to her. Annie looks up from her menu with a confused expression, as if she doesn't realize what she's just said. And she probably doesn't. She's so conditioned to throwing out bits of snark and backhanded jabs that she does it without thinking about it anymore. I learned to tune it out a long time ago.

"I'm sorry, Blake," Annie offers. "I didn't mean that to sound so—snarky."

I give her a smile. "It's fine, Annie. I deserved it for being late."

Annie reaches across the table and takes my hand, giving it a gentle squeeze. Ever since we had our little—tiff—and then talked things out, Annie has been really trying to be better. To not be so judgmental and more accepting of the choices both

Maisey and I make. The best thing to come out of this is that for the first time in her life, Maisey is feeling both heard and supported. Annie has even started getting to know Maisey's boyfriend, Marco. I'm glad that my cousin no longer has to hide her relationship from her mother.

For my part, I'm doing better about making time for Annie and Maisey. Carving out time to have dinner or just hang out with them. And I have to admit, it's been nice. It's not always easy and there have been plenty of bumps along the way—and there will likely be more—but things are better than they used to be. For the most part.

"So, what kept you so late tonight?" Maisey asks, a maniacal gleam in her eye. "Chasing down a serial killer?"

Maisey has always been a fan of true crime. She eats it up, reading every book and watching every documentary. It's a fascination I don't think Annie is ever going to share or understand, but at least she's not giving Maisey as much grief about it as she used to.

I laugh. "Serial killers are a very small part of our case load," I tell her. "Most of the cases we handle are boring, garden-variety crimes."

"What kind of crimes could ever be considered garden variety?" Annie gasps.

"Rape. Fraud. Drugs," I say. "We chase down—"

"That was rhetorical, dear," Annie rolls her eyes.

"Oh. Right. Sorry," I say with a chuckle.

"So, what were you doing tonight then?" Maisey presses.

"Astra and I had to meet with a couple of gangsters we thought killed a man—"

"Oh, that sounds exciting!" Maisey squeals.

"Do we have to do this at the table, girls?" Annie interrupts.

"Your drinks, ladies," the waitress says as she arrives at the table.

"I took the liberty of ordering a drink for you," Annie says with a smile.

I'm about to thank her, but freeze with my mouth hanging open for a moment as the waitress sets a glass of red wine down in front of me. My stomach churns as I look at the red liquid. My mind flashes back to when I was just a kid and walked in on the bodies of my parents lying in a thick pool of red, congealing blood. Ever since that day, I've sworn off the color red. I won't wear it, eat or drink anything of the color, or have it in my home. I know it's irrational; it's a ridiculous emotional response to trauma. But I can't help it. It's something I've not yet been able to overcome.

"Oh, God. Blake, I'm sorry," Maisey says then turns to the waitress. "Can you please take this away? Blake, what do you want to drink?"

"Just an iced tea, please," I reply.

The waitress scoops up the glass of wine and gives me a patient smile before turning and walking away. Annie looks at me strangely for a minute and then the realization seems to dawn on her.

"I'm sorry, Blake. I wasn't thinking," she frowns. "I didn't realize you were still having—issues—with the color red."

I grit my teeth and try to stuff down the annoyance that flashes through me. "That's certainly one way to put it, I suppose."

"Well, how would you put it?" Annie asks.

"I wouldn't put it any way," I tell her. "It's —complicated."

The tension in the air is growing thicker and I'm just barely hanging onto the thin threads that are controlling my temper. I don't want to have a blowout with my aunt here—I don't want to have a blowout with my aunt at all. But sometimes it seems as if she makes no effort to understand my problems, acting as if

I can just wish them away. That's not how it works. No matter how much she thinks it should.

The waitress arrives again and drops off my tea, defusing the moment. "Are you ready to order?" she asks brightly.

"Yeah, but start with them, please," I say.

As they place their order with her, I snap up the menu and take a quick look through it. I settle on the chicken cordon bleu simply for expediency's sake, which seems to offend Annie's delicate sensibilities, and I groan to myself. We seem to be stuck in that place where nothing I do can please her. I take a couple of beats to tamp down my irritation. I'd rather not spend the night fighting. I want to enjoy the evening out, but she doesn't make it easy to do.

"So, how are things at work, Annie?" I ask, trying to take a different tack.

"The same. Nothing ever changes much there, really," she shrugs. "But I suppose it's better than chasing gang members and getting shot at."

I'm about to open my mouth to deliver a scathing reply, only to see the corners of Annie's mouth curling upward. That was her idea of a joke and a way to call a truce between us—which I'm all for.

"Maisey and Marco are going on a vacation," Annie announces.

Her smile wavers and I can tell she's trying to be alright with it. But at least she's not entirely shutting Maisey down out of hand and is trying to be open to the idea. That marks a big shift in the relationship between them. Six months ago, Annie would have forbidden it and Maisey would have gone along with what she wanted. Seeing this turnaround in their relationship makes me stupidly happy.

"Well? Where are you two going?" I ask.

"We're going to Jamaica," Maisey announces, absolutely beaming.

"That sounds amazing," I reply. "I'm so happy for you, Maisey."

Annie reaches over and takes Maisey's hand, giving her a gentle smile. Maisey looks back at her mother with an expression of pure happiness on her face—something I've seen all too infrequently in her life.

"I'm happy for you too, dear," Annie says. "Marco is a good man."

My jaw practically hits the table, and I find myself gaping at my aunt. I can't believe she's come this far in such a short amount of time. And it makes my heart swell with joy. The fact that Annie is trying so hard to change her behavior and be somebody different than she's been for so many years—somebody her daughter needs—is amazing. I couldn't possibly be happier.

Sure, I may have my gripes with her, but I know she's trying. Maybe I've been too harsh on her myself. Despite the fact that she's a second mother to me, this is all uncharted territory. There will probably be road bumps on the way—but as long as Annie is willing to try, I will, too.

Our meals arrive and any tension that had been lingering evaporates. The conversation is light and fun with lots of laughter, and I can honestly say I haven't enjoyed a night out with my aunt and cousin more in a very long time. And as I think about how much my aunt has handled her own issues and has changed as a result of it, I start to wonder if I can do the same. I start to wonder if I can handle my own issues with as much ease and aplomb as my aunt.

After clearing all the dinner plates, the waitress comes back to take our dessert order, and I look at the photo in the menu of the strawberry crepes. I look at the red glaze and sliced strawberries, red and plump on the plate, covering the crepes, trying to work up the nerve to order them. To conquer my own fears and issues with something as simple as ordering a dessert.

But as I sit here, looking at the menu, I see the dull, lifeless eyes of my parents. I see their pale, waxy skin and the wide pool of thick, viscous blood all around them. In my mind's eye, I can see that ocean of red, so sharp and vivid. I can't do it. My courage flees and I know it's still a bridge too far right now.

"I'll take the flourless chocolate cake with the chocolate ganache, please," I tell the waitress and close the menu, feeling disappointed in myself.

TWENTY

Registrar and Records Office, Washington State University; Pullman, WA

"Can you give us his class schedule, please?" Astra asks.

The woman behind the counter eyes our badges with wide eyes and a look of concern on her face. She's probably a fresh graduate in her mid-twenties, with long blonde hair and a bookish air about her. She's also obviously not used to dealing with law enforcement. The woman licks her lips nervously and glances around, perhaps hoping somebody will come save her from us.

"I'm not sure if I can give out that information," she says.

"Fine. Then get us somebody who can," Astra replies.

"My boss isn't coming in today," she tells us.

I slap my forehead and try to keep myself in check. We've been standing here for ten minutes dickering with this woman about whether or not she can give us a class schedule. I hate getting the run-around, and my last nerve is stretched way too thin.

"We're not asking for the nuclear codes or state secrets," I tell her. "We just need Ben Davis' course schedule. I'm pretty sure that's something you can give us. There isn't a law or a school policy that says you can't give that to federal agents."

"Look, I just got this job and I really need it. I'm not trying to get myself fired," she says. "I was told we don't give out personal information."

"Listen—Jackie," I start, after clocking her nametag. "You're not giving out personal information. It's a class schedule. We're conducting a murder investigation, and right now, you're interfering with it. So, unless you want to get hit with obstruction of justice charges and spend a couple of years in prison for it, go and get us the damn schedule."

Her eyes grow wide as I speak, and when I'm finished, she turns and hustles away with the promise of getting the information we're asking for. Astra turns to me and grins.

"Pretty good. I always knew you had the heart of a BS artist in you," she chuckles. "Obstruction charges. That's pretty good."

"Got the ball rolling."

"That it did."

A moment later, Jackie comes back to us with a sheet of paper that's still warm, obviously fresh out of the printer, and thrusts it at us.

"Thank you," I say as I snatch the paper out of her hand.

The girl fires off about a thousand questions, but Astra and I turn and walk out of the registrar's office, ignoring her completely. I scan Ben's list of classes, and aside from a couple of general ed courses, most of his time was spent in the biology department and science building in general.

"What do you think?" Astra asks. "Where should we start?"

I tuck a strand of hair behind my ear and frown as I think

about it for a minute. That the drug-and-gang angle didn't pan out was a bit of a blow. It was a definite setback. I'd been so sure that's where this was all headed. And that's not to say another street gang in Seattle didn't murder Ben. It's an avenue of investigation I'll keep open. Yes, I'm fairly certain the Kings and the Playboys didn't do it, but there's still the possibility that another gang murdered Ben to either send a message or make a name for themselves.

But we really are back at square one again. The only difference is that now we know Ben's name and his story. We can open new lines of investigation, which is helpful. The wider you cast a net, the quicker you can usually haul in the truth. Usually. There's a sinking feeling in the back of my mind telling me that this case isn't going to be easy or straightforward. I just have a feeling we're in for a bumpy ride.

"I guess we head over to bio department over in Macpherson Hall," I shrug. "Might as well start with the basics."

"Fair enough."

We head out and try to find our way across the large, sprawling campus. All around us is the hustle and bustle of students busy dashing to and from class. Here and there we can see small groups sitting over in the green areas or at picnic tables. I get that familiar buzz I always feel whenever I'm on a campus. There is just a special energy on college campuses you don't find most anywhere else. I think of it as a vibrant optimism. All these kids are so looking forward to their futures and achieving their dreams, it creates a physical energy you can feel. Or at least I can. But then, maybe that's because I loved my college experience, and the time I spent on a campus a lot like this one.

We have to stop half a dozen times and ask students for directions, and after about half an hour of walking, we finally find it. Like the rest of the buildings on campus, it's large, and made of red brick with large windows bordered by white trim. I won't say Washington State is the most beautiful campus I've ever been on, but it has a certain charm to it, I suppose. It's a very colorful campus with trees and green spaces everywhere, somehow making the red brick buildings seem more vibrant. I imagine in the fall this place is something to see.

We make our way to the fourth floor, where we find the office of Dr. Henry Avila—he taught one of Ben's human anatomy courses. The door is partially open and so I knock on it.

"Come in, the door's open," he calls out.

I push the door open and let Astra step in before me. I follow and close the door behind me, then turn to find Dr. Avila seated behind a large, ornately carved desk made of some dark wood I can't identify. A pair of matching bookcases flanks Dr. Avila on the wall behind him, and in between is a plethora of degrees and awards he's garnered. He's obviously very proud of his education and achievements.

He gets up, a frown upon his lips as he looks at us. Dr. Avila is about five-seven, with a slight build and thick, dark hair that's graying at the temples, along with a neatly trimmed beard. He has a tawny complexion and hazel eyes behind round, frameless spectacles that seem to lend him a scholarly air . As we introduce ourselves, he shakes our hands, his touch light and delicate, rather than giving us a firm grip. It makes me notice how long and smooth his fingers are. A surgeon's hands, I seem to remember their being called.

"Please, have a seat," he gestures to his chairs.

"Thank you," we both reply as we take our seats in front of his desk.

Dr. Avila leans forward, his hands folded together, his eyes intently focused on us. He looks uncertain, perhaps even a little nervous, which I think is understandable. It's not every day you get visited in your office by a pair of FBI agents.

"So," he says then clears his throat. "What can I do for you, Agents?"

"We need to talk to you about one of your students," I start. "Ben Davis."

His face immediately lights up, but then as the realization that we're FBI agents dawns on him again, his expression darkens, and he frowns.

"May I ask what this is about?" he asks. "Has he done something? I mean, I know about his past—he told me all about it—but Ben is a wonderful person. Bright. Charismatic. Passionate. He is going to make a fantastic surgeon. He has a gift. I'm sure whatever you think he did, Ben couldn't have done. He's not that man anymore."

"You two seem very close," I note.

He nods. "I'm his faculty advisor. I've gotten to know him very well over the last year or so. I think the world of him. He's a good kid."

His words hit me like a punch to the gut. After having to watch Ben's mother break down, I wasn't expecting to have to watch his faculty advisor do it as well. But I can see by the look on his face that this news is going to hit Dr. Avila hard. And I wouldn't tell him at all if I didn't think he might have some bit of information that would be helpful. But the fact that he and Ben are as close as he says they are suggests to me that Ben would have confided in him. Perhaps something innocuous to him, but something that can help break the case open.

"Dr. Avila, I'm not sure how to say this, but Ben Davis was found murdered," I tell him. "We're looking into his death and—"

"Wh—what?" he gasps.

"He was murdered, Dr. Avila," I repeat.

Dr. Avila slumps back in his chair and seems to physically deflate right in front of us. His face sags, his eyes go glassy, and tears spill from the corners of his eyes. He sniffs loudly and sits up, shaking his head.

"This can't be. There must be some mistake," he says. "Ben would never do anything that would lead to—that. He was a good man. He had a good heart."

"Even people with the purest of hearts get themselves into bad positions, Dr. Avila," Astra says. "That old saying is true—sometimes bad things happen to good people."

He forces his hands, which had been balled into fists, back open, and lays them flat on the top of his desk. I can see them trembling, though, and watch as a tear splashes on the blotter. He's still shaking his head, trying to deny the truth of what we're telling him.

"Do you know if Ben was having trouble with anybody on campus, Dr. Avila?" I ask. "Did he mention any altercations or—"

"No, never. Nothing like that," he replies. "Ben is—was—very well thought of by faculty and other students alike."

And the myth of Saint Ben grows. I know that people often say a victim was beloved by everybody. But that's never true. There are always going to be some people out there who just don't like a person, for whatever reason. Maybe it's jealousy for how much that person is liked by others. Maybe it's for some weird reason a perpetrator's got bubbling in his head that would make sense to nobody else. Maybe it's even for no reason at all. But the fact of the matter is that nobody is ever beloved by everybody. There's always an enemy somewhere. The only question is whether that enemy is violent enough to actually cause harm.

"Dr. Avila, did Ben owe money to anybody? Did he have a problem with gambling, perhaps?" Astra offers.

"Ben? No, of course not. He wasn't a gambler," he replies.

"How about drugs?" I ask. "I mean, given his background, was it possible he was dealing or perhaps using and put himself in a financial hole—"

"That's preposterous," Avila snaps. "He was clean. Even when he was running around with that street gang, he never used."

"And how do you know that?" I counter. "Because he told you?"

Avila sighs and nods, apparently conceding the point. When somebody reveals his background, even if he tells you the lowdown, shady things he did, he still might not have been one hundred percent truthful. Most people will always hold something back. Something they're too ashamed to admit, or something they just want to keep to themselves. It's a universal truth that nobody is ever fully and completely open about everything in his or her life, no matter how much you might want to believe the person has told it all.

"I'll only say then, that in the entire time I've known Ben, I've never seen evidence of drug use. I never once suspected he was high or strung out," Avila admits. "And I'm certain I would know if he was using. I would have been able to tell. I'm a doctor, after all."

"Fair enough," I acknowledge.

"So, no beefs with other students, no drugs, and no gambling debt," Astra recounts.

Avila shakes his head. "No."

"Is there anything you can tell us you think might be relevant? Any change in behavior. New friends. Anything like that?" I ask.

"No, Ben kept to himself mostly. I mean, he had friends in the lab, but I don't believe those friendships extended beyond the lab," he shrugs. "Ben was focused and driven. He was serious about his goal and didn't have time for extracurricular relationships."

This has been highly unproductive, unfortunately. He hasn't been able to give us a single thing that could lead us to another bread crumb on the trail. But that often happens when you're being thorough—you tend to run into a lot of blind alleys and dry holes.

"Okay, well, thank you for your time, Dr. Avila," I say as I get to my feet. "If we have any other questions, we'll give you a call."

"Please find who did this. Find them and punish them," he says with steel in his voice.

"We're doing our best," I reply.

TWENTY-ONE

Macpherson Hall Medical Labs, Washington State University; Pullman, WA

"Do me a favor and shoot Rick a text," I tell Astra as I hold the door open for her. "Ask him to do a deep dive into Ben's financials. Your question about a possible gambling addiction was a really good one. I think we need to see if there's a money trail."

"What makes you think I didn't ask him to do that already?" she chirps.

I arch an eyebrow at her. "Did you?"

"I was just about to."

"Uh-huh," I say. "Still, good idea. Good question."

"I honestly doubt it's going to come to much. It was a shot in the dark," she tells me. "But you never know. And to quote you, that's why we do our due diligence."

We share a laugh as we walk down a flight of steps that takes us down into the basement of the science building. We pass different labs for prosthetics, robotics, and biology. They're all filled with students working on a hundred different projects.

If what Avila said about Ben's friendships not extending outside the lab is true, I doubt we're going to find much here. Just another dry hole, but that's the job. We're paid to run down as many dead-end corridors as are necessary until we find the one that leads us to the truth.

It takes us a minute and several very literal dead-end corridors until we find the anatomy lab Ben most often worked in. The doors slide open with a pneumatic hiss, and all eyes turn up to us as we step inside. There are half a dozen students in white lab coats huddled around various machines and implements that look absolutely alien to me. I couldn't tell you what ninety-nine percent of the equipment in here does.

"Can I help you?"

I turn around and find a tall, thin Asian man approaching us. He's lean and has straight dark hair that falls to his shoulders, dark almond-shaped eyes, warm, fawn-colored skin, and a little feather duster of a mustache on his upper lip. Of course, his apparent inability to grow a full and thick mustache makes him look more like a little kid who's desperately trying to look older.

Astra and I badge him, stopping him in his tracks. He suddenly looks nervous, caught in that moment between fight or flight.

"You alright?" I ask.

"Fine. I'm good," he says. "I just haven't dealt with the police that much in my life, let alone the Feds."

At the mention of the word "Feds," everybody seems to stop moving all at once—as though it was choreographed. All eyes turn back to us and there is a palpable tension in the room. I look at each student in turn, eyeballing them closely as I search their eyes for signs of something—guilt, maybe? I'm not sure. But this crowd looks as if their worst crime is not eating their vegetables with dinner. I refuse to tease them or call them nerds, though, since it's entirely possible that at some point in the future, my life will very literally be in their hands. And I'd hate to think they'd remember a snide remark from twenty years earlier.

"I'm guessing nobody in here has ever had to talk to the Feds, huh?" Astra asks.

They all shake their heads in unison, but nobody speaks. It's so ridiculous I want to laugh, but I manage to hold it in. Just barely. As long as I have their full attention, though, I should probably take advantage of it.

"How many of you were friends with Ben Davis?" I ask.

"Were?" a blonde in the corner pipes up. "You said 'were'. Is he dead or something?"

A hush falls over the lab and everybody exchanges glances as the weight of the moment settles down over everybody. They're somber but not sad, telling me that Avila was right—Ben really wasn't close to anybody here. Which will make trying to get any useful information out of them an exercise in futility.

"I'm not sure any of us are really friends with him. Lab buddies maybe, but that's about it," the tall Asian guy offers. "I'm Monty, and I guess you could say I'm the closest to him. We worked together in here a lot."

"Alright, well, is there someplace we can talk, Monty?" I ask.

"Uhh, sure. Yeah."

"Astra, can you go talk to the others? See if they have anything that can help?"

"You got it," Astra nods.

I follow Monty over to a long, rectangular contraption. It's a stainless steel box of some sort set atop a pedestal, bringing it up about waist high. It's hollow in the middle with a reflective black plate at the bottom of the box and the sides are studded with dozens of—sensors, I guess. Safe to say, I've never seen anything like it before.

"What is this?" I ask.

Monty smiles. "This is our 3-D operating table."

"A 3-D operating table?"

He nods excitedly, the smile on his face stretched from ear to ear, as if he's thrilled to be showing off his new toy to somebody.

"Wow. I guess you and Ben really weren't friends, were you?" I ask, a bit jolted by his lack of concern for our victim.

He shrugs. "I mean, it's a bummer. He was a cool guy. But how can you be sad if you didn't really know somebody? If I broke down and was all boo-hoo about it, I'd be a hypocritical, disingenuous douche," he replies. "I mean, I feel bad for the guy. But he didn't really occupy an important space in my life. He came in, we worked in here, said goodbye, and that was it."

"Huh," I say. "Well, that was refreshingly honest, I suppose."

He chuckles. "That's me. Refreshingly honest," he says. "Now watch."

He goes to the head of the table where there's a computer set up attached to the table. He punches in a series of keys, and a moment later, the inside of the box flares to life and I find myself staring at a holographic body. He picks up an instrument that looks like a scalpel and comes to stand next to me at the side of the table, grinning like a fiend.

"Check this out," he says.

He leans down and slides his pseudo-scalpel along the torso of the body, and I watch with morbid fascination. It really looks as though he's making an incision—minus the streams of blood, of course. I'm glad the designer of this contraption opted to not go for hyperrealism.

"This gadget allows us to practice our incisions and even delicate surgeries on a hologram. No more having to go out and dig up fresh corpses for the lab." He beams, but then seems to recall that he's talking to a Fed and quickly adds, "I was kidding. I've never had to dig up a corpse. People donate their bodies all the time. It's just that this thing is more practical now."

I give him a small smile. "Don't worry. Grave robbing isn't really within my purview, anyway."

Astra walks into the side room we're in and peers down at the holographic body inside the box with a strange look on her face.

"What in the hell is that?" she asks.

"It keeps them from having to go dig up fresh corpses," I say.

"Hey, want to see me remove a malignant tumor from a lung?" Monty offers.

"Oh, that's so tempting," Astra says. "But I'll pass."

I laugh, but Monty looks kind of bummed. Clearly, he enjoys having an audience who will "ooh" and "aah" while he works. With that kind of narcissism and need to have his ego stroked, he's going to make a great surgeon.

"Alright," I say and hand him one of my cards. "If you think of anything you think might help, give us a call."

"Will do," he nods as he tucks my card into his pocket. "And for what it's worth, I am sorry to hear about Ben. As I said, he was a cool guy."

I purse my lips and nod then follow Astra out of the lab, waiting until we're out of Macpherson Hall before I speak.

"Get anything from them?" I ask.

"Squat," she replies. "Nobody knew him other than to say hi, and they didn't have a feeling about him one way or the other. You?"

"Same. Monty had nothing to offer other than that he's bummed Ben's gone, but not really all that sad about it," I say.

"Those are some strange kids."

"I guess you have to be kind of detached from humanity to do the work they want to do," I say. "I mean, it takes a certain kind of person to go rooting around in somebody's insides, I think. I imagine you have to be kind of—cold."

"Huh. Funny," she says. "That's what they say about cops and FBI agents, too."

"Nobody says that about cops and FBI agents."

"They really do," she tells me with a grin. "You need to read more."

"Yeah, sorry, Buzzfeed and Reddit aren't really high on my reading list."

"What, you don't want to know which "The Office" character you are, based on your taste in desserts? You're missing out."

"I think I'll survive," I say. "Come on, let's hit the next stop on this magical mystery tour."

TWENTY-TWO

Garden Village Apartments; Pullman, WA

Using the key his mother gave us, we let ourselves into Ben's apartment and walk around in silence for a few minutes. The air inside is heavy, with the fading trace scents of cleaning solutions and a jar of dried-out potpourri that's sitting on the bar that separates the small kitchen from the living room. Ben's place isn't big, and it's sparsely furnished—couch, flatscreen TV sitting on top of a stand, a bookcase, and a coffee table. None of the furniture matches, but like his mom's house, it feels comfortable. Well lived in.

"I will say, he knew how to keep an apartment," Astra observes as she snaps on a pair of gloves. "Not a speck of dust to be found anywhere."

"I think we know exactly who he got that from," I remark as I put on my own gloves, then walk into the kitchen.

Astra remains in the living room, going over to the coffee table to look at the closed laptop sitting there alone. She opens the machine, boots it up, then watches as a log-on screen materializes. "Damn," she says softly. "I'm not surprised it's password protected, but I'd hoped we might get lucky."

"Not in the cards," I say. "We'll just have to take it in." Turning to my search area, I open up his refrigerator and notice that the plastic containers that hold his leftovers are all marked with dates and contents. Everything is organic and healthy. No empty pizza boxes or Chinese food cartons anywhere. I close the refrigerator and open the pantry door. Everything is perfectly lined up and obsessively organized—each can has a sticker with the expiration date clearly marked. The man's body was very clearly his temple.

I wander from the kitchen and into his bedroom, gently pushing the door open, and see that it's as clean as everything else in the house. His bed is neatly made, the hamper is half-filled with clothes, and his drawers are all as well organized as his pantry—everything is folded with military precision and the stacks of clothes are spaced apart equally inside the drawers. Same with his closet—all his hangers are one uniform color, all of them spaced equally apart. He obviously had a touch of OCD to his personality.

I don't know exactly what it is we're looking for in here. I doubt we're going to find a signed confession from the killer. We're more than a week into this now, and not only do we not have a viable suspect, but we also don't even have a real direction to steer the investigation. I'm starting to get impatient, but I have to remind myself to slow down. It's just as important to get to know the victim as it is to profile the killer. That's just the basics. I'm just frustrated that I took us pretty far afield by pouring so much of our energy into the idea that we were looking at a gang hit or a drug deal gone wrong.

Unfortunately for us, I don't think his almost-obsessive cleanliness is going to be a factor in helping us find his killer. Of all the killers I've caught, I've never had one say to me that it was his victim's housekeeping habits that marked him out for death. I look around the bedroom again and realize it's what I don't see that's striking. I walk back out into the living room and scan the area with this new insight in my mind.

"What is it you don't see?" I ask.

Astra, who's busy combing through the books on the shelves—mostly medical texts—looking for things tucked inside the pages, looks up at me. She sets a book down and turns in a circle, a frown on her lips. Finally, she stops and looks at me.

"I don't know. What is it that I'm supposed to be not seeing?"

"Anything personal," I explain. "You couldn't go a foot in his mom's house without seeing a picture of Ben, or a photo of them together. Her walls were covered in personal mementos. But here? Not a thing."

Astra looks around again and seems to notice what I'm saying. Aside from a few cheap prints that add some color to the walls, there is absolutely nothing in here. Not a single trace of his personality. It might not mean anything. Not everybody is going to have his mother's overwhelming desire to cover her walls with captured moments. But knowing how close Ben and his mother were, it strikes me as more than a little strange.

"Huh. You're right," she says. "This does not feel like a twenty-five-year-old dude's apartment—and trust me, I've seen plenty. There's no dusty Xbox, or sneaker collection, or abandoned set of dumbbells. Or anything. Do you think it's significant?"

I shrug. "It might be. It might not be," I say. "It shows that his personality with the other students in the lab—distant, aloof, drab, even—extended to his apartment. It's almost a forced effort to hide his personality from everybody."

"Maybe he felt he had something to hide," she postulates.

"Could indicate shame. But shame about what? He got out of a bad situation and was making something of his life."

"That's the million-dollar question."

As Astra turns back to the books, I walk into the bathroom. Just like everything else, the bathroom is excessively neat. Not a streak on the mirror or stray hair on the floor to be seen. The towels are all hung up on the bar and are evenly spaced, of course. I walk over to the cabinet and open it up, looking at the small collection of medicines—aspirin, antacids, melatonin, multi-purpose vitamins, Pepto—nothing too out of the ordinary. And like the food in his kitchen, everything is labeled with a bright sticker and the expiration date written in his hand.

I look at the cup and at the pair of toothbrushes inside, then at the bottles of contact lens solution, and a box of condoms that's still unopened. If Grace was right and it was a girl who convinced him to get out of the gang life and into school, it doesn't seem as if the two of them were having sex very often. That's when my eyes drift back down to the toothbrushes—two of them. One with a blue grip, the other with a pink one. So, there was a girl in the picture.

I turn to walk out of the bathroom to talk to Astra when my eyes fall on a tapestry hanging on the wall in the corner, tucked discreetly behind the shower. I didn't notice it when I walked in, because the door partially obscures it from view. But now that I see it, the tapestry strikes me as wholly incongruous with the rest of Ben's apartment, which is bland and impersonal to the point that somebody could walk through and think it was a display unit shown to prospective tenants. The tapestry, though—a brightly colored mosaic that features a silhouette of the African continent—stands out like a sore thumb. It's the only touch of personalization in the entire apartment.

I pull the tapestry aside and feel my eyes widen and my

pulse start to race. This might be what I'm looking for to help bring the stereogram that is this case into focus.

"Astra, I think you should get in here," I call.

As I take down the tapestry, she comes in, looks as I point,, and whistles low. "My, my my," she says. "A secret room. How intriguing."

"Right?" I reply.

"What do you think is in there?" she asks.

"Won't know until we go in."

"Do we need a warrant?"

I shake my head. "Grace gave us permission to search. That would include any hidden rooms we might find, I assume."

Having taken down the tapestry, we are standing here looking at the door that was hidden behind it. I feel my adrenaline kicking into high gear but try to stave it off. There's no point in getting excited until we see what's in there. It could be nothing more than storage. We might go in there and find nothing but empty boxes. On the other hand, we could possibly go in there and find a treasure trove of stuff that will help us make a case.

But I've found it's always best to temper your expectations and not get your hopes up too high, because when something doesn't pan out, the crushing fall always sucks.

"Shall we find out what's behind door number one?" Astra asks.

"Absolutely."

I reach out and turn the knob, only to find that it's locked. I try again, using a little more force this time, but the knob still won't turn.

"Easy there, Wonder Woman. Wouldn't want you ripping the door off the hinges or anything," Astra cracks.

I step back, laughing, as she pulls a small leather case from her inside jacket pocket and kneels down in front of the door.

She takes a couple of instruments out of the case and sets to work on the lock.

"Are you kidding me? Where did you learn how to pick a lock?" I ask.

"Same place I learned to hotwire a car," she offers.

"You can hotwire a car?"

"In less than thirty seconds."

"You're lying," I say.

"Want to bet on that?"

I look at her and hear the click of the lock. "I'm going to pass on that bet," I say.

"Wise choice."

She turns the knob and pushes it inward, and we are immediately overcome by the smell of pot. It's thick and earthy. I'm getting a contact high already.

"Holy cow," she gasps.

She stands up and I follow her into the room. It's not a large room—eight by eight at best. But there is a very sophisticated hydroponic trough system set along three of the walls, with large, lush, marijuana plants growing. There are powerful grow lights stationed above each of the troughs, making sure the plants get the light they need to thrive. And on the fourth wall, on both sides of the door, racks have been mounted to dry the weed. The racks are currently full of product, and although I'm no expert, I'm assuming the thick, bushy plants in the troughs are ready to be harvested.

"This is—something," I note.

"This is every college kid's idea of paradise," Astra replies. "Do we have a drug test at work coming up anytime soon? If so, we're screwed, because I think I'm stoned."

I flash her a grin and walk over to a small desk stashed in the corner. The thing that catches my eye first is a picture in a small silver frame. It's a photo of Ben and a woman who is half a foot shorter than him. She has long dark hair, golden skin, and wide, dark doe eyes. And the way she's leaning into him, with his arms around her, tells me this is the mystery girl Ben's mother told us about.

Besides the picture, there is a ledger on the desk that lists out the planting dates, harvest dates, yield of his crop, and estimated value. Ben was as meticulous about keeping his records as he was about keeping his house. And judging by the figures I'm seeing in his ledger, he was making a very good living. Scholarships paid for his schooling and I'm assuming a piece of his apartment as well, which means the money he was making from his weed business went straight into—something. He probably invested some of it back into his business, but I really want to look at his financials now. I want to see where all his money was going.

"You realize this puts us back at the possibility that Ben's murder was the result of a drug deal gone wrong, don't you?" Astra asks.

"Yeah, the thought crossed my mind. That means we're going to need to speak to the Kings again to see if they were keeping anything from us."

"B—Ben's dead?"

I pull my weapon and wheel around in one fluid movement, training the end of my pistol at the face of the man standing in the doorway.

TWENTY-THREE

Garden Village Apartments; Pullman, WA

ASTRA PACES behind the couch and I pace in front of it, keeping the intruder from focusing on either one of us. It's a common tactic we use that's meant to keep a suspect on edge and unable to keep both of us in sight at any one time. My gut tells me this kid isn't a threat to us. He's tall and lanky—looks more the type to collect Pokémon cards than to gun down federal agents for fun. But my gut isn't one hundred percent, and my experience has taught me that anybody can be a threat. All it takes is for your focus to slip for a nanosecond, and you're bleeding out on the floor.

"What's your name?" I ask.

"Dwight. Dwight Feeley," he replies, a tremor in his voice. "And who are you? And what are you doing in Ben's apartment?"

I flash him my badge. "I'm SSA Wilder. The woman behind you is Special Agent Russo, and I should inform you she is not only the fastest draw in all of Washington but is also the best shot as well. She could put a dot dead center in the back of your head before you fully get off that couch, so think before you act."

"Or don't," Astra says. "It's been a few weeks since I shot somebody and my trigger finger's getting a little itchy."

"See, now I know you guys are just messing with me. You're just trying to intimidate me. Federal agents don't run around just gunning people down. That's not how it works. I'm not an idiot," he says.

"Funny. I wasn't there, but I heard that's the same thing they said down in Waco. And at Ruby Ridge," I snap.

The man on the couch shifts in his seat and looks at me, then tries to turn his head.

"Eyes forward," Astra snaps, her voice cold as ice.

He snaps his head forward again. I have no reason to be torturing the kid this way other than the fact that he sneaked in and got the drop on us. And that irritates me. I don't like getting caught unaware like that. And neither does Astra, so we mentally rough him up a bit before we launch into our questions, just to make ourselves feel a little better.

"So, what were you doing in here, Dwight Feeley?" I ask in my best official FBI voice.

"I—I saw the door was open. I thought Ben was home and I wanted to talk to him," he stammers. "I haven't seen him in a few days."

"And you two are friends?" Astra asks, and when he starts to turn around to answer her, she barks at him. "Eyes forward."

He turns to face me again, his face a mask of confusion and fear. He clearly has no idea what's going on here. We've got him on edge.

"Can you tell me what's going on here?" he asks.

"When was the last time you saw Ben?" I ask.

"I don't know. It's been like—a week? Something like that. I don't know for sure," he says. "And to answer your earlier question, yeah. We were friends. At least, to the extent anybody could be friends with Ben. He always kept most people at an arm's distance, you know?"

"But you're good enough friends that you can just walk in unannounced?" I ask.

He nods. "Well, yeah. I live next door. Met him the day he moved in," he says. "We hang out pretty regularly."

"You buy your weed from him?" Astra asks.

He opens his mouth to reply, then closes it again as if something had just occurred to him. "I uhhh... I think maybe I should talk to a lawyer."

"Relax," I tell him. "It's legal. We couldn't care less if you smoke weed or not. We're not looking to jam anybody up over something like pot. That's not why we're here."

"Then why are you here?" he asks.

I hold the picture frame I'd taken from the secret room out so Dwight can see it. He looks at the photo and I see the flash of recognition in his eyes I was looking for.

"Who's the girl?" I ask.

"Ben's girlfriend."

"Don't get cute," Astra snaps. "Because I know where to hit you so it'll cause you pain but not leave a mark."

Astra is clearly still annoyed by the fact that he sneaked up on us and is unwilling to let it go just yet. I have to fight to keep the smile off my face.

"His girlfriend. What's her name?" I ask.

"It's Chloe. I don't know her last name," he says.

"Sounds like you two were real tight."

He finally turns around, glaring at her. "Ben is a good guy and he's my friend. But he's secretive, okay? He has like this double life, and if you aren't in the circle, you don't get all the details," he snaps back at her. "And so far as I know, only he and Chloe are in that circle."

Astra gives him a nod, then turns away and starts to pace again. It's obvious Dwight has some measure of friendship with Ben, which I can respect. But I also get the idea that he's withholding. That he's got some information he's not sharing with us. Probably because Ben asked him to keep it to himself. I can tell that he's not the type who goes around spreading other people's business for sport. He's loyal. But that also tells me I need to give him something to get something back from him.

"Listen, Dwight. I have some bad news," I say. "Ben's dead. He was murdered. So it's—"

"What?" he gasps. "No. You're wrong. It can't be."

"I'm sorry, but it's true."

"The DNA is conclusive," Astra adds.

"DNA? You had to match him through DNA?" Dwight asks and I can see him turning it over in his mind. "That means you couldn't ID him physically?"

"Criminal Justice major?" I raise an eyebrow.

He nods. "How'd you know? Are you guys watching me, too?"

I shake my head. "No, just an educated guess," I say. "But listen, we're trying to find out who did this to him. Do you know of anybody who might have wanted to hurt Ben? Anybody he had a problem with? Did he mention any fights or—"

"No, nothing like that. Everybody—"

"Liked Ben," I finish for him. "Yeah, so we've heard."

"It's true. He was quiet and, you know, private and all. But he was a good guy," he says.

"Even though he had a double life?" Astra asks. "How do you know he wasn't some hardcore thug in his other life?"

"Because I know he wasn't. I may not have known everything about him, but I did know him well enough to know he wasn't like that," he snaps. "His double life revolved around Chloe. He was insistent they keep it all on the down-low. Swore me to secrecy about her."

I find that bit interesting. He led a double life primarily, it seems, to keep his relationship with this girl out of the public eye. He was secretive about her. That explains why he had her photo hidden away in that secret room. It was his way of maintaining that mirror life he was living. I don't know what it means yet, but I know it's significant.

"Alright, what do you know about this Chloe?" I ask. "I know she was a secret, but surely you know something about her."

He shakes his head. "All I know is she goes to some private school somewhere around here. It's why he chose Washington State—he said he wanted to be close to her."

"That's good, Dwight," Astra tells him. "That's very helpful. Do you know anything else about her? Anything at all, no matter how small or insignificant you might think it is."

He screws up his face, trying to think about it. But I know he's struggling with his grief, which makes thinking a Herculean task. Been there, done that, and it sucks. He finally shakes his head.

"I really don't know anything about her. I never really spoke to her other than to say hi in passing," he shrugs. "She's pretty and they were totally in love. That's about all I know."

"How do you know they were in love?" Astra asks.

"You could see it in the way they looked at each other. You just know," he says, then his eyes widen as fear washes across his face. "Oh, God. Is she alright? Was she—"

I shake my head. "We don't know. We know she wasn't with him when he was found," I tell him. "But other than that, we don't know."

"But we will be looking into it," Astra adds.

Dwight buries his face in his hands and rocks back and forth on the couch. "I can't believe it. I can't believe he's gone," he repeats over and over to himself.

I feel bad for the kid. He genuinely seems to have had some kind of connection to Ben. Strange and tenuous, given how secretive Ben apparently was, but still. Friendships come in all different shapes and sizes. Who am I to judge? Nobody, that's who. I've certainly had a few unconventional friendships in my day.

Dwight stops rocking and looks up at me. His eyes are rimmed red and are shimmering with tears. I feel terrible for him.

"Listen, this is probably going to be a stupid question, but—I already gave Ben some money for the weed that's drying on the rack. Would it be possible for you two to look the other way for a few minutes? Today just turned out to be a crapfest and I'd kinda like to just—go somewhere else. For a little while, anyway."

I look at Astra, who seems to be fighting to keep from laughing out loud. She just gives me a shrug. I mean, I know I shouldn't. All the weed in there should be tagged for evidence. On the other hand, nobody even knows it's in there right now, so it's not as if it's cataloged or anything. As a law enforcement officer, I should say no. I absolutely know that. But as a human being who has been known to self-medicate once in a while—though only with booze—I get where he's coming from.

"Astra, do me a favor and call the field office," I tell her. "I want a crime scene unit out here on the double. And make sure they snag that laptop and get it to Rick."

"Yeah, I can do that," she nods. "I'll make the call downstairs though. The reception here sucks."

"Good thinking. And I'll start trying to track down this

Chloe," I say, then turn to Dwight. "Hey, can you do me a favor and make sure the front door is locked up tight behind you when you leave? Also, make sure there is nothing missing that shouldn't be."

Dwight nods and gives me a faint smile. "Thank you, Agent Wilder. I appreciate that."

"You're welcome."

TWENTY-FOUR

Registrar and Records Office, Oakmont University;
Richland, WA

"The trip isn't very conducive to a relationship," Astra observes.

"It is if you're trying to keep it on the down-low," I reply.

"Takes some dedication to make this run every weekend."

I shrug. "Well, if they're as in love as Dwight thought they were, I'm sure they thought it was well worth it."

"Yeah, but my question is, who were they trying to hide their relationship from?" she responds. "And why?"

"Good question. Let's just hope we can get some answers here."

After badging our way through the security gates at the front, we pull into the parking lot outside the administrative offices of Oakmont University. It's a private liberal arts college—which is a nice way of saying it's a school where rich people send their kids to keep them away from the big, bad world. It's a bubble for the wealthy, and the high cost of tuition ensures it stays that way. But it's nestled in some absolutely beautiful forest country. Built in a Gothic style, the buildings on campus all have soaring towers, tall arches, and high gables. It's gorgeous, to be honest. If I'd had the money, I might not have minded going here.

I called the only other school within driving distance from WSU last night, Wellington College, and was told the same thing I was told when I called Oakmont—they can't give out private student information over the phone. So, with no other options, we had to make the hour-and-a-half drive from Pullman to Richland. We've got a fifty percent chance of being right, and I really hope we are. Because if we're wrong, we're going to have to turn around and head back the other way, which means a four-hour trip to Wellington, something I really don't want to do.

Private security pulls their golf cart next to the car as soon as we get out. The two men, one black and one white, look hard at us. I look over at Astra and smile.

"At least we know the student body is well protected here," I comment.

"No wonder the cost of tuition is so high. Private security isn't cheap."

"Can we help you ladies?" asks the white guy as he slips out of the golf cart.

He's tall and thin, but carries himself like a man who's confident in his ability. His hair is crew-cut short and he's got blue eyes. His partner has dark umber skin, is a few inches shorter than his partner but still has a few inches on me, and is wide and brawny. He's bald underneath his ballcap and has a neatly trimmed beard. He carries himself like his partner—with confidence. I'd guess that both are either cops or military. They just give off that naturally authoritative vibe.

I pull out my creds. "SSA Wilder. That's Special Agent Russo," I say. "We're on our way to the registrar's office."

"Can we ask what this is about?" asks the black guard, his voice higher pitched than I would have expected of such a burly man.

"We're conducting an investigation and need information on one of your students. I'm afraid that's all I can tell you right now," I say.

"If it involves one of our students—"

"Our investigation does not involve the school, so you're not exposed legally. That's all you need to know," I tell them.

Astra and I walk away from the guards before they can ask any more questions, and follow the signs that lead us to the registrar's office.

"This campus really is stunning," Astra remarks as we climb the stairs to the office.

I nod. "It really is. Oh, to have rich parents."

"Yeah, tell me about it."

The doors slide open and we step into the office. There's a sitting area immediately to our left, with a sofa and a pair of plush chairs. To our right is a wall that holds several bulletin boards and glass display cases. There's a door in the wall that leads back to some of the administrative offices. And further inside on the left is a long counter with winding rope lines in front of it. Everything is done in a soft cream color trimmed with white. It's all very sleek and clean inside.

Other than Astra and me, the entire office is empty and there is only one older woman behind the counter. She scrutinizes us closely from behind her black horn-rimmed glasses as we approach the counter. She's a couple of inches shorter than me and is thin. Her steel gray hair is pulled back into a tight bun that sits at the nape of her neck, and her face is softly lined around the eyes and mouth.

"May I help you?" she asks.

We step to the counter and flash her our creds. "Yes, we need to verify whether or not you have a student named Chloe on campus—we unfortunately don't have a last name," I tell her. "We do have a photo of her though. And you are?"

"My name is Alice. Is there some trouble?" she asks.

"To be honest, we're not sure yet. Her name came up in the course of an investigation and we just need to speak with her," I say.

"We ordinarily are not permitted to give out our students' information. The families of our students have an expectation of privacy."

"We understand that completely. But we are in the middle of a homicide investigation," Astra says. "And we need to speak with Chloe. If you could just do us a favor and look through all the information on your computer and compare it against this photo. We only need to know where to find this one girl."

Alice frowns and looks from us to her computer. "I suppose if we can help solve a homicide, we're morally obligated to do that," she says as if speaking to herself. "Integrity and duty are two of our founding principles. Yes, I suppose in that narrow scope, it will be alright."

"That's fantastic. Thank you," I smile, sliding the picture of Chloe over to her.

"Do you know what year she's in?"

I shake my head. "All we have is the name Chloe and this photo."

"Well, that's alright. How many Chloes can we have on campus?" she giggles to herself.

Her fingers fly over the keys then pauses for a moment and frowns.

"Is there a problem?" I ask.

"No, it's just that I didn't know we had so many girls named Chloe here," she replies and gives me an apologetic smile. "This should only take a couple of minutes, though."

Alice hums to herself as she pecks away at the keys, glancing at the photo every time she pulls up a new student—they apparently have quite a few Chloes on campus. I can see the student ID pictures she's pulling up in the reflection off her glasses, and after half a dozen different student files, Alice nods to herself and smiles.

"There we are," she says brightly, then looks around furtively, making sure we're still alone. Alice leans forward anyway and pitches her voice low to avoid being overheard. "You're looking for Chloe Diamatta. She's twenty-one and a third-year student."

"That's fantastic. Would you mind printing—"

Alice comes out with a printed page and hands it to me. I take it from her with a smile and quickly look it over. It's got a picture of Chloe as well as her class schedule and dorm assignment.

"This is perfect," I say. "Thank you so much, Alice."

"Of course. Just don't tell anybody where you got that if you're asked," she says with a conspiratorial smile. "And I hope you catch the criminal you're after. Good luck and be safe out there, Agents."

We thank her for her help and walk out of the registrar's office and back into the sunshine of the afternoon. We walk to a coffee cart and order a couple of cappuccinos then head for the dorms, because, according to her schedule, Chloe is in class right now. If her roommate is in the dorm, we're likely going to get more out of her than anybody else. It takes us ten minutes to get directions to Wembley Place, the all-female dorm where Chloe lives.

Once we get firm directions, we walk across campus. I can't help but notice the difference between campus life here and at Washington State. The atmosphere at WSU was lively and energetic. Here it's staid and low-key. There is no music playing from a dozen different speakers, nobody throwing frisbees across the lawn, no spontaneous jam sessions—it's much quieter here. The buzz I feel on other college campuses is muted.

We follow the signs that lead us to Wembley and head inside. We garner quite a few strange looks from the students, but it's mere curiosity rather than the open hostility we usually get in places like the Kings' bowling alley. Astra and I take the elevator up to the fourth floor and find Chloe's room. There's a whiteboard attached to the door with a combination of crude and cutesy notes written all over it.

"Nice to see they still know how to be kids," I say.

Astra nods. "I swear to God, walking across campus felt like we were walking through a retirement complex."

"I had the same feeling."

She laughs as I knock on the door. A moment later, a blonde girl opens the door with a wide smile on her face. The instant she sees us, her smile drops, and she quickly slams the door. Through the door, I can hear the sound of things being hastily shoved into drawers and I glance over at Astra.

"Get the feeling something's going on in there she doesn't want us to see?" I ask.

"Pretty sure she's not just hiding a boy under her bed."

Knowing she didn't think to lock the door, I turn the knob and push the door inward. The girl is standing in the middle of the room with a can of air freshener in her hand, spraying furiously with the window standing wide open. She's a petite five-three, with honey blonde hair and wide green eyes. Wearing nothing but boy shorts and a t-shirt and with her hair sticking out in a hundred different directions, it's obvious she just rolled out of bed.

"You do realize you're only making your room smell like lemon-scented pot, right?" I ask.

Astra laughs as she closes the door behind her. "Nothing like a little wake and bake, huh?"

"I prefer coffee," I say as I show the girl my creds. "SSA Wilder. This is Special Agent Russo."

The girl's eyes are wide and she's gaping at us with fear etched into her features. She sets the can of air freshener on the small table beneath the window and quickly tries to smooth her hair down. She straightens up and puts a haughty look on her face, trying desperately to recapture some of her dignity.

"Y—you need a warrant to be in here or something," she starts. "You're like violating my Second Amendment rights or something."

I turn to Astra. "Clearly, fifty thousand dollars a year doesn't buy you the kind of education it used to."

"Clearly," Astra agrees.

The girl cocks her head. "What's that supposed to mean?"

"Maddie Jergen?" I ask.

She nods. "Yeah?"

"Chill. Pot is legal in this state. I don't know the college's policy, but we're not in the business of busting you for your extracurricular habits."

She lets out a long breath of relief and sags down onto the bed. I look around the room and see that only her side looks lived in. Her bed is unmade and the desk at the foot of it is cluttered with empty cans of Red Bull, notebooks, textbooks, and her laptop. Clothes are strewn about the floor and are hanging out of her dresser drawers.

The other side of the room has been stripped clean. The bed and desk are bare and the dresser is empty. Astra opens the closet on that side of the room, and I see there's nothing in there. It's been cleaned out entirely.

"We're looking for Chloe Diamatta," I explain.

"She's not here."

"Where is she?" Astra asks.

The girl shrugs her shoulders. "She said she's taking some time off school. Went home."

"When was this?"

"A few days ago," Maddie replies. "I—is she in trouble?"

"Where is home?" I ask. "Where did she go?"

She shakes her head. "I have no idea. All I know is that her dad came and picked her up."

"You were her roommate, and you don't know where she's from?"

"We were roommates. It's not as if we were best friends," she says defensively. "I mean, we were friends, but we weren't super tight. We ran with different crowds."

"I see. And what crowd did she run with?"

"I have no idea. Not mine, though."

I sigh and glance at Astra, who gives me a small shrug. This is beginning to look like another dry hole. Or maybe just a really stoned one.

"Did you know her boyfriend, Maddie?" I ask.

She nods. "Sure. I met Ben a few times. He was nice. Good-looking."

"Did she ever mention anybody hassling them? Anybody have a problem with them?"

"No, she never mentioned anything like that."

I cross my arms over my chest and frown, thinking about my next question for a minute. When I have it, I look up at her again.

"Do you know why she was keeping her relationship with Ben a secret?" I ask.

"I didn't know she was. I mean, I guess I just figured they weren't like, one of those couples who were overly affectionate or something," Maddie says. "They weren't like, all over each other or anything. I assumed they just weren't into the whole PDA thing."

"Do you know anything about Chloe's home life?" Astra asks.

Maddie shakes her head. "No, she didn't tell me much about it. She was pretty quiet and kept to herself mostly. She didn't spend a whole lot of time with me. Like I said, we ran in different crowds."

"Yeah, I get that," I say.

We ask her a few more questions without getting anything useful from her. But at least I can say that we did our due diligence. After finishing with Maddie, we track down a few of her friends on campus and get much the same story—she kept to herself and didn't invest a lot of emotional energy into her relationships on campus. All that energy was saved for Ben.

Once we finish up, we climb back into the car and drive back to the shop, since neither of us feels like waiting for a plane. It's only about three hours from where we are now, but I'll bet I can trim that to two hours and fifteen minutes, tops.

Neither of us speaks for the first half-hour of the trip. I know we're both tired and anxious to get home. I'd like a hot shower before I crawl into bed, though. I never feel as clean showering in a hotel room as I do when I'm at home.

"These two," Astra finally breaks the silence. "Committed. I'll give them that."

"Committed? Or co-dependent?" I raise an eyebrow.

"She shrugs. Maybe a little from column A and a little from column B."

I nod. "Yeah. That sounds about right."

We were able to get a lot of information overall, but I don't yet know how those pieces fit into the puzzle. But given Ben's sideline business, it seems as if a drug deal gone bad is back at the top of our list. There's still a lot more work to do before we decide it's the theory we should be investing yet more energy into pursuing. And there's still the laptop to be investigated.

For now, we just have to keep digging.

TWENTY-FIVE

Criminal Data Analysis Unit; Seattle Field Office

"Okay, well our trip east wasn't entirely fruitless," I start as I pace at the front of the bullpen.

"But the pickings are pretty slim," Astra points out.

"That's true," I acknowledge. "Did CSU deliver the evidence from Ben's apartment yet?" I want Rick to get that laptop.

"Negative, boss," Mo says. "They say it's going to be another day or so before they're finished processing it."

"How did things go in Bremerton?" I ask.

She nods. "They went well. I think I've managed to track down the source of the opioid crisis there. A Dr. Eugene Hastings," she says. "His finances had a sharp spike about a year and a half ago and he's maintained that higher income level since. I checked with the hospital, and his standard of living is well beyond his salary."

"Excellent work, Mo," I say. "Absolutely excellent. So, are you going to pick him up?"

She gives me a strange look. "I thought you—"

"This is your op and you're running point on it. You identified this case, you put in the legwork, and I'm sure you've documented everything extensively," I tell her. "This is your collar. Take a SWAT team and go snatch him up."

The flush of pride and excitement on her face is unmistakable. I can see it in the way she's suddenly sitting a little bit straighter, and in the smile stretched across her lips.

"Thank you, boss," she says.

"Don't thank me. You put in the work. I need to thank you for that," I tell her. "Make sure you get warrants for both his house and office, though."

"On it already."

I give her a nod, proud of the agent she's becoming. "Of course you are," I say. "Then go get him."

Mo gets to her feet and heads for the shop door, but I stop her. She turns around.

"Be careful out there. Let your SWAT team go in ahead of you," I tell her. "Everybody comes home tonight."

"Yes, ma'am," she says.

Mo walks out of the shop with a spring in her step that makes me smile. She's growing into an excellent agent. Talented, instinctive, and doggedly determined. I'm so glad to have taken the chance on her.

"I do believe you made her day," Astra says. "Who knew she had it in her to be a door smasher?"

"I did," Rick replies. "It's all she talks about. She's stoked to be in the field. So yeah, I think you did make her day."

"She's earned everything," I admit. "I really am impressed."

"Then why do you look like a mother who's watching her little girl go off to kindergarten for the first time?" Astra asks.

My laughter echoes around the bullpen. "I do not."

"You do. Totally," Rick cracks with a grin.

I shrug. "Well, I guess I kind of feel that way. I'm proud of her. And scared for her."

"She'll be good," Astra says firmly. "She is good. This will give her some solid field experience. She needs it."

I nod and try to refocus my thoughts. Astra's endorsement makes me feel slightly better about sending Mo out there to run point. Granted, the guy is a doctor and probably won't pose much of a violent threat, but you just never know. But if Astra, who's been hard on Mo, thinks she's ready to run her own op, then I should probably ease up. I need to let her get some experience running her own team in the field. After all, if things go well and we end up expanding my unit, I'm going to need experienced leaders out there I can lean on.

"They grow up so fast, don't they?" Astra quips.

"Shut up," I smirk at her, then turn to Rick. "Okay, since we're still waiting for the evidence to be processed, and we don't have Ben's laptop yet, I want to know about Chloe Diamatta. What can you dig up on her?"

"Give me a minute," he says.

I continue pacing back and forth in front of the monitors as I wait for Rick to pull up some information. The facts of the case are still swirling around in my mind, but I can't get the complete picture to resolve yet. I don't even have enough to put together a viable profile of the suspect we're looking for.

"Why do you think Ben was so secretive about Chloe?" Astra wonders. "That's something I haven't quite been able to figure out yet."

I shake my head. "My best guess is that somebody in her life—likely her father—didn't approve of Ben for some reason," I say. "They had to keep their relationship a secret from him."

"Why her father?"

"Her father came to pick her up from school, and given how hastily she withdrew from classes for the semester, I'm imagining he's a little domineering," I explain. "And for her part, I'm guessing Chloe jumps when he tells her to. I'm getting a picture of somebody who's a bit on the meek side."

Astra nods. "That makes sense."

I honestly don't know if it makes sense. I'm thinking on the fly and speaking off the cuff. I've got absolutely nothing to back any of these theories up. But as I speak, I feel as if the words coming out of my mouth are right. They just have that ring of truth to them.

"So, how does Ben's little weed farm factor into all of this?" Astra asks.

"Whoa, Ben had a weed farm, and you didn't bring me a sample?" Rick calls over with a chuckle. "How thoughtless are you?"

"She couldn't bring any back for you," Astra says. "She was too busy satisfying Ben's client base."

"And you leave me out," Rick scoffs. "Man, that's cold."

I shoot her a look, which makes her laugh as if she just made the best joke in history, which prompts Rick to join her. Allowing Dwight to take what he'd paid for is not only against Bureau protocols, it's illegal. That was evidence. I don't know why I did it, to be honest. I just saw how shaken up Dwight was and thought he needed something to calm himself down, I guess. Not my finest hour and not the smartest thing I've ever done. But what the Bureau doesn't know won't hurt them.

"Anyway," I say, cutting into their laughter. "I still think Ben's weed farm is the primary reason he's dead. I've come back around to thinking that it's a deal gone bad."

"I don't get that. Over weed?" Rick asks. "It's legal here, for crying out loud."

Astra arches an eyebrow. "The way that room smelled, I'm pretty sure Ben was cultivating better stuff than you can get at the dispensary."

"I don't know about that. I've gotten some really good stuff at the dispensary," Rick counters, then seemingly remembers he's a federal employee, adding, "I mean, gotten, um, that info from a friend who told me about it."

Astra laughs. "I'm no expert, but I'd put Ben's stuff up against the dispensary product," she says. "And I have a feeling he was probably undercutting them by selling it cheaper."

"Yeah, but he wasn't growing enough for mass distro," I say. "He wasn't going to put anybody out of business. My guess is he was only selling to the kids on campus. Maybe some of the townies, but I'm willing to bet his primary customers were students."

"Like Dwight."

I nod. "Yeah. Like Dwight."

"Some of these dispensary guys are more territorial than those gangsters you talked to," Rick adds. "I mean, they're like crazy territorial. You don't have to be threatening to put them out of business. Some of them take any dip into their profit pool as a major personal offense. Might be a bit of a stretch, but I think there's a possibility there."

"You sure do know a lot about the world of weed, Tech Analyst Jenkins," Astra says.

"I read a lot."

"Uh-huh," she replies. "You better be reading up on how to beat a pee test."

They continue trading barbs with each other as I clasp my hands behind my back and walk back and forth, letting it all crystallize in my mind. Nothing about this makes sense.

"You look troubled," Astra notes.

"Just trying to put it all together," I say. "We've got about a thousand disparate pieces but no idea how they all fit together."

"I think we need to take another run at the Kings," she tells me. "Maybe the Playboys, too. We rattle their cages and see if anything falls out."

"I'm just having trouble seeing any of them as the killer."

"Why is that?"

"Whoever murdered Ben is a highly organized offender," I say. "He wasn't killed by some street gangster or angry dispensary owner in the heat of the moment. Whoever murdered him was efficient. Methodical. And had a good enough sense of human anatomy to perfectly disarticulate the body. This wasn't a spur-of-the-moment kill. This was planned out and it took a long time."

"You're not thinking that maybe one of the geeks in his lab might have done it, are you?"

I shake my head. "I don't want to rule them out yet. But they're not at the top of my suspect list," I say. "I'll go out on a limb and say Monty was one of Ben's regular customers. It's possible they got into a beef over money."

"Possible but not likely," Astra responds. "At least, I don't think so."

"No, I don't think so either. But it's something we need to factor in, anyway," I acknowledge. "I just wish we had a primary crime scene to look at. I want to know where he was killed."

"Whoa," Rick gasps, his eyes fixed to his computer screen. "This might just change everything."

"What is it?"

"Chloe Diamatta isn't exactly Chloe Diamatta," he says.

"What are you talking about?"

Astra and I walk over to his workstation and look over his shoulder. On the screen, we see her driver's license photo and then on another monitor, he pulls up a copy of the application she filed to change her name. A few years back, Chloe dropped her paternal surname and adopted her mother's maiden name.

"So who is her father?" Astra asks.

On the monitors at the front of the bullpen, an image appears. The man in the photo has cold, pale skin and dark, intense eyes. His hair is salt-and-pepper, trimmed neatly, as is his beard. He's got a strong jawline and high cheekbones. He's a handsome man, but I don't see anything distinctive about him. I haven't the first clue who he is.

"So? Who is he?" I ask.

"Ladies, you are looking at Sarvan Petrosyan, also known as Stephen Petrosyan—he changed his name upon gaining citizenship thirty years ago," Rick explains. "Petrosyan is the head of the Elezi crime family. He is the Armenian mob."

Astra whistles low and we exchange a look.

"You're right," I say. "This does change everything."

TWENTY-SIX

Avenue Four Luxury Condominiums; Downtown Seattle

"Swanky," Astra whistles as we approach the doors.

"Very swanky," I confirm. "Makes sense, though, if your daddy is the head of a crime family."

"Hey, if I got to live in a place like this, I might not mind if my daddy was mobbed up."

I laugh as the doorman opens the door for us and we step into a large marble foyer. It's sleek and modern in design, with lots of glass and burnished steel. There's a fountain with a sitting area to our right, and to our left is a counter that looks like a hotel check-in desk. A woman in a bright blue blazer is flashing us a smile bright enough that it should require eclipse glasses.

"May I help you ladies?" she asks.

We walk over to the counter and show her our creds. "We need to find Chloe Diamatta's apartment."

"Oh, I'm afraid I can't furnish—"

"You actually can. We need to speak with Ms. Diamatta

immediately," I cut her off, my voice cold. "Tell us which unit is hers unless you want to find yourself looking at federal obstruction charges."

The woman quickly types something into her computer then looks up at us. "Seventh floor. Unit number 17-B."

"Thank you for your cooperation," I say.

Astra and I turn and head for the bank of elevators, and from the corner of my eye, I catch her grinning at me. We step into the waiting car and the doors slide closed behind us.

"Federal obstruction charges—that old chestnut again, huh?"

I shrug. "It seems to work. Might as well use it until it doesn't."

After doing some preliminary digging into Chloe, we were able to find that her father bought this condo for her after she graduated high school. We also found the OC unit has an active but sealed file on her. I tried to get hold of Hobbs for some help, but he's doing some undercover work and is unreachable at the moment.

So we asked Rosie to flex her muscle and get the file for us. I want to know what the Bureau has on her. Bureaucracy works slowly; I'm sure it's going to be a while before we get the file. I further realize that if and when we do get that file, it's likely going to be heavily redacted. Especially since it's still an active investigation—which I have to assume is into her father.

But with all those factors weighing on me—and not being the most patient person ever born—Astra and I decided to have a sit down with Chloe ourselves. I'm pretty sure OC is going to be pissed and Hobbs will likely chew my backside for it, but Chloe's being the secret girlfriend of a murder victim makes her somebody I really think we need to talk to. I'll deal with the fallout when it comes.

The bell chimes and the doors slide open, a mellow robotic

voice announcing that we've arrived on the seventh floor. Because apparently, the gigantic embossed "7" that's mounted to the wall across from the elevator isn't enough to tell us which floor we're on. We find our way to Chloe's unit and knock on the door. She has one of those doorbell camera units attached to the door and I know she's looking at us, so I hold up my creds.

"Y—yes?" her voice issues through the speaker, quavering and uncertain.

"Ms. Diamatta, we need to have a word with you, please."

"O—okay. Just a moment please."

We wait and then we hear the sound of the door unlocking. It opens a crack. The girl staring through the small gap stares at us with wide eyes that are bloodshot and puffy. She's obviously been crying.

"Chloe Diamatta?" I ask.

"Yes?"

"SSA Wilder and Special Agent Russo," I announce. "We need to speak with you. May we come in for a moment."

She hesitates but opens the door to us. We walk inside as she closes the door, then leads us to the living room. Her condo is a loft-style unit. Done in red brick and light hardwood, it has a look that's both modern and old-world at the same time. The entire rear wall of the unit is glass, and a staircase leads up to the bedroom area. The kitchen, done in black and white subway tile with brand-new stainless steel appliances, is separated from the living room by a tall bar with black stools lined up in front of it.

The living room is warmer, with a plush sofa set across from a pair of deep, well-cushioned chairs and a glass and wood rectangular coffee table between them. It's all set on a large area rug that's colorful and vibrant—my gut tells me Chloe picked this out. Against the red brick wall is an entertainment center with a large flatscreen TV flanked by a pair of bookcases stuffed with books of every genre, along with personal knick-knacks. Photos crowd every surface and hang on the walls in a way that reminds me of Grace Davis' house.

There are pictures of Chloe with her mother and friends. Pictures of her in various vacation spots, engaging in a variety of activities from skydiving to snorkeling. She appears to be an avid skier and seems to enjoy the outdoors, if the photos tell the whole story. But what I don't see is what strikes me the most. Not only are there no pictures of Ben anywhere, there are no pictures of her father, either. I assume that ties into why she took on her mother's maiden name rather than using her father's surname.

"Wh—what is this about?" she asks.

"Please, have a seat," Astra says.

Chloe is a small girl. Five-five at most, and petite. She's got silky-smooth dark hair, eyes like chips of amber, and deep olive skin. She obviously takes after her mother, as I see no trace of Stephen Petrosyan in her face. She sits down on the couch and seems dwarfed by it. The way she's drawn into herself makes her look even smaller than she is. Almost child-like.

Astra and I take the two chairs across from her and exchange a look. Judging by the pillows and blankets surrounding her, Chloe has been sleeping on the couch—when she's managed to sleep at all. She looks exhausted. Wrung out. She's dressed in pajama bottoms and a hoodie, and it's not hard to believe she's been wearing the same thing since her father yanked her out of school and dropped her here.

"Are you alright?" I ask.

Chloe pulls one of the pillows into her lap and hugs it to her tightly, avoiding my eyes. She bites her bottom lip and nods. She looks up at me, meeting my eyes for just a moment, then drops her gaze back down to her pillow.

"I'm fine. Thank you," she says, her voice soft. "What is this about?"

"We need to speak to you about Ben Davis," Astra says.

Chloe immediately tenses up and I see her eyes shimmer with fresh tears. She manages to fight them off and looks up at us with a carefully crafted expression of neutrality. She's obviously been schooled in keeping her face blank and giving nothing away—probably especially when she's speaking with law enforcement. Given who her father is, I'm sure that's been ingrained in her from an early age.

"Who?" she asks.

I frown. "Chloe, we know Ben was your boyfriend. We wouldn't be sitting here if we didn't know, so let's not play games, alright?"

I say it as gently as I can, but Chloe recoils as if I'd slapped her across the face. A single tear spills from the corner of her eye and races down her cheek and she angrily scrubs it away.

"He *was* my boyfriend," she says. "We broke up some time ago."

"Some time ago?" Astra asks.

She nods. "I haven't seen him in months. It was for the best."

The answers she's giving sound robotic. As if these were the lines she's been fed and is expected to speak on command.

"Chloe, why are you lying to us?" Astra asks. "We know you were at Ben's apartment in Pullman a week ago."

She shakes her head. "That's not possible. We broke up some time ago. I haven't seen him in months," she repeats. "It was for the best."

Astra and I exchange another look. It's obvious she's more afraid of somebody—her father, probably—than she's afraid of us. She has obviously been fed these lines and is dutifully reciting them back to us.

"Chloe, is it your father forcing you to say these things?" Astra asks. "We can—"

"My father has nothing to do with this," she interrupts. "I broke up with Ben. I couldn't be with somebody who deals drugs and runs with a gang. That's beneath me. He's beneath me."

Her words ring completely hollow, and I can see the toll it's taking on her to say them. Tears roll down her face unabated, and this time, she doesn't even try to wipe them away. She looks down at the pillow in her lap again.

"Chloe, did your father force you to break up with Ben?" I ask.

"No, my father has only ever wanted the best for me," she replies. "He protects me. Keeps me safe."

"Chloe, we know who your father is," Astra adds. "We know what he does. And I think you do, too. Did he kill Ben? Did he kill your boyfriend?"

She shakes her head but says nothing. It's obvious to me that she knows what happened to Ben. Or at least, she knows he's dead, even if she doesn't know the exact manner of his death—which is probably for the best.

I'm just about to open a new line of questions when the front door opens and a man in a stylish, very expensive three-piece suit enters. He's about six feet tall, very fit, with blue eyes, perfectly coiffed hair, and a ten-thousand-megawatt smile. He looks as if he belongs behind an anchor's desk gleefully reciting the day's horrible news, but he'll most often be found in a courtroom defending scum like Stephen Petrosyan.

"Palmer Tinsley," I say. "Attorney to the criminal underworld. How are you today?"

"I'm well, thank you. And when you say 'criminal underworld', I say, 'well-paying clients'," he says, his voice rich and cultured. "And as I am on retainer to Mr. Petrosyan, I'm here to inform you that this interview is over."

"Interview?" Astra asks. "We were merely having a conversation with an obviously distraught young lady."

"Relationship stuff," I add. "A little girl talk, so if you don't mind..."

"Actually, I do."

"Oh, good," Astra pipes in. "We were just about to discuss menstrual cycles, so if you have a perspective you'd like to share, we'd be happy to hear it."

He laughs softly. "Charming. To the last," he says. "But, as I assume you have no warrant, you have no right to be here."

"Counselor, we were just having a conversation," I say.

"A conversation that is now over," he replies. "So unless you are planning on charging my client with something, I think it's best that you leave."

I look at Chloe and see her sinking further and further into herself. She looks absolutely miserable. Her face is red and splotchy and the tears running down her cheeks glisten upon her skin. I've never had a maternal instinct in my life, but right now, all I want to do is hold her and let her cry.

"Chloe, you're an adult. You can make him go away," I tell her. "If you want to talk to us, just tell Mr. Tinsley here that he's fired and send him packing."

Tinsley's expression darkens and he casts a meaningful glance at Chloe. She sits up on the sofa and uses the sleeve of her hoodie to wipe the tears from her face. She sniffs loudly and looks at me. I can see the fear sharply etched into her face, but she shakes her head.

"I have nothing to say to you," she says, her voice trembling. "Please leave."

"Well, there you have it," Tinsley immediately announces. "Time for you to go, Agents. Thanks for stopping by."

I get to my feet and stand toe-to-toe with Tinsley, my eyes boring into his. He's a cool customer, though, not seeming rattled in the least. A smile curls one corner of his mouth upward.

"Send our regards to Mr. Petrosyan," I say.

"And tell him that we'll see him soon," adds Astra.

"Good luck with that," Tinsley replies.

We walk out of Chloe's place, and I feel a fire burning in my gut. The direction of the investigation is shifting—again. But I fear I might also be running down another blind alley. This is just another confusing point on this muddled, indecipherable stereogram.

"What are you thinking?" Astra asks as we emerge from the building and back out onto the street.

Light rain has started to fall, and a cool wind buffets us. It feels nice against my skin, which is burning hot with anger.

"I'm thinking that Chloe has a lot to say," I reply. "A lot she's not being allowed to say."

"I agree," she nods. "But it's maybe a stretch. I mean, breaking Chloe's heart by pulling her out of school to kill a relationship is one thing. Killing her boyfriend is something else entirely."

"People have killed for far less," I remind her.

"That's true. But we have nothing linking Petrosyan to Ben directly. I'm still thinking the drug angle is more likely."

I nod. "Alright. Why don't you go back and talk to the Kings," I tell her. "See if you can get anything out of them."

"And what are you going to do?"

"I'm going to see about finding a link between Petrosyan and Ben."

TWENTY-SEVEN

Jade Pearl Billiards House, Chinatown-International District; Seattle, WA

"It's lovely to see you again, Blake. But if you keep coming around, people will say we're in love," Fish says, doing a passable impersonation of Anthony Hopkins' Hannibal Lecter.

"I forgot that's your favorite film," I say.

"It's cinematic brilliance," he replies. "I dare you to find a better film."

"I don't know. I was pretty hyped up about Captain Marvel."

"Heathen. What is wrong with you?" he says, making me laugh.

"That's right. You identify with Lecter—the misunderstood and tortured genius."

He shrugs. "I do not consider myself tortured," he says. "Nor am I a cannibal. I could never eat a human—too much fat and far too many chemicals. It would only pollute my pristine body. It is a temple, after all."

A smile crosses my face. "I'm glad to know you draw the line somewhere."

Fish, otherwise known as Huan Zhao, a Chinese immigrant turned underworld kingpin turned confidential informant, sits behind his desk across from me. He's an intriguing man of many different hats who has his own code of morality—which, as much as I hate to admit it, doesn't entirely differ from my own. Fish is self-educated and self-made. He got his start selling drugs while he worked as a fishmonger down along Pike Place—hence the moniker.

He's a complicated man. He did unspeakable things during his rise to power. But he's also done incredible good in the community. He's perhaps the smartest, savviest person I've ever known and has charisma for days. It's easy to hate the dark and criminal side of his world, but it's almost impossible to not like him as a person. It makes for a very complex relationship between us that I'd describe as something of a tenuous friendship.

Perhaps best illustrating that duality in Fish is the fact that just outside his office doors where we're sitting right now is an illegal gambling hall. Fortunes are being won and lost as we sit here. And yet, down below us is a perfectly legal billiards hall and bar. And I know for a fact that he uses one hundred percent of the profits of the billiards hall to fund half a dozen programs around Seattle—most of them aimed at providing food and shelter for children.

I only know this because I've done some serious background research on him over the years. He doesn't publicize his charitable endeavors and never talks about them. He only confirmed it for me when I pressed him on it, and he's refused to speak of it since. For all the bad he does, Fish does twice as much good. How can you truly hate somebody who does something like that? Or for that matter, write him off as an unredeemable criminal?

"So, what can I do for you today, Blake? Not that I don't enjoy your company," he says.

My smile slips and a feeling of dread settles down over me. "What can you tell me about the Armenian mob? Specifically, the Elezi crime family and Stephen Petrosyan?"

Fish whistles low and a shadow crosses his face. "I can tell you two things with absolute certainty," he says. "First, without Petrosyan, there is no Armenian mob in Seattle. He is the Armenian mob."

I nod. That's about the extent of what I've heard. "And second?"

"Second is that you do not want to tangle with Petrosyan. He is, hands down, the most violent and brutal man in the entire Pacific Northwest. He had to be, or he was going to be wiped out by the Russians and Italians," he says. "I do not know what sort of case you are working on, but I would suggest that you walk away from it."

"You know I can't do that."

"Then pass it on to somebody else, Blake," he says. "I genuinely fear for your safety if you try to lock horns with this man. He is cunning and he is dangerous."

The fact that Fish fears Petrosyan sends a cold chill down my spine. The man is usually as fearless as he is unflappable. Nobody scares him. At least, I don't think anybody scares him. But as he talks about Petrosyan, I can see genuine fear in his eyes. And I find that unsettling, to say the least.

"Blake, I generally don't believe people are pure evil. I believe we're more complex than that. It's a delicate balance. All people are capable of good—and bad," he says, though I don't think he's referring to himself. "But that man comes as close to that line as possible. He has the darkest soul I've ever seen. He has very few redeeming qualities. If any."

I sit back in my seat and ponder what Fish has told me so far. It's not great news for the home team, that's for sure. Anybody who can rattle Fish's cage is somebody to be incredibly wary of, that's for sure.

"May I ask what he did that's prompting your investigation?" Fish asks.

"He murdered a kid," I say. "At least, I believe he did. The boyfriend of his daughter."

Fish nods, a knowing look in his eye. "Yes, he would certainly do something like that."

"This kid—he used to run with the Eighth Street Kings, but got out of it," I explain. "He was pre-med at WSU and was going to do something with his life."

"But Petrosyan did not approve, I take it."

"I can't prove that Petrosyan even knew about the relationship," I tell him. "Ben—that's his name—and Petrosyan's daughter kept it a secret. A deeply buried secret. Very few people knew about it."

"And what does the lovely Agent Russo think?" he asks. "She's very smart and intuitive. I'm surprised you're coming to me rather than leaning on her."

"Between Ben's gang ties in the past and the fact that he was a small-time weed cultivator and seller, she thinks somebody in one of the gangs hit him," I explain. "She very well could be right, but this reads more mob hit than street gang hit to me."

"And why is that?"

"The body was found completely disarticulated. The joints were surgically sliced," I reply. "This wasn't some crazed dude with a machete hacking a man to pieces. This was methodical. Practiced. And that doesn't read 'street gang' to me."

Fish steeples his fingers in front of him as he looks at me. I watch as he processes everything I've told him. But his face is a complete blank. I can't get a read on what he's thinking, one way or the other.

"As for the girlfriend, Petrosyan's daughter, we paid her a visit, and she is an absolute wreck. I know she knows what happened. But before we could get anything out of her, Petrosyan's thousand-dollar-an-hour mouthpiece showed up and put the kibosh on everything. Kicked us out of her place."

A wide smile crosses Fish's face. "And how is Mr. Tinsley?"

I chuckle. "Yeah, I guess I should have figured you'd know him."

"Of course. In my rarified line of work, it is wise to have somebody of his skill and talents on retainer," Fish says. "As you Americans like to say, my mother did not raise a fool."

"No. No, she did not," I say with a hearty laugh.

We sit in silence for a long moment, each of us seeming to be thinking about the situation. The trouble is, the more I think about it, the angrier I get. I hate what Petrosyan is doing to Chloe. She's terrified. And she has to suffer through the murder of her boyfriend, a man she was purportedly deeply in love with, all alone. Even worse is the fact that she has to cope with her father is the one who murdered him. I can't even imagine what that must feel like or what it does to a person. Chloe is never going to be the same after this. How could she be?

"Why would this man murder a boy his daughter loved?" I ask. "To keep her under his thumb? To keep his boot on the back of her neck? Is controlling her that important to him?"

"With all due respect, I believe you're asking the wrong question," Fish replies. "The question you should be asking is: what lengths would a father go to keep his daughter from making what he believes is a terrible mistake?"

"I don't understand."

"If you were to ask me if Petrosyan is capable of killing a boy to keep his daughter from making what he feels is a mistake, then the answer is yes. Without a doubt," Fish clarifies. "But believe me when I say it would be as much for him as it would be for his daughter. And I believe he knows that. He guards his daughter so zealously because he knows without her he would be lost."

"What do you mean?"

"Chloe is Petrosyan's humanity. She keeps him tethered to the world. Without her, he would be even more of a savage beast than he is now. He would unravel. And believe me, that would be good for nobody," Fish goes on. "She stung him once by refusing his name. He might not be willing to allow her to sting him a second time by being with somebody of whom he does not approve. There was something about this boy Petrosyan rejected, and I doubt it had anything to do with the weed he was selling."

"Huh," I say, gnawing on my bottom lip as I think it over.

"All of this is conjecture, mind you. Based on the idea that you are right and that it is Petrosyan behind the killing of this boy. Which I cannot have an opinion of one way or the other at this point."

"Right. Of course," I nod. "I'm not even one hundred percent sure of anything in my own mind right now."

"With all things being equal, the simplest explanation tends to be the right one," he quotes.

"Occam's Razor," I reply.

"Quite right," he says. "Don't overthink things. It's one of the most often cited theories for a reason."

"Yeah. But I don't know what the simplest explanation is right now."

"Oh. I think you do."

A weak smile touches my lips. "I'm glad you have faith in me."

"I always do, Agent Wilder," he says. "And I always will."

TWENTY-EIGHT

Wilder Residence; The Emerald Pines Luxury Apartments, Downtown Seattle

I SHUT the door behind me, lock it, and drop my keys, badge, and gun on the table, feeling spent. I drop my bag next to the table, then kick off my shoes, letting them rest where they fall next to my bag. All I want is a glass of wine, a hot shower, and eight hours of uninterrupted sleep. I think that would be heavenly. It would have me feeling like a new woman in the morning. Hell, if I get that much sleep in one go, maybe I'll even wake up with the answers in my head already.

My meeting with Fish left me with more questions than answers, but at least he gave me a lot to think about. I also managed to extract a promise from him to squeeze his sources to see what he could find out about the murder and whether it's related to Petrosyan or not. It's something I appreciate, as he's obviously reticent to get involved with the Armenians.

If Occam's razor is correct this time, the simplest explanation is that Petrosyan killed Ben to keep him away from Chloe.

He didn't approve of Ben for a variety of reasons—his ties to the Kings, his dealing weed, and most especially, because Ben is black. The Armenian mob, like most mob families, tends to be insular and virulently racist. They only approve their offspring marriages to members of the same ethnic group, be they Italian, Russian, or Armenian. The crime families do not like bloodlines being mixed—or, as they put it, diluted.

It's a sick way to live and to see the world, but it is what it is. Racism has a long and sordid history. I'd like to believe people are capable of looking past something as trivial as skin color, but all around the world—America included—it continues to be a major problem. It's thoughts like these that sometimes make me wonder what it is we're fighting for. If the people of the world are going to continue to separate themselves by their ethnic tribes and murder those who don't look like them, are we even worth saving as a species?

It's a depressing thought and one I just don't even want to think about anymore. But we need to start getting some answers. It's time to drill down and figure out which explanation is the simplest—the Kings or Petrosyan. I'm firmly convinced one of them murdered Ben Davis. I feel the truth of it down in my bones.

I flip on the stereo and put on some smooth jazz—something a little mellower to settle my nerves. After that, I walk into the kitchen and pour myself a glass of Chardonnay, then leave the bottle on the counter, because I know I'll be needing a refill soon. After that, I pull out my phone and call Astra. It goes to voicemail after a few rings—she's probably enjoying her evening with Benjamin. The thought prompts me to look around my empty apartment and, for the first time, feel a twinge of self-pity.

It would be nice to come home to somebody, I have to admit. No, I'm not softening my stance on Mark. Astra was right—he's not the right fit for me. But it might be nice to find someone who is. Maybe once we've put Ben Davis' case to bed, I'll be a little more proactive about looking for somebody. Maybe I'll even let Astra set me up with Benjamin's friend.

The beep sounds on her voicemail. "Hey, it's me. Not sure how things went with the Kings today, but I'm thinking we need to bring them in as well as Chloe Diamatta. We need to have a formal sit-down and get them all on the record. Somebody's lying to us and I'm tired of it, so it's time to go full-court press and crack them. We'll hook up in the shop tomorrow morning to talk strategy. Hope you and Benjamin are having a good night."

I click off the call and drop my phone on the counter, then take a long swallow of wine as I try to clear my mind of all the garbage of the day. I drain the glass then pour another and head down the hall toward my bedroom. The siren song of my war room pulls at me, though. I try to resist it but realize it's futile, so I promise myself that I'll just take a peek and let my subconscious do the work while I sleep.

I turn on the light—and have just enough time to process the fact that somebody is standing right in front of me before his fist smashes into my face. Pain exploding in my head, I stagger backward, barely registering the sound of the wine glass shattering on the floor. I somehow manage to keep my feet as the dark figure rushes out of the war room. I'm stunned, but still coherent enough to lash out with my foot and trip him up. The figure goes down hard and then I'm on him.

But the exact instant I grab hold of his left arm, intending to twist it up behind his back, his right elbow crashes into my temple. Bright bursts of light flare behind my eyes and I'm rocked to the side, but I keep hold of his wrist. I drive my fist into his kidneys, and when I hear the grunt of pain that bursts from his mouth, I realize it's not a *him* at all. My intruder is a woman.

We both get to our feet, facing each other. A balaclava conceals her face, which only allows me to see her eyes. And as my gaze bores into hers, I'm overcome by a wave of familiarity. I recognize those eyes, though I couldn't say from where. Nor do I have time to think about it as she presses forward, moving with the practiced, graceful ease of a highly trained martial artist. She feints to the left, making me bite on it, but comes through with a right that smashes into the side of my face.

Pain radiating through every nerve ending in my face, I stagger but keep my feet. I dart back out of the hallway to grab my firearm, and she lopes after me. It's all I can do to avoid her swift fists. She's on my tail, but I manage to make it back to the table, grab my gun, and whip around. I lift my arm to fire—but before I can even squeeze the trigger, her foot is on me in a rapid blur. She knocks the gun out of my hand with an incredible spin kick. It flies out of my grip, banging against the wall and clattering onto the floor with a loud bang as the round I had chambered goes off.

I take advantage of the distraction and launch myself forward, throwing a dizzying array of punches. I'm fast but she's faster. She parries my every punch, deftly turning them aside, then delivers a vicious hook to my side, driving the air from my lungs. I grunt and fall to a knee, gasping for air. My attacker turns to run, but I hook her ankle with my hand and send her sprawling again as I lunge forward and deliver a series of body blows to her sides and back that makes her cry out.

She arches her body and throws me off. I land on my butt and hit the couch with my back but ignore the pain and struggle to my feet. She's already back up, closing in on me and blocking my path to the gun. I block her first punch, realizing too late that it was a distraction—a point driven home when her fist crashes into my side. Stars burst behind my eyes as if a sledgehammer just rammed me. I manage to land an uppercut that connects with the bottom of her chin. I hear the satisfying sound of her teeth clacking together as her head snaps back.

The satisfaction is short-lived, though, as my attacker lunges forward again and drives her foot into my exposed midsection. I double over, then feel something hard and blunt smashed into the back of my head. I collapse onto my stomach, my entire body a live wire of pain. I feel something warm and viscous spilling down the back of my neck and realize that I'm bleeding. My thoughts are fuzzy and I can see the darkness creeping in at the edges of my vision.

Before it claims me though, I see my attacker lingering around me. I hear her as she walks into the kitchen and vaguely wonder what she's doing. Then I hear her voice. It's low and muffled, as if she's trying to disguise it somehow. Her words sound mumbled to me. I'm stupidly reminded of the way Charlie Brown's teacher sounded in those cartoons. I might laugh if I didn't think it would be agonizing to do so.

Then my attacker's feet come into my field of vision. She stands in front of me—hovers over me—and I wonder if this is it. If this is how I go out. Strangely enough, I'm not scared of death. I don't welcome it, but I'm not scared of it. My only regret is that I didn't find the monster who killed my parents and abducted my sister. If not for that, I wouldn't have a single regret about dying before my time.

As I stare at the tips of her shoes, the darkness crashes down and pulls me under, and I know no more.

TWENTY-NINE

Seattle Community Medical Center; Downtown Seattle

The first thing I'm aware of is the searing pain in my body. I'm not sure there's a square inch that doesn't hurt. The second thing I realize is that if I'm in this much pain, then I'm not dead. But with the amount and intensity of the pain ravaging my body right now, I kind of wish I was.

"Well, look who's rejoined the land of the living."

I hear Astra's voice but cringe when I open my eyes. The light in the room hurts my eyes and makes my head start to throb.

"Lights," I croak.

"Crap. Sorry."

I hear her rushing around the room and the rattling of the window blinds for a moment before she speaks again.

"Sorry about that. You should be clear now," Astra says.

I cautiously open my eyes and find her standing at the foot of my bed, her smile wide, her face twisted into a mask of relief.

"I never thought I'd live to see the day when the great and

unbreakable Blake Wilder got her ass handed to her," Astra teases.

"You should see the other guy," I manage.

"I would but he apparently left after kicking your ass."

I shake my head and wince, silently cursing myself for being stupid enough to move. My throat is dry, and my mouth feels gummy and gross. I try to sit up but groan, and then Astra's there beside me, gently pushing me back down onto my pillows.

"No moving," she admonishes me. "Doctor's orders."

"Water," I rasp.

She picks up the cup from the table and holds the straw to my lips. I drink deeply, relishing the sensation of the cool liquid as it spills down my throat. My eyes closed, I pull back and nod to her. Astra takes the cup away and I hear her set it back down on the table. I take a moment to gather myself—focusing on not moving in any way that's going to hurt—then lean forward again and open my eyes.

A weak smile crosses my face and I look up at her. She looks as though she's been here all night. There are dark circles under her eyes, her hair isn't fashionably styled, and she's got no makeup on. She's dressed in a green sweatshirt and yoga pants—and Astra is never seen outside of the house in yoga pants. Unless of course, she's going to yoga. But it's as if she rolled out of bed and got here.

"Have you been here all night?" I ask.

"All night? Babe, you've been here a day and a half," she says. "Everybody's already come by at least twice—I had to use a crowbar to get Rosie out of here. Even Fish stopped by. That guy's a character."

"You don't even know the half of it," I say.

"He's definitely got a style all his own, and damn if it's not kind of sexy," she says with a giggle as I roll my eyes. "Anyway, he brought you those."

I sit up and immediately regret it. My body screams in agony and I slump back against the pillows again. I look over to where she's pointing and see a large vase holding an assortment of sunflowers. I have to admit, the bright colors make me smile. But then the reality of my situation settles down over me again and I frown.

"What's wrong with me?" I ask, certain that I've got internal bleeding, a broken spine, or some other life-threatening condition.

"Wrong? Nothing, other than you're really milking this asswhoopin' you got," she laughs.

"What?" I ask. "I feel like hell. Everything hurts. Surely something has to be wrong."

She shakes her head. "You were brought in and had a concussion. You have a cracked rib and of course—that," she says, gesturing to my face.

"What's wrong with my face?"

She goes to her bag and pulls out a compact. Walking back over, she opens it and thrusts the mirror toward me. I take it in trembling hands and groan. I look like a monster. My eyes are black and still swollen, I've got abrasions on my forehead and cheeks, and my nose is red and puffy. Probably broken. Though it looks as if they might have reset it.

"I look horrible," I mutter.

"That you do," she replies as she takes her compact back. "But the important thing is that you're alive. You're going to be alright and make a full recovery."

"Why was I out for a day and a half?"

"The nurse said you were exhausted and apparently needed the sleep," she shrugs. "As I said, you were milking it for a little extra sleep."

I laugh softly and grimace as the pain grips me. Astra is staring at me. She's obviously being flippant, but I can see the worry in her eyes. I reach out—slowly—and take her hand, giving it as firm a squeeze as I can.

"What happened, Blake?"

"I don't know. I came home and flipped on the light and she was just there. Right in front of me. Sucker-punched me before I was even ready," I say.

"Wait—she?"

"Yeah, it was a woman," I nod. "And even though she was hitting me plenty hard, I got the impression she was pulling her punches a bit. I remember thinking that she's got so much more fighting skill than I do that she was toying with me. Either that or she didn't want to actually hurt me. Girl did some sort of jumping tornado spin kick move that took my gun out of my hand. Definitely highly trained."

"You got banged up plenty, so don't think she went easy on you."

"Maybe not. But she didn't go as hard as she could have. I'm sure of it," I say. "But that doesn't make sense. If Torres sent somebody to kill me, why would she not do the job?"

"Whoa. What makes you think it was Torres?"

"Who else could it have been?" I ask.

She scoffs. "Let's see, there are the Kings, the Playboys, and let's not forget the Armenian mob. There's a long list of people who might want to put a hurtin' on you."

"It wasn't the Kings or the Playboys. Neither gang has any reason to want to hurt me," I tell her. "Speaking of which, how did your meeting go with them?"

"It was fine. We'll talk about it when you're back on your feet," she brushes me off. "My point is that there is a list of people who might not mind knocking you around a bit. It might not have been Torres at all."

"Occam's razor," I mutter.

"What about it?"

"Simplest explanation is usually the right—"

"Yeah, I'm familiar with the theory. How does it apply here?"

"Torres is the only one who's truly motivated to want to hurt and/or kill me," I point out.

Astra shakes her head. "You're forgetting about the mob boss whose daughter you tried to convince to flip on him."

"Hey, you were there, too."

"Yeah, but you're the boss. You get all the credit and all the beatdowns," she offers. "And I'm suddenly feeling very okay with that."

I chuckle, it's a dry raspy sound. "Gee, thanks."

"Where did you go that night?" she asks.

"I went to see Fish. I wanted him to dig into Petrosyan."

"Then there's your answer," she says. "It had to be Petrosyan."

"No. Too fast," I say. "There's no way he would have known I asked Fish to dig into him that quickly. Which means it was Torres."

Astra frowns and folds her arms over her chest. "It's possible. But I'm questioning it because Torres is a sexist pig. Why would he send a woman to do a job he believes a man can do better?"

That's an angle I hadn't considered. And I have to admit that she has a point. Torres *is* a sexist pig. He only puts men in certain positions while shoehorning women into other less dangerous and less important positions. I seem to recall that Mo has a grudge against him, which tells me she was one of those women who got shoehorned. Astra's right: Torres would never trust a woman to put a beating on me. Never in a thousand years. So, who, then?

I push those thoughts aside to focus on something more practical and immediate. I look up at Astra.

"How did I get here?" I ask. "The last thing I remember is blacking out. My attacker was standing over me. I thought for sure she was going to kill me."

"Somebody called 9-1-1," she tells me. "I heard the tape. It was a woman and she said you required medical assistance. Hung up right after giving your address. But after doing that, she called me and left the line open. I knew something was wrong."

"A woman?"

She nods. "We assumed it was one of your neighbors who came across you—your door was standing wide open when we got there. But the fact that you were attacked by a woman puts a new spin on this."

"That makes zero sense. Why would she beat me half to death—"

"More like a quarter to death. Let's not be dramatic," Astra interrupts with a smile.

A quiet laugh escapes me. "Fine. But why would she beat me and then call for help?"

"That's a good question. And one we can answer once you're back up on your feet," she tells me. "The doctors say you can go home in the next day or so and then back to work in about a week."

"A week? That's crap," I sigh. "If I was only beat a quarter to death then that means I can come back as soon as I get out of this bed."

"Yeah, not going to happen," she shakes her head. "Rosie's putting orders in at the door that you're to be turned away if you show up."

I groan and press my head back against the pillows. But then the door to my room opens and when I look up, I see Mark standing in the doorway. Astra immediately stiffens—as do I. He looks at me with mournful eyes and worry on his face.

"This might not be the best time for you to be here," Astra tells him.

He nods. "I know. Probably not. But I was worried and needed to make sure you were okay. I just needed to see you."

"Okay, you see her and see that she's alright," Astra says. "Thanks for stopping by, but you can go now."

"Actually, I was hoping we could talk," he says then turns to Astra. "Alone. I'd like to have a word with her in private."

Astra looks down at me and I can see that with her eyes, she's telling me to stand firm. But I give her a small nod.

"It's okay. I'll text you later," I tell her.

"You sure?"

"Yeah. It'll be fine."

She nods. "Okay."

"Thank you, Astra. For everything," I tell her. "I owe you."

She gives me a smile. "I'll just put it on your tab. Love you."

"Love you back."

Astra walks out, eyeballing Mark the whole way. I can see the warning flashing in her eyes, and Mark stands there with his hands in his pockets, nodding as if he understands. When the door closes behind her, he steps over to the edge of the bed and takes my hand.

"Look at you," he says softly. "This is what I was worried about."

"She could have killed me if she wanted to," I tell him simply. "But she didn't."

"She?"

I nod. "Yeah, it was a woman."

"Any idea who it was?"

I shake my head. "No, she wore a balaclava. But if I had to guess, I'm thinking it was Torres sending a message. Though admittedly, there are some problems with that theory," I admit with a quiet laugh. "But that's what I'm running with today."

He sighs. "I just—I think it was this thing with your parents. They were sending you a message for sure," he says. "And this might be the only warning you get, Blake. I'm scared for you. This is why."

"I know. And as I said, your concern is appreciated," I tell him. "But if—and I'm not convinced it was—but if this was the Thirteen sending me a message, then that means I must be getting close to something. That means I can't back off."

"Blake—"

"Let me rephrase that. That means I won't back off," I clarify, my voice firm. "This is too important to me."

He runs a hand through his hair. "I understand that. I do. And this time apart from you—I've had a lot of time to think about it. I see now that I wasn't as supportive as I could have been. Should have been, maybe," he says. "But you have to understand, I'm a doctor. I'm not from your world. I don't chase fugitives with guns. I never get shot at. And I certainly don't try to run down shadowy figures who assassinate Supreme Court Justices. This is all new for me. New, and if I'm being honest, terrifying."

"And I do understand that. But this is my life. This is who I am. And that's something I'm not going to change. I can't," I tell him. "That's why I thought it best that we go our separate ways. I know this isn't your world. But it is mine. For good or bad, this is how it is. And I'd rather be alone than be with somebody who doesn't get that. It wouldn't be fair to either of us."

"I've missed you, Blake."

I give him a soft smile. While it's true that in the days immediately after our split I didn't feel much, over time I did miss him. Mark is a lot of fun to be with. We have great conversations, and we laugh a lot together. That's something I love and something I've missed. In a lot of ways, he's a fantastic partner. It's just in that one way, perhaps the way that matters the most, he hasn't been.

"I've missed you too, Mark. But I'm not going to back away from this investigation. Not for anybody. It's too important to me, and I need it to be important to whoever I'm with, too," I tell him. "Not to mention the fact that by being with me, you're making yourself a target as well. If the Thirteen is going to take me out, they won't hesitate to take anybody around me out as well."

"Then we go down together. You're important to me, Blake. And your finding a sense of peace and closure are important to me, too. That's something I've learned during our—hiatus."

" Are you telling me you want to get back together?"

"Yeah. I'm telling you I want us to get back together." "I can't promise I'm not going to have a freak-out now and then. But yeah, I want to be here for you. I want to help you in whatever way I can. Even if it's just being here to listen."

I look into his eyes and see the earnestness and sincerity there. His smile still puts a flutter through my heart, as does his touch. I appreciate his newfound support, but I worry about his ability to cope with what I'm doing. I fear it's going to get worse before it gets better. And that makes me worry for him.

"I don't know if you understand what you're getting yourself into," I say.

"I probably don't. I mean, I know it could be dangerous."

"It could be fatal."

"Look, if there's one thing I learned during our hiatus it's that, without you, my life isn't nearly as worth living. If they're going to take you out, then I'd rather go out with you than live a life without you in it," he says.

"That's a little dramatic."

"No. That's just the truth."

The EKG machine I'm strapped to starts to beep incessantly as my pulse races and I can't do anything to stop it. We both look at it, then laugh together.

"Is that a yes?" he asks, his tone hopeful. "You'll give me another shot?"

"That's a yes."

His smile stretches from ear to ear. "That's a great answer."

And as he leans down to kiss me, the EKG machine chimes wildly.

THIRTY

Wilder Residence; The Emerald Pines Luxury Apartments, Downtown Seattle

Day four of my involuntary imprisonment starts the same way the previous three did—with nothing happening. I've put my house back together. Cleaned it from top to bottom. Tried to watch TV, only to lose interest in seeing supposedly real housewives behaving like real spoiled asses. And have tried at least half a dozen new juice smoothie recipes. To say I'm climbing the walls and going out of my mind would be a massive understatement.

The guards they posted out front aren't even talking to me. Rosie must have specifically asked for the two surliest, straightest-laced sticks in the mud in the whole field office. Their heads kind of look like thumbs and their personalities do, too. Every few hours they call a cursory, "Switching shifts, Agent Wilder," through the door, and those are about the only words they say to me.

I found out yesterday that Astra wasn't kidding when she

told me that Rosie had put a block on my ID, disallowing me from entering the field office. I went in and was told that I was temporarily restricted from access, then sent back home. I've tried calling Rosie more times than I can count. She could probably get a restraining order for stalking by now. But she's not taking my calls.

It sucks because I'm feeling better and am ready to get back to work. The longer I'm sitting on the bench, the colder my case is getting. Timing is everything in this game, and sitting on the sidelines is only letting the other team get that much further ahead of us. I can practically feel the case slipping away from me as I sit here twiddling my thumbs.

I take a bottle of water out of the refrigerator and wander into the war room. As I take a long swallow, I look at the wall before me, my eyes drifting to the photos of the dead Supreme Court Justices once more. I'd told myself the other night that I needed to get to work, delving into the replacement Justices.

I've done a light survey of their backgrounds and didn't find anything that particularly popped with me. About all I can say is that none of the three is a political firebrand. They all avoid issuing controversial opinions, and unusually, none has an overwhelming amount of experience on the bench. But they were apparently centrist enough to garner support on both sides of the aisle and achieve confirmation.

In fact, all of them were confirmed with broad bipartisan support, which is really surprising, given the times we're living in. And because I don't think this conspiracy is that wide and far-reaching, I can't say that every member of the Senate who confirmed these Justices is involved. Also, two were appointed by one Presidential Administration, the third by another, which makes it all the more unlikely there was an orchestrated conspiracy, unless there would be a way to get both sides of the aisle to go along with it. And that would mean a conspiracy that encompasses all the movers and shakers on Capitol Hill. Which is so far out there, I think the possibility is pretty much a non-starter.

So, why these three Justices? It just feels too significant that we lost the three previous Justices over the last few years. Too coincidental. I open up my laptop and start to look through some of the cases the SCOTUS has decided since Justices Karen Witkowski, Sherman Havers, and Benjamin Pearce ascended the bench. I'm not sure exactly what it is I'm looking for and I'm certainly no legal expert, but I'm hoping that something stands out to me. Something I can cling to and start to unravel this Gordian knot.

I've just gotten into it when my cell phone rings. I glance at the caller ID and see that it's Astra, which brings a smile to my face. I answer the call and press the phone to my ear.

"Hey, what are you doing?" she asks.

"Reviewing Supreme Court decisions and trying to make conversation with those beef slabs outside."

She groans. "Yeah, okay, I'll talk to Rosie. See if she'll lift the embargo and let you back into the building before we need to fit you for a padded room," she replies with a laugh.

"I'd appreciate it. But I still need to review these cases."

"They tie into your side project somehow?"

"They might. Hard to say just yet," I tell her. "I'm only now getting into it."

"Fair enough," she says. "I just wanted to call and check on you. We miss you down here."

"I miss you guys. I never got a chance to ask how Mo's raid went."

Astra laughs. "I'll let her give you the details, but she did a good job. Guy tried to run, and she went full Terminator on him."

"Good girl. I knew she had it in her."

"Yeah, she's riding pretty high right now," she says. "Also, I brought Blade and Demone in for a formal sit-down yesterday. Got them on the record. They even waived their rights to a lawyer."

"Yeah? How'd that go? They pissed?"

"Not at all. They had a good time in here," she says, her voice tinged with amusement.

"What makes you say that?"

"They asked for applications."

"Clowns."

"Totally," she says. "But as far as the case goes, they copped to buying weed from Ben from time to time, but it wasn't a regular thing. They admitted that they don't sell weed on the streets—no profit in it since it's legal, you know?"

"That makes sense."

"And I really don't think these guys had anything to do with Ben's death. When I pressed them on it, they got real upset," she says. "They said when they find out who did it, they're going to give whoever it is the same business. Said it on tape."

"Yeah, that's not smart."

"But it kind of tells me they were being honest."

"Unless it was an act," I counter. "If whoever the killer is turns up jigsaw-puzzled like Ben, their lawyer can always argue that the tape means nothing, since no rational person would make that argument when he's knowingly being filmed."

I frown and tap my finger against my lips, thinking. I mean, it goes along with what I've been saying all along—that I don't feel the Kings are involved in Ben's death. They actually liked him, and I don't see as the types to do what was done to Ben. But I know that was my opinion beforehand, so maybe this is simply a bit of confirmation bias.

"What do you think? What does your gut tell you?" I ask.

"My gut tells me these two are innocent," she says. "Of this, anyway. I'm sure they're guilty of a host of things we don't know about. But I don't think they murdered Ben. They don't have any clue who did. Their story yesterday didn't change from the one they told us in the bowling alley."

"Yeah, I don't think so, either," I reply. "Which means we're down to Petrosyan as our sole survivor."

"Occam's razor," she sighs. "Looks as if you were right."

"I certainly hope so. We've been jerked around so hard from the start, I'm taking nothing for granted," I tell her. "I won't be satisfied until we have somebody in custody. I'm hoping it's Petrosyan, but at this point, I won't be surprised if it's somebody else entirely."

"Your lips to God's ears," she says with a bitter chuckle.

I stand up and pace the room for a minute, trying to put a plan together. To draw Petrosyan out and get him to come in, we need bait. We need to make him want to sit down with us. The logical choice is his daughter. We need to use Chloe.

"Alright. As soon as I'm allowed back in the building, we're going to bring Chloe in for a nice little chat. That might be enough to rattle Petrosyan," I say.

"Sounds good to me. The sooner we can put this to bed, the better. This case is giving me migraines," she replies.

"Tell you what, I'll take your migraine, you can take this broken rib."

"Hardy har har. I'll go talk to Rosie."

"Please do; she's not even taking my calls."

"She's pretty hardcore."

"Yeah, she is," I say. "Oh, and I meant to say thanks."

"For what?"

"For telling Mark about what happened," I reply. "He and I had a long talk and—"

"What are you talking about?" she cuts me off. "I didn't talk to him. Remember? I was the head cheerleader for the 'dump Mark' campaign?"

"You didn't tell him I was in the hospital?"

"Definitely not."

"Huh. Okay, sorry."

"So does that mean you two are back together?"

I shrug. "I'm not sure what it means yet. But we're talking."

"Well, as long as he lets you be your own woman, I'll support you."

"Thanks, Astra. Love you."

"Love you back."

I click off the call and set the phone down. My mind churns as I pace the room, a million different thoughts spinning through my head. If Astra didn't call him to let him know I was in the hospital, who did? How did he know I was in the hospital at all? We weren't at the hospital where he works, so he wouldn't have heard through the grapevine there. And I doubt anybody else I know would have called him, either. So how in the hell did he know to come?

A creeping feeling of dread wraps its icy tendrils around me as I recall something Gina Aoki said to me during our meeting. It was something I brushed off at the time, thinking it was the sort of paranoia she'd had to cultivate over her lifetime. But all of a sudden, I'm second-guessing that. I think back to that meeting I had with her and replay what she said in my head:

You'll never see them coming, Blake. They won't be ham-handed about putting surveillance equipment in your home. They'll insert people into your life to keep tabs on you. And these people will stay with you for years. That is how committed they are to their cause."

I look around the room, wondering if there is any surveillance equipment in my house right now. Wondering if Mark is somebody inserted into my life to keep tabs on me. It would explain his near-obsession with getting me to drop this case. His job might have been to watch me and deter me from following this path. He's been so insistent about it that I have to wonder about his motivations now.

Was it really because he's afraid for me? Or because it's his job to deter me? And that leads me to wonder what his orders are if I get too close. Would he hire somebody to rough me up so I'd think twice about pursuing this? Would he be ordered to kill me? Was that what the woman was doing in my place? Was she planting bugs? Cameras? Did I come home in the middle of her operation? But then, if she was hired to rough me up, why in the hell would she call the paramedics for me?

Nothing about this is making any sense, and it's frustrating me. More than that, it's starting to scare me. I hate the creeping feeling of paranoia stealing over me, but I can't help it. I know I'm playing in some high-level political machinations right now, and I know it's dangerous. But how dangerous is it really? Dangerous enough that I have to worry about the man I'm sleeping with?

There's only one way to get the answers I need. I grab my phone, punch the button, and hold the phone to my ear. It's picked up on the second ring.

"Hey, Brody, it's me," I start. "Got a minute?"

"For you, I have two," he replies. "I heard about what happened and I'm glad you're okay."

"Thanks," I say, casting a wary eye around the room. "I'm doing better and I'm ready to go back to work."

"Of course you are. You're just like Pax that way," he says with a chuckle. "Anyway, what can I do for you?

"Actually, can you do me a favor and meet me somewhere?"

THIRTY-ONE

Interrogation Suite Alpha-4; Seattle Field Office

A COUPLE DAYS LATER, once I was finally allowed back into the field office, Astra and I made our plans. The following morning, we executed our search warrant on Chloe's place and brought her down to the interrogation room. Now, we're letting her cool her heels for a little bit. She's sketchy and jumpy as it is. Letting her stew in there might make her more likely to say something she probably shouldn't, before her father's mouthpiece can stop her.

Astra and I are standing behind the glass in the control pod, watching her and her father's attorney, Palmer Tinsley. She's huddled down and sunken into herself, playing with the ends of her hair, looking like a young girl, rather than the twenty-something woman she is. Tinsley, on the other hand, exudes his smarmy arrogance even just sitting there. He looks at his nails, no doubt thinking about scheduling his next mani-pedi.

"I really hate that guy," I mutter. "He's just so—"

"Cocky. Greasy. He makes a used car salesman look ethical in comparison."

"Yeah. All of the above."

"So, are you ready?" I ask.

"You know I am."

"Good. Let's go shake the trees and see what falls out."

We walk through the door in the control pod that lets us into the interrogation suite. I close the door behind me and we take our seats across the table from Chloe and Tinsley. I set down the folder I'm carrying and watch as her eyes flick to it, concern crossing her face. Tinsley looks at me with a smile that makes me want to go shower.

"Lovely to see you again, SSA Wilder," he starts. "And you as well, Special Agent Russo. Fine weather we're having, isn't it?"

I shrug. "I've always enjoyed the rain."

"Well, let's go ahead and wrap this up quickly so you can go outside and play in the puddles, shall we?"

I smirk at him. "As much as I'd like to, I don't think this will be wrapped up that quickly. We've got quite a few questions that your client is going to need to answer before she's allowed to go home."

"And just to make it official, this is your notice that this interview is being recorded, both audially and visually," Astra says, then adds gently. "Have you been read your Miranda rights, Chloe?"

Tinsley interjects. "She doesn't need—"

"Actually, she does need to be Mirandized," I cut him off. "As a suspect in the murder of Benjamin Davis, Chloe has rights. So I need you to affirm that you've been properly Mirandized."

Her eyes flit from mine to Tinsley's then back again. She looks around the interrogation suite in silence and I can see her fear growing. It's as if she's only just now understanding where she is and what's happening—and is terrified. Her lips tremble and she's growing paler by the minute. The interrogation suites are designed to be uncomfortable and build anxiety within a subject, and it seems to be working on Chloe.

I feel bad for her. She's just a pawn in this game, caught between us and her father. And on top of that, she no longer has Ben to turn to. He'll never again be able to comfort her. I feel terrible for having to use her like this, to get at her father, but these are the cards I was dealt, and I have no choice but to play them.

"Chloe?" Astra asks. "Were you properly Mirandized, or do you need me to read you your rights again?"

She shakes her head. "No, I understand my rights. I was properly Mirandized."

"Very good," Astra says. "Thank you."

"You think she murdered Mr. Davis?" Tinsley asks. "You've lost your mind, haven't you? Look at her. Does this look like somebody who's capable of murder?"

"Mr. Tinsley, I've been doing this for a while now, and let me just say, anybody is capable of murder given the right circumstances. Anybody at all."

"Even you?" he asks, arching an eyebrow as if he thinks he's scoring a point.

"Even me. Even you. If the right—or wrong—things coalesce, it can make for one deadly and toxic stew. It can make people do the most horrible things," I say.

"Nobody is immune to anger," Astra adds. "We're all human and have human emotions. We're all capable of snapping."

He frowns and leans back in his chair. "Fine. Whatever. Let's get this over with. What do you want to know?"

"Chloe, why did you keep your relationship with Ben a secret?" I ask.

She looks at me and I see her eyes shimmer with tears. The mere mention of his name can make her cry. I hate that we're going to have to go hard at her, but we have no choice. I know she knows something, and until we can shake it out of her, we can't treat her with kid gloves. A man was murdered—a man she loved—and we need to know who did it and why.

"I told you. We broke up—"

"I know what you told us, but we know you're lying," I interrupt. "We have a witness who put you at his apartment in Pullman less than a week before Ben's murder."

"You know how unreliable eyewitness testimony can be," Tinsley counters.

"Not in this case. Our witness actually spoke with her," Astra says. "And given that he'd known Chloe for more than a year, I'd say that makes him pretty reliable."

She looks up at me, her eyes wide, looking like a wounded girl. I can see her silently pleading with me to stop this. To let it go. But I'm sure that, even though she's grieving and scared —and apparently terrified to grieve openly—she knows I can't let it go.

"Did you kill Ben Davis, Chloe?" Astra asks.

"That's preposterous," Tinsley cuts in.

"Is it?" Astra presses. "Because right now, what we know is that your client was seen with our victim and she was having a secret relationship with him. That makes her a viable suspect in any book, Counselor."

"I'll ask you again, Chloe. Why lie about the relationship?"

"Was it because your father didn't approve?" Astra asks. "Did he force you to break up with him?"

She shakes her head. "I told you. I broke up with him months ago—"

"Yeah, and we know that's a lie," Astra says. "Did the suit here feed you those lines, Chloe? Is he making you say these things? Or is it your father?"

Her eyes widen for a moment and she pulls back, crossing her arms over her chest. She looks away, unable to meet our eyes.

"Unless you have any specific evidence tying Mr. Petrosyan to this despicable crime, I would suggest you refrain from attempting to sully his good name."

"Good name," Astra says with a snort. "That's cute, Counselor."

"I would remind you that we're here as a courtesy," Tinsley says.

"Actually, you're not. You're here because Chloe is a suspect in a gruesome murder, and we need some answers. So, Mr. Tinsley, if you want us to cut your client loose, I would suggest instructing her to give us some answers."

"Were you keeping your relationship with Ben a secret because you feared your father would find out, Chloe?" I press. "And did he find out anyway? Is that what happened?"

"No, I—I mean, I broke up with Ben weeks ago. We weren't together," she says, her voice tinged with desperation.

"Weeks ago, Chloe?" Astra asks. "A moment ago, you said months ago. So, which is it? Did you break up with him weeks or months ago?"

"Agents, I would ask you to stop badgering my client. She's obviously in a fragile emotional state and—"

"I would be, too, if my secret boyfriend was found cut to pieces and stuffed in a barrel," I snap. "I'd be in a very fragile emotional state. Especially if I knew my father—"

"Once again, Agents, if you continue attempting to tarnish Mr. Petrosyan's name, this interview will be over," he says. "We are here doing all we can to assist your investigation and to prove that Chloe had nothing to do with it. However, if you continue with this absurd witch hunt, I'll have no choice but to pull the plug. We're trying to be fully transparent."

"Is that so?" I ask. "Then why has Mr. Petrosyan refused to return our calls? Why will he not sit down with us?"

"Because he had nothing to do with this crime," he replies smoothly. "Therefore, there is no reason for him to come in for an interview."

Chloe is looking down at her hands, refusing to even acknowledge us. I can see she's pretending that none of this is happening. She's probably somewhere else in her mind—somewhere with Ben. She's content to repeat the lines she was coached to say and let Tinsley do the rest of the talking. She's just going to run out the clock—probably as she was instructed to do by her lawyer. Or her father. Or more likely, by both.

Which means if I want to get anything out of her, I'm going to have to shock it out of her. My eyes flick to the folder, and although I really don't want to use it, I'm starting to think there's no way around it. The last thing I want to do is further traumatize this girl who's obviously been traumatized her entire life. But I need to do something to shake her out of this. I glance at Astra and she gives me a subtle shake of the head, silently telling me, not yet.

"You loved Ben a lot, didn't you, Chloe?" I ask.

She doesn't answer and starts to chew on a nail. She's so beaten down and worn out that she's reverting back to some of her childhood behaviors. She doesn't look anything like the confident girl some of her friends said she is. She looks like a scared little child. And she probably has good reason.

"I know he loved you a lot. He kept your pictures and all of your keepsakes locked away in his special room," I go on. "It was his way of keeping you safe. Protected. But you knew that, didn't you? He did that because of how much he loved you."

She looks up at me for a moment and nods. It's not much, but it's enough of an acknowledgment for now. At least she knows what I'm talking about.

"I know you can't keep him safe or protect Ben anymore, but don't you want justice for him?" I ask. "Don't you want the people who did this to pay?"

"I thought you suspected her of doing this?" Tinsley asks.

I look over at him. "How about you do your job your way and I'll do my job my way?"

"In other words, unless you have something to add to the conversation, zip it," Astra says.

"Did you do this, Chloe?" I ask. "Or did somebody else murder Ben?"

"Now is the time to get ahead of this," Astra presses. "We know you've been lying about your relationship with him, so to us, you're looking good for this. If it wasn't you who murdered him and stuffed him into a barrel, now's the time to tell us."

"Are these graphic details cleverly phrased in the form of questions necessary, Agents? Do you need to traumatize this poor girl any more than she already is?"

Ignoring Tinsley, I lean forward and tap the file on the table. "Do you know what's in here, Chloe?" I ask, and I see her eyes flick to the folder again. "There are photos in here of what was done to Ben. The man you love. Do you want to see them?"

"SSA Wilder, that is gratuitous. There is no need—"

"I'll conduct my interrogation any way I see fit," I snap at him.

"No, that's it. I'm taking my client home."

He shoots to his feet and takes hold of Chloe's arm. She looks at me, her eyes wild, as if she's even more terrified than before. She obviously doesn't want to go with him, so I get to my feet and stare at him.

"Actually, you're not going anywhere," I say. "Or at least,

Chloe's not. We can hold her for seventy-two hours and we intend to do just that. Now, take your hands off her and you can see yourself out."

Tinsley stares at me as if I've gone mad. "Do you have any comprehension of what you're doing right now?"

"Yeah. Trying to solve a murder," I say.

"You have no idea the can of worms you're opening."

I shrug. "Not the first can I've opened. Won't be the last, I'm sure. Tell your client—your other client—where to find me if he wants to talk."

THIRTY-TWO

Criminal Data Analysis Unit; Seattle Field Office

"I did not see that coming," Astra comments as we walk back into the shop.

"Yeah, sorry. I didn't mean to sandbag you like that," I say. "But I feared that if she left that interrogation room, we were never going to see her again. She looked absolutely terrified."

"You don't think Petrosyan would—"

"No, nothing like that," I reply. "But given how close she seemed to cracking, I wouldn't put it past him to stick her on a plane and send her back to Armenia. Or maybe some boarding school in Switzerland."

She nods as she drops down into her chair. "Smart thinking. Except that we can't talk to her without that walking snail trail present."

"Officially, no. But I've got an idea," I say.

"Oh, I like it when you get that twinkle in your eye. It's so —devious."

"Welcome back, boss," Mo chirps. "Glad to see you upright again."

"Thanks. Glad to be upright again."

"Wow, somebody really did a number on you," Rick says.

"Yeah, thanks, Rick."

He chuckles. "Sorry, I didn't mean it like that. It's just kinda like seeing Superman with bruises on his face. It's just one of those things you never expect to happen."

"Yeah," I shrug. "Well, I'm not a daughter of Krypton after all. The bruises will fade. Now, can we get to work?"

I hate being reminded of my own frailty. The fact that somebody got the drop on me. I hate being reminded that I'm not a superhero after all and can be hurt and killed like any mortal. That brush with mortality has had a lasting effect on me, as much as I hate to admit it. Just one more trauma to add to a life filled with them.

But I'm going to channel that into something good. Something positive. I've got a black belt in Tae Kwon Do, but it's been a long while since I've actively trained. And judging by the beating I took, I've obviously forgotten much of my training. Which means I need to keep trained and in shape. I've already scheduled my sessions at the local dojo and am going to get back on that train. I'll never allow myself to be caught unaware and defenseless again.

As good as I think I am, there's always somebody better. And the woman who jumped me was excellent. The next time I see her—and I am sure I'm going to see her again—I'm going to have a surprise for her. Vengeance and humiliation are always solid motivational tools, I've found. If nothing else, this beatdown I took is going to make me more physically fit and better able to fend off an attack I never saw coming.

"Actually, I have to go," Mo says. "I'm meeting with Hastings and his lawyer for some follow-up questioning."

"He causing you problems?" I ask.

"Nothing I can't handle. I just need to reiterate that we've got him cold, and his best play is to confess."

I nod. "Excellent. Well, go get him, then."

Mo gives me a smile, and as she hustles out of the shop, I see the stacks of boxes on a cart in the corner by the door I didn't notice when we walked in. Good thing it wasn't a masked woman, or she would have beaten me down again. It would have been nice if CSU had told me they were done processing, but whatever. I push the cart to the tables, grab the first box, and set it down. Astra gets up and takes another one. I take the lid off and start pulling out and sorting the evidence that's been gathered.

"Oh, I forgot to mention that Rosie was by earlier. She said the file on your girl is with OC. They're not down to give it up because they're working on a RICO case against her daddy," Rick says. "But Rosie said she saw it and there's nothing that relates to the case you're working on, so it's moot."

"Yeah, I didn't think it would yield much, but it was worth a shot," I shrug. "Thanks, Rick. Have you been able to come up with anything on her?"

"Negative, boss. She's clean as a whistle. By all accounts, she's just a normal kid," he says. "She gets good grades, has excellent credit, does a lot of volunteer charity work."

"Obviously trying to atone for the sins of her father," Astra mutters.

I nod. "Could be. If what Fish said is true, I imagine that girl has seen some things," I say. "With no son and heir to his empire, I've got to think Petrosyan has been grooming her to take over for him once he's dead."

"Sure would be a shame if that happened sooner, rather than later."

I grin. "Now, now, let's not wish ill upon him," I protest.

"Not until I have him in cuffs and looking at the needle for his laundry list of crimes."

"If OC is building a RICO case against Petrosyan, you know this is going to create some blowback. He's not going to be happy about our targeting him," she says.

I shrug. "It shouldn't matter who collars him, so long as he gets collared," I say. "And statistically speaking, going away for murder will keep him in a cage longer than if they manage to make a RICO case stick. And that should be our goal—to get and keep this animal off the streets."

"I don't disagree at all," she says. "But you know better than anybody how alpha dog Hobbs can get when you step on his toes."

I nod. "Yeah, I'll give him a heads up. But there's no way in hell I'm backing down from this case. If we can send Petrosyan to prison for murdering Ben Davis, then that's what's going to happen. Period."

"That's my girl. Balls of steel," she says. We sift through the boxes of evidence but don't find anything of much value. Nothing that definitively ties Petrosyan to Ben. Not that I expected anything, really. Ben was obsessively careful, and Petrosyan is so careful, he borders on paranoid. It's how he's managed to avoid prison all these years. But still.

"Is it too much to ask for a signed confession every once in a while?" I ask. I look among the evidence, but don't see Ben's laptop. "Rick," I ask, "have you seen the laptop CSU brought from Ben's apartment?"

"Yeah, I got it a few days ago. I cracked the password right away, and sifted through everything on the machine. Nada, boss. All I saw were files related to his studies, just term papers and class notes. I couldn't make heads or tails of most of it, with all the medical jargon, but there was nothing suspicious. Nothing that would seem to relate to his murder."

"What about online activity and social media?" I ask.

"Again, boss, no dice. His search history involved mostly stuff tied in with his lab work. On social media, he was a ghost. No presence, which is almost unique for someone his age. There were a few photos of Chloe in his Pictures folder, but nothing else of a personal nature."

Another dead end, but it's that due diligence thing. Ben was exceedingly careful.

The doors to the shop open and a twenty-something Asian man comes in with a manila envelope. I recognize him as one of the clerks who works in the mailroom. He gives me a smile and hands me the envelope. I immediately look at the postmark and see that it's from the King County Medical Examiner's Office.

"Thank you," I tell him.

He nods. "Not a problem."

I show it to Astra, who groans. "Are you even kidding me right now?"

"This has Torres written all over it."

"Yeah, it really does."

I shake my head as I tear the envelope open. The fact that they mailed copies of the reports rather than simply emailing them over to us, ensuring they spent at least a few days in transit, is just Torres' latest double-middle-finger salute to me. We could have had this information a week ago. *Should* have had this information a week ago. The fact that we didn't infuriates me, because as I scan the reports, I see things that could have altered the course of this investigation earlier.

"Something really needs to be done about Torres," I say.

"Uh-huh. Something really bad," Astra adds.

I hold up the page I'm reviewing and look at Astra pointedly as I start to read.

"The contents of Ben's final meal: grape leaves and pork,

lamb meat, ghapama, and manti," I say. "Also, there were still traces of oghi in his stomach."

Astra stares at me with disbelief on her face. "Armenian food?"

I nod. "Armenian food."

"Son of a—"

"His last meal was Armenian food. If we'd known that a week ago, we would have been able to pivot from the Kings to Petrosyan sooner," I say. "If nothing else, we might have been able to get to him before he had a chance to terrorize his own daughter into silence or destroy any potential evidence."

"Torres needs to go down for this," she says.

"Yeah, but how are we going to prove it?" I ask. "We can't prove he slow-walked this. We can't prove anything. He's too careful to leave his fingerprints on anything."

"Hey, boss," Rick calls.

"What is it?"

"I'm looking at Ben's credit card statements that we finally got. The night he went missing, or at least, three days before his body was found, he used his card at a restaurant called Rose of Armenia. It's in the Capitol Hill district," he says. "But get this, the charge is for two dollars and twenty-five cents—an iced tea."

"And yet, he had a full meal in his belly," Astra says.

"Sounds to me as if he was invited to dinner on somebody else's dime," I say. "And Ben wanted to make sure anybody looking could trace him back to that restaurant."

"It's almost as though he knew what was going to happen to him," Astra says.

"Why would he even go, then?" Rick wonders.

"Hope," I say. "I think he had hoped he could talk Petrosyan into letting him see his daughter. Hope that Petrosyan might see how much he's changed. Wanted to show him that he wasn't the same gang member he used to be. Maybe he wanted to show Petrosyan that he genuinely loved Chloe."

"That's sad," Astra says. "Really sad."

"Not to mention that it's eerie as hell," Rick adds. "Knowingly going to your death like that but leaving breadcrumbs for other people to follow? Sad and eerie."

"For maybe the first time ever, I agree with the nerd," Astra shrugs.

"Do I need to guess who owns Rose of Armenia?" I ask.

"If you were going to guess Stephen Petrosyan, you would be correct."

"That's our nexus," Astra says. "That's where they crossed paths."

"Yeah, but we need to put them there together," I say. "It's a popular restaurant. Ben's having dinner there doesn't prove that he saw, let alone spoke to, Petrosyan."

"So, what do we do?"

"Good work, Rick. Keep digging. See if you can find anything that puts Ben and Petrosyan together," I say.

"Not to state the obvious, but can't the girl you have in a cell do that?" he asks.

"She's not going to talk just yet. I think part of her is trying to convince herself that her father didn't do it," I say. "No, we need something to prove to her that her father killed her boyfriend," I say, then look at Astra. "Up for some Armenian food?"

"Absolutely. Let's do it."

As we head out of the shop, Rick calls after us. "Hey, can you bring me back a couple of kabobs? I'm kind of hungry."

THIRTY-THREE

Rose of Armenia, Capitol Hill District, Seattle, WA

With a vaulted ceiling, high arches, red brick, and polished light wood, the Rose of Armenia has an old-world charm to it. There are curtains and room dividers made of plum-colored velvet cloth, sheer pink silk swags, and mosaic tile on the floor. All the tables are made of the same light wood as the arches, and recessed lighting lines the entire dining room. It's dim and atmospheric, and the air is redolent with the aromas of spices and cooking meats. Soft Middle Eastern music issues from speakers discreetly tucked around the dining room.

"Is it wrong that I'm suddenly really hungry?" Astra asks.

"I was thinking the same thing, actually."

"Table for two, ladies?"

We turn and see a young woman who couldn't be more than twenty-two or so standing behind us. She's wearing flowing skirts that are burnt orange, with a white tunic top. She's got silver chains around her waist that make me think of a belly dancer or a gypsy. She's got midnight-black hair and dark eyes set into a round face.

"Yes, please," I say.

"Very good," she nods, her voice colored slightly by a Middle Eastern accent.

She leads us to our table and sets the menus down in front of us before she smiles and turns in a swirl of skirts and walks away. A busboy is suddenly there, setting a pair of glasses filled with ice water on the table before he scampers off. I look around and see the dining room is half-filled withpeople casting furtive glances at us. The clientele looks primarily Armenian—and they don't look exceptionally pleased to see us.

"I think we've been made," I say.

"You think?" Astra replies with a grin.

I know that ethnic communities can sometimes be insular places that don't trust outsiders. Especially when those outsiders come wearing badges. Trusting law enforcement isn't something most of these folks are apt to do, and I can't say I necessarily blame them. In a lot of cases, the countries some of these folks fled from are rotten to the core. The police, who were supposed to be there to protect them, were often their worst oppressors. In some Eastern European countries, the police are merely arms of the local warlord, who send them to beat, torture, and even kill the citizens. Little wonder that they have learned to distrust anybody who's a cop.

The waitress stops by and takes our orders, and I remember to pick up a few kabobs for Rick. We sit back and chat idly as we wait. The whole time, though, I'm casing the place, looking around and seeing where the security cameras are set up. I see half a dozen that are visible—mostly near the bar area, with only a few covering the dining room. I have to believe there are other cameras that I can't see, though. In this day and age, it pays to have hidden surveillance.

"Do you realize Ben might have eaten his very last meal right here at this table?"

I look up at Astra. "My God, you are morbid."

"Like the thought didn't cross your mind," she says.

"It didn't, actually."

"Liar. I saw the way you looked at the table when we sat down."

I shake my head. "Morbid. Twisted and morbid."

"Two of my better qualities."

We sit and talk for another ten minutes or so, then I see Petrosyan step out of the back of the restaurant. He walks out of the kitchen carrying a white plastic bag full of Styrofoam containers, his gaze locked onto mine.

"Yeah, we've definitely been made," I mutter.

Astra says nothing but sits up in her seat a little straighter. I see her slip her hand beneath the table, obviously moving it closer to her weapon just in case things go sideways. Petrosyan stops at our table and sets the bag down. He takes a long moment to look at each of us, obviously not liking what he sees, judging by the sneer on his lips.

Petrosyan is slim and athletic, standing about six feet tall. He looks exactly like the photo Rick had pulled up for us in the shop. He's a handsome man. What the photo didn't convey was the fact that he has a presence about him. He's not the largest man in the room, but he's got such a gravitas about him you might think he was.

"What's this?" I ask.

"On the house," he says, in his accented voice. "But I think it best if you take this to go. Your presence is upsetting my customers."

"I'm sorry, have we done something to offend you?"

A smirk curls a corner of his mouth upward. "I know who you are, SSA Blake Wilder," he says then turns to Astra. "And I know who you are as well, Special Agent Astra Russo. Police are not warmly welcomed here."

I give him a nod. "Well, I suppose we don't need to waste time with introductions, then."

"No, we do not," he says. "And I know what you are doing to my daughter. She does not belong in a cage."

"See, I don't think so, either. But we've got a problem," I tell him. "We've got one dead male, twenty-five years old. Was involved with your daughter—and she lied to us about it. That creates an issue we need to resolve."

"She broke up with him months ago," he repeats the same lie. "She has not seen him in a very long time."

"See, but that's a lie," Astra says. "We know for a fact that Chloe was with him just days before he was killed."

"This is not possible."

"And yet, it is," I shrug. "Tell me something, Mr. Petrosyan—those security cameras around the restaurant, do they work?"

He shrugs. "Of course."

"Good. Then we're going to need the tapes going back the last three weeks," Astra says.

He shakes his head. "This is not possible. My system deletes the surveillance camera files every seven days."

"Well, that's convenient," Astra notes.

He shrugs. "I know very little about technology. The installation man set it up for me. I trusted his word."

"Uh-huh. You strike me more as a man who needs to control everything, Mr. Petrosyan," I say. "As in, every single minute detail."

He flashes me a grin. "Then I think you have a wrong impression of me."

"Did you know Chloe's boyfriend?" Astra asks. "Did you know Ben Davis?"

"No, we never met."

"And yet, you didn't like him," she presses. "Did you?"

"I told you I never met him. How could I not like somebody I've never met?" he asks. "These are silly questions."

"I think you didn't like him because he was black," I comment.

"This is not true. I am not racist," he protests. "I did not like him with my daughter because he was in a gang. Because he does bad things. I did not like him for being lazy. But you know those people....all they do is be lazy and kill each other. That is not the way for my daughter."

Astra gives me a dry look. "But remember, he's not racist."

"How dare you," he snaps. "My lawyer said you two were crude and crass. That you were trying to smear my good name. I see now that he is right."

"So, you really didn't know Ben Davis?" I ask.

"This is what I have already said."

"Well then, would it surprise you to know that the very last meal he had on this earth was right here at Rose of Armenia?" I ask.

He hesitates for a split second. He covers it well with a quick shrug, but not before I notice it. He hadn't expected that we'd be able to trace it back to his restaurant.

"When are you going to release my daughter?" he growls. "You know she had nothing to do with that boy's murder."

"Do we?" I ask. "How would we know that? And how can we reconcile that with the fact that she's already lied to us?"

"You have spoken with my daughter. You know she is not a killer," he says, as if that ends the debate.

"You know what I think?" I ask.

"No, but I have a feeling you are going to tell me anyway."

"She does that," Astra says.

"I think that you met with Ben. Right here, in fact. Over dinner, you told him to stay away from Chloe. That you wouldn't permit her to see him," I say. "I think that Ben told you he loved her and had no intention of staying away from her. I think things went bad from there, and you killed him. Chopped him up and put him in a barrel, drove him out past Tukwila, and dumped him there. Except, you didn't check the currents and didn't realize the Green River flows back this way. How'd I do?"

He chuckles. "That is a good story. Almost as good as some of the stories my grandmother used to tell me when I was a boy."

"I'll bet," I say.

"And do you have any proof of this wild tale you are saying?"

"Not yet. But we're getting there," Astra says.

"Well, please be sure to tell me when you do have evidence," he replies with a smirk. "I would not want to miss it."

"Believe me, you'll be the first to know," I say.

"So, when will you be releasing my daughter?"

"When our investigation has concluded," I tell him. "She knows more than she's telling us, and I would prefer if she didn't suddenly have a burning desire to go visit the old country before I'm done with my investigation."

Petrosyan leans down, planting his large hands on the table. He leans close enough to me that I can smell his cologne, which I hate to admit has a pleasant aroma. Say what you will about the man, but he's got good taste.

"Be careful, Agent Wilder," he whispers. "You are playing a very dangerous game."

I stare back at him unflinchingly. "Yeah, I get that a lot."

His smirk darkens. He points at the bruises that are coloring my face and I feel my anger bubbling up inside of me.

"I can see that is true," he says. "And it looks to me as if you lost the last time you played. Believe me when I tell you it can be much worse than that."

"Are you threatening me?"

"No. Just pointing out a fact."

"Uh-huh," I say. "I'm coming for you, Petrosyan. I'm coming and I will bring you down, because it's you who is playing a dangerous game. I'm not a woman to be trifled with."

He shrugs and stands up straight again. "It looks to me as if you have been trifled with plenty," he says. "Please, take your food and go. Have a good night."

He turns and walks away, chatting amiably with his customers in their native tongue—no doubt talking about us. Astra grabs my hand.

"Come on. Let's go," she says. "The last thing I want to do is spend the rest of the night filling out paperwork because you shot the man in his own restaurant."

Gritting my teeth, I get up and follow Astra to the door. Before I walk out, though, I turn back and find Petrosyan staring hard at me. Then he grins and turns away.

THIRTY-FOUR

Field Office Holding Cell 22; Seattle Field Office

I CARRY the tray into the pen and set it down on the table against the wall across from the holding cell. I pull out the chair, set it next to the cell, and sit down. Chloe is sitting on the bunk, her knees drawn up to her chest, her arms wrapped around her knees. She stares at me but says nothing. I turn and grab the fast-food bag and the soda I brought for her and set them on the pass-through tray in the bars.

"I thought you might be hungry," I start.

She looks at the food but doesn't move. Chloe just sits there staring at me, silently judging me. I know she's angry and doesn't understand what's going on, but truthfully, I don't think there's anything I can say that's going to change that. She's got a lot of anger in her, and I'm sure most of it isn't even directed at me. Having a father like Stephen Petrosyan is going to do that to you. But I'm a convenient outlet.

"Listen, I'm sorry this is happening," I say.

"Then why am I in a cell? You know I didn't kill Ben."

She says it with such heat and force, I'm taken aback for a moment. It's basically the first thing she's said to me, and I'm going to take that as a good sign. She seems to have finally snapped out of her catatonia.

"Do you know who killed Ben?" I ask.

She gnaws on her bottom lip and looks away. Maybe that was too direct. I know I shouldn't be in here talking to her without Tinsley present. Nothing that's said in here is ever going to be admissible in court. But that doesn't mean I can't still glean some valuable information without tanking the case. I just need to tread delicately.

"You loved him a lot, didn't you?" I ask.

Her eyes glisten and she wipes at them with the back of her hand. And though she doesn't say it, she nods. The pain in her face is heartbreaking, and it makes me hate her father all the more. She shouldn't be going through this. She's young. She should be enjoying college life. She should be finding love and reveling in it. She shouldn't have to mourn her dead boyfriend in secret for fear of her father.

"How long had you two been together?"

"A couple of years," she says softly.

I open up the bag and pull out the burger, fries, and fried apple pie I'd picked up for her, then set the empty bag down at my feet.

"You really should eat something," I tell her. "I know it's not the best food around, but it'll fill the void."

She hesitates but finally gets off the bunk. She walks over to the pass-through tray and takes the food, then sits down on the ground because she has no chair. Not wanting her to feel excluded, and trying to build rapport with her, I slip off the chair so I can look her in the eye as we talk. We sit in silence for a few minutes while she eats.

"Thank you for the food," she says.

"You're welcome. I know it's not as good as the food your dad serves, but as I said, it'll fill the void in a pinch," I say. "It's also way better than the stuff they serve here. I've tried it before, and let me tell you, it's like eating warm cardboard."

She giggles and covers her mouth with her hand. "Can I tell you a secret?"

"Sure."

"I hate Armenian food. Always have," she says.

That was so unexpected, it gets a genuine laugh out of me. She smiles and takes another bite of her burger. And in that moment, I can see the real girl underneath all the pain. I already know she's compassionate and intelligent. But she's also charming and sweet. I can see why Ben fell for her so hard that he was willing to change his entire life to keep her.

We chat about inconsequential things for a little while, just getting to know each other. I'm trying to loosen her up a bit and show her that she can trust me. That I'm not some bad, horrible person or a monster, regardless of the lies her lawyer tells her. I think, deep down, this girl is a fighter. But because her father truly is a monster, I can see why she chooses to stand down. I can see the spark in her, though. I can see that she's got a little fire in her belly, and I like it. I like her. She's a sweet girl, and away from her father and his mouthpiece, she's completely different. She's just a normal twenty-one-year-old.

"Ben was the love of my life," she says quietly, picking at her burger. "I was going to marry him one day."

"Yeah?"

She nods, and I see a dreamy look in her eyes. "Once we both got done with school, he was going to start his residency and everything, then we were going to get married."

"What about you? What were you going to do?"

She smiles. "I was going to start teaching. Literature," she says. "Eventually, I wanted to get my Ph.D. and teach at a university."

"You say 'was' and 'wanted,' in the past tense. As if it can't happen now," I say gently.

She shrugs and her smile fades. "What's the point anymore? Those dreams are over," she sighs. "Ben's gone and my dream died with him."

I shake my head. "You can still be a professor of literature. If that's what you always wanted to be, you can still do that, Chloe," I press. "And I can't think of a better way of honoring Ben's memory than to chase your dream and live a full, happy life. I know that I didn't know him, but I am positive that's what he would want for you—to live a full life and be happy."

"I don't know if I can ever be happy again," she says.

"I used to think that, too," I tell her. "When I was young—a kid—I found my parents dead. Murdered. And I was so angry and hateful for so long. But the truth is, I was only in pain. And when that pain faded, so did the anger and the hate. And it turned into purpose. It's because of that purpose that I'm here right now."

"I'm sorry you went through that," she says quietly. "Nobody should have to endure that kind of loss."

I meet her eyes and hold them. "No. Nobody should. But here's the thing—we can either be held captive by our pain and grief, or we can channel them into something better. We can choose to take control of our lives—even if we've lived for a long time feeling that we have no control over our lives. That's a choice we make every single day," I tell her. "So, you can choose to let your grief, as entitled to it as you are, define you. You can choose to let it snuff out that fire I see in you. Or you can choose to harness it. You can choose to let it temper you and make you stronger than steel."

"I wish it was that easy," she says.

"It can be."

She shakes her head miserably. "Not with my father. He controls everything," she tells me. "As in, everything."

"Is that why you took your mother's maiden name?"

She nods. "I'm not naïve. I know who and what my father is," she says. "And I didn't want to go through life attached to that name. He thinks I'm going to take over for him when he steps down. But I won't. I'm not like him. I'll never be like him."

I nod and find myself admiring the courage this girl has. It couldn't have been easy to stand up to somebody like Petrosyan and declare even that bit of independence from him. To guys like him, family names and traditions are everything. So, knowing that his daughter, the only viable heir to his throne, didn't want to be associated with that name or those traditions….it had to hurt. Had to make him angry. And probably made him double down on his control over the other areas of her life.

"Did he try to control your relationship with Ben?"

She hesitates for a moment then nods. "Yeah. That, too."

"Did he tell you that you weren't allowed to see Ben again?"

She nods. "Yes."

"I know this is hard and painful. I'm so sorry you're going through this, Chloe," I say. "I wish there was something I could do to take away the pain."

She gives me a shaky smile. "It's not your fault."

"No, but I know this whole thing isn't easy for you."

"I know you're only doing your job," she says. "Want to hear something weird?"

"Absolutely."

"Being here in this cell? It's the safest I've felt in a long time," she says. "Isn't that like, super bizarre?"

"I actually think I get it." At this point, I think it's time, so I ask, "Do you know who killed Ben, Chloe?"

A lone tear spills from the corner of her eye, but she lets it run. She just shakes her head.

"I don't know who did it," she admits. "But I'm sure my father was involved. He knew it was the only way to keep us apart."

We sit in silence for a few moments, everything we've said swirling around between us. And as I look at her, I see the core of strength in her. No matter how this plays out, I know she's going to bear the scars of her ordeal. She'll carry that grief around with her maybe for the rest of her life. She didn't ask to have a father like Petrosyan. She's done everything she can to distance herself from him. She didn't ask for this kind of life. All she wants is to be happy. To love. To live life to the fullest.

Things will be tough for a while after this. She's going to go through a minefield of pain and grief. But I want to believe she's going to be alright. In time, she's going to come out the other side of this stronger for it. I have to believe that for her.

THIRTY-FIVE

Criminal Data Analysis Unit; Seattle Field Office

"So, what do we have?" I ask.

"Nothing," Astra replies. "At least, nothing we didn't have before."

"Rick, have you been able to find anything?" I ask.

He shakes his head. "Nothing yet."

I growl in frustration as I pace the floor at the front of the bullpen. I'm pretty sure it won't be long before they have to replace the flooring up here since I'm wearing a groove in it. But I think better when I'm moving.

"What about the security cameras?" Mo asks.

"He said they delete everything after seven days," I reply.

"Wait... do you know what kind of system they use?" Rick asks.

I shake my head. "I don't. Why, do you have an idea?"

"I might. Let me do some digging before you all get excited. This may be nothing."

Astra is looking through the evidence boxes again, just for

lack of anything better to do. We know Petrosyan did it. We know why he did it. We just can't prove it. Tinsley has been down in the holding cells with her all morning, so I haven't gotten to talk to Chloe today. Tinsley is a lot of things, but he's not stupid. I know he knows I spoke to her last night, so I'm sure he's doing some damage control down there. He's probably pumping her for information, trying to find out what she told me and figure how to contain or spin it.

But she's a smart girl, and I think she's hoping we can nail her dad for this, so I'm not worried about her revealing the details of our conversation. Not that we got into any details. I was careful to avoid talking about anything specific enough to tank the case. Although I did want some information from her, I also wanted to make sure she knows she isn't alone. And that she has other options in her life. She just needs to find the courage in herself to take them.

"Chloe is positive her dad is somehow involved with Ben's death," I say.

"Which is great, but we can't prove it," Astra replies. "Unfortunately, we can't convict the guy just because his daughter hates him."

"It would make things a lot easier," I mutter.

"Wouldn't it, though?"

"Hey, wait, did you guys see this?" Mo asks.

I turn and see her holding one of the picture frames that were taken out of Ben's secret room. It's covered in fingerprint dust. I recognize the frame and recall it was a picture of Ben and his mom. But Mo's taken it apart and is pulling out a slip of paper from between the photo and the backing. It's been taped to the picture, so even if the frame is opened, the paper will likely be missed.

"Wait, wait," I say. "We need to document it for the chain of custody and evidence preservation."

"Right," Mo nods.

She sets it down and takes some pictures with her phone. After that, she snaps on a pair of black nitrile gloves and uses a pocketknife to slice the tape, then carefully lifts the paper out of the frame. We're huddled around her as she sets the frame aside and unfolds the page. I'm holding my breath as I watch her reading it, and when I see her eyes widen, I feel a spark of hope ignite inside of me. I try to temper it, reminding myself of the cost of crushed hopes.

"What is it?" I ask, forcing myself to stop feeling such a wave of hope inside of me.

"It's a travel itinerary," she says.

I quickly put on a pair of gloves before I take it. Astra, thinking her usual two steps ahead, has an evidence bag out and ready. We're going to need to get this printed just for the official record and to avoid claims of tampering. I hold it up so we can all read it. Sure enough, it's a travel itinerary.

"Two tickets to Florida," I say.

"Look at the date," Astra points. "Unless I'm mistaken, they were going to leave right after the semester ended."

"Do you see that?" I ask.

"What?" Astra replies.

"These tickets are one way," I announce. "They weren't coming back."

Mo and Astra both draw in a sharp breath as the full import of the moment settles down over us. This piece of paper might be what got Ben killed. This could be why Petrosyan murdered him. It suggests that he found out Ben and Chloe were leaving for good. But it brings a question to mind that I need to answer before I'm completely sold.

"Mo, can you run a search? I need to know if Ben was transferring schools," I say.

Mo sits down and starts banging away at her keys, and I can

feel the excitement starting to fill the room. If we're right, this is our motive. Is it a smoking gun? No. But this could potentially take things out of the abstract and make the scenario more concrete. It makes me wonder why Chloe didn't mention it to me last night. Or maybe she did—when she talked about her dreams dying with Ben. And maybe she's smart enough to know that if she'd told me outright that it would taint the evidence, because it was elicited without her lawyer present. She may not have known where Ben hid the itinerary and was trusting me to find it. There are still so many questions floating around, irritating me. I need concrete proof.

"Bingo," Mo chirps, unable to keep the excitement out of her voice. "His application to the University of Florida medical program was recently accepted. Once this semester ended, they were going to get the hell out of here."

"That's the motive. Petrosyan was not about to let his daughter go. Especially not with Ben," I say. "This is why he murdered her boyfriend."

"That's great but how are we going to prove that?" Astra asks.

"We'll need to get Chloe to confirm it. She knew better than to tell me about it directly last night. But now that we've found it, I know she'll testify to it," I say.

"Hey, guys, that's great and all, but I am about to be a hero to all of you," Rick cuts in, a wide smile on his face.

"And why is that?" I ask.

"Tell me something—does finding a key piece of evidence, perhaps the most critical piece of evidence to date, come with a raise?"

"Hey, I bought you kabobs the other day," I offer.

"That's true. And they were really good," he acknowledges. "Fine, fair enough. I'd like to direct your attention to the monitors at the front of the bullpen, please."

We all turn, and a moment later, the screen fills with a video feed. And as I look at what I'm seeing, then at the date and time stamp, my eyes widen and my mouth falls open. There in the center of the screen, we see Ben sitting with Petrosyan. They're talking and sharing a meal together. I turn around to find Rick leaning back in his seat, his hands folded behind his head, grinning like the cat who ate the canary.

"Tell me, who's the best tech analyst in the world?" he asks.

"Well, Brody Singer. But you're a close second," I tease.

"You wound me so, madame."

"How did you get this, Rick?" Astra asks. "Petrosyan said his system auto-deletes after seven days."

Rick grins and I can tell that, like a magician explaining his secret, he's about to draw this out and wow us with his skill. But hey, he just put a smoking gun in our hands, so he can do a tap dance for all I care right now.

"And after finding out which system he uses, I can say that is true. But most subscribers to this particular system don't read the fine print—I always read the fine print—"

"Of course you do. Most nerds thrive on the fine print," Astra quips.

"This is true. Anyway, this fine print tells them the footage is uploaded to a cloud-based storage service every twenty-four hours," he says. "So, while the hard drive in the machine will auto-delete, unless the user physically goes into the cloud and deletes the files by hand, they will stay up there forever. All I did was use the date range on the ME's report and sifted through the footage until we found this."

"Rick, you are an absolute genius."

"Yes, I am. And so under-appreciated in my time," he says.

"Nice work, nerd. I mean it," Astra says brightly. "Gold star for you today."

"That's almost as good as a raise," he replies.

My cellphone rings, and I'm so jazzed about what's happening, I connect the call and put it on speaker without thinking about it.

"Wilder," I say.

"SSA Wilder, this is Palmer Tinsley."

I look at my phone then turn around to make sure he's not standing behind me. "Tinsley? Aren't you still down in the holding cells?"

"No, I left a little while ago," he says. "And let me just say, if you go down there and talk to Chloe again, without my presence, I will file a report with SAC Espinoza. What you're doing is—"

"I brought a hungry kid a burger," I cut him off. "You really want to make a federal case out of my feeding a hungry girl? I mean, if you really do, have at it. I'm not stopping you. But don't waste my time with idle threats."

"You violated her Miranda rights—"

"No, I actually didn't. I solicited zero information pertaining to the case," I tell him. "We mostly talked about her."

I cringe, though, knowing just how close to the line I was treading. But the important thing is that I did not cross the line.

"Also, before you go running to the media to prop up this crazy notion that I acted improperly, I'll pull the security videos from her cell and they will prove that we didn't talk about anything inappropriate," I tell him. "Or actually, on second thought, please go to the media with this story, because I would love to release those videos and make you look like an enormous jackass. That would make a good day even better."

"A good day?" he asks, his voice suddenly filled with the ring of suspicion.

"Maybe I should say a great day," I add. "See, we have the smoking gun evidence that is going to bury your client. And I'm not speaking of Chloe. We're about to bury Petrosyan so deep, it's going to make the Mariana Trench look like a crack."

"What is it you think you have?"

"You'll get it at discovery before the trial, I'm sure," I reply.

"You're bluffing."

"Am I?"

The silence that follows is telling. He's calculating the odds that I'm bluffing against the possibility that I'm not, and what that means for his client.

"Give me a preview. Call it a professional courtesy," he finally says.

"Fine. Your client lied to us. He told us point-blank that he had never met Ben Davis before," I say. "We can prove conclusively that was a lie. Not only that, but we can prove conclusively that your client was with Ben the night he died."

Another silence follows. I can almost see Tinsley pacing his office in a near panic as he thinks about one of his cash cows going down in flames. I only wish I could see it in person. And when he finally speaks, I feel a rush of satisfaction at hearing just how tight and worried the tone in his voice is.

"Before either of us does something rash, let me propose something," he says.

"I'm all ears."

"Let me bring Mr. Petrosyan in for a conversation."

"Will this conversation include a confession?" I ask.

"It will include an explanation."

I look over at Astra and she nods, a wide smile on her face. Mo is doing a silent happy dance with Rick back by his workstation.

"Be here in an hour," I demand. I disconnect the call and give Astra a high five.

Everyone gives out a whoop.

"Sooo...about that raise?" asks Rick.

THIRTY-SIX

Interrogation Suite Alpha-4; Seattle Field Office

Astra and I sit across from Tinsley and Petrosyan. The man sits there staring at me stone-faced. His jaw is clenched and his eyes are filled with hatred.

"Thanks for the kebabs, by the way," I tell him. "I heard they were outstanding."

I see Petrosyan's body tense, and I'm half convinced he's going to come over the table at me. But Tinsley puts a hand on his arm and whispers something in his ear. He looks at his lawyer, then back at me, and says nothing, but his jaw is clenched so tight, I'm sure he could split steel between his teeth right now.

"Be advised that this session is being recorded with both audio and visual equipment," Astra says. "Mr. Petrosyan, do you acknowledge that you have been properly Mirandized?"

He says nothing but continues grinding his jaw as he stares at me. I look at him and flash him my best smile.

"Mr. Petrosyan," Astra repeats. "Do you acknowledge that you have been properly Mirandized?"

"Stephen?" Tinsley prompts.

It seems to break the man out of his hate-induced stupor as he looks away from me and nods, waving Astra off.

"Yes. I acknowledge this. Fine," he says.

"Excellent," Astra says. "Then let's begin."

"You said you had an explanation," I start. "Would that be an explanation for why Benjamin Davis was found disarticulated and stuffed into a barrel, then fished out of the Green River by the Tukwila Police Department?"

"Yes."

"And you know how Benjamin Davis came to be in this condition?"

"Yes."

"Is that because you murdered Mr. Davis?" Astra asks.

"No," Petrosyan says with a small, smug smile.

"No? Are you telling me you didn't murder Benjamin Davis?" I ask, staring at him completely dumbfounded. "You're honestly sitting there trying to convince me that you didn't turn him into a human jigsaw puzzle?"

"That's what my client is saying, yes," Tinsley says.

Tinsley looks at me with a small, knowing grin on his face that, frankly, makes me nervous. I don't like it when worms like Tinsley feel they have the upper hand. That means more often than not, they do. And he looks like a man with something stashed up his sleeve. I exchange glances with Astra and can tell she's thinking the same thing.

"What motive would I have to kill this man?" Petrosyan says.

"What motive did you have when you lied to us?" I counter. "You told us point blank that you had never met him before."

"I lied because I knew you were trying to pin his unfortunate death upon me," he says. "And I lied to protect somebody I care about."

"We know Chloe had nothing to do with this."

"I was not speaking of my daughter," he says flatly.

"Then who were you speaking of?" I ask.

"First, I want you to answer his question," Tinsley says. "I want to know why you're so hellbent on trying to prove he killed Mr. Davis."

"He didn't approve of Chloe's relationship with Ben," Astra says. "And he's a man who has to control everything—including his daughter's love life."

Tinsley smirks. "That seems a little thin as far as motives go."

I open the folder in front of me and take out the photocopy of the travel itinerary, then slide it over. Tinsley picks it up and they both look at it.

"Mr. Petrosyan learned that his daughter was leaving. That she was going away with Ben Davis and was not coming back," I explain. "And he could not countenance that after he had forbidden her from seeing him again. So he killed him."

Tinsley flicks the page back to me, clearly unimpressed. He's still wearing that smug smirk. It's getting harder and harder to keep myself from slapping it off his face.

"That still seems very weak as far as motives go," he says.

"People kill for less all the time," Astra chimes in. "And you should know, considering defending scumbags like that is your stock in trade."

He laughs gently. "Charming."

"But not untrue," she replies.

I open the folder and take the still photo we took from the security footage and slide it over to them.

"This is proof that you and Mr. Davis had dinner the night

of his death. You lied to us and said you had never met him before," I say. "And the fact that he was murdered mere hours after this doesn't bode well for you, Mr. Petrosyan. I think the best thing you can do for yourself is to get out ahead of this. Tell us what happened and—"

"I think you're putting the cart before the horse here, SSA Wilder," Tinsley cuts me off. "What you have evidence of here is two men having what looks like a very cordial dinner together. Last I checked, that isn't a crime."

"The preponderance of evidence we have will guarantee that a jury—"

"Oh, this will never go to a jury, SSA Wilder. That much, I promise you."

I can feel the unease wafting off Astra like waves of heat from the sun. I can't help but feel that we just walked into a trap. Tinsley has been baiting us this whole time, and now that we're in the cage, he's ready to spring it on us. As if he's reading my mind, he gives me a knowing smile.

I gather myself quickly and steel my nerves. We have Petrosyan. I don't know what slick legal maneuver Tinsley is trying to pull, but the evidence is on our side. Granted, much of it is circumstantial, but a jury will be able to see through that. We have him cold.

"And why do you think this won't get to a jury?" I ask.

"Because Mr. Petrosyan will never be charged with anything. And this case—if that's what you wish to call it—will never see the inside of a courtroom," he says.

"Enlighten me, Counselor. What is it you think you have that can help your client wriggle out of a murder charge?"

"A confession," he says. "From Azad Mushyan."

I feel my entire body tense up and my jaw clench tight. I stare at Petrosyan and watch the grin spreading across his face as my hands ball into fists. This can't be happening. We have him dead to rights. There is no way he can get out of this. I open my mouth to speak but find that I can't form a coherent word.

The case we've worked so hard to build is crashing down around us in flames. This man, who I know beyond the shadow of a doubt either killed or at least participated in the killing of Ben Davis, is going to walk out of here a free man. My stomach churns and I can taste the bile in the back of my throat. Petrosyan remains silent and just stares at me with a glint in his eye that tells me he's enjoying this. He's amused by watching this house of cards come tumbling down around me.

"And who is Azad Mushyan?" Astra asks.

"He has served as Mr. Petrosyan's personal bodyguard for the last fifteen years," Tinsley says as he pulls a sheet of paper out of the file in front of him.

He slides the paper over to Astra and she picks it up. She makes a snort of disgust as she reads it, then hands it over to me. I read the words. Then read them again. And a third time. And as I read them again, I feel the disgust in me welling up, blending with the pure, unabashed hatred I feel for the man sitting across from me.

"So, you convinced one of your men to take the bullet for you," I growl.

"No. Mr. Mushyan freely admits that he acted alone and without direction from anybody," Tinsley replies and taps the page in my hand. "You can see that he admits to having been in love with Chloe. When he learned of her plans to run away with Ben, he just lost it. Snapped. He admits to killing him and disposing of his body the way you so eloquently described earlier. What was it? Oh, that's right. A human jigsaw puzzle."

"This is absolute crap. Garbage," I snap, crumpling the paper into a ball and throwing it across the room. "That confession, if you want to call it that, is a work of pure fiction."

"Don't worry, I have copies. I'll make sure you get another one," Tinsley says. "And you can see for yourself that the document is signed, witnessed, and properly notarized. It's all very legal and binding, I assure you."

"This is garbage," I growl.

Tinsley shrugs. "Love makes men do some very crazy and sometimes distasteful things," he says. "Would you agree, SSA Wilder?"

"Nobody was more shocked than I was when Azad confessed to such a barbaric crime," Petrosyan adds. "I did not think him capable of such violence. I suppose that old saying is true—you just never truly know somebody, eh?"

"We will coordinate with the King County DA to arrange for Mr. Mushyan to surrender himself," Tinsley says. "Which I suppose ends our business here."

Tinsley and Petrosyan get to their feet and start for the door. The rage in me boils over and I launch myself at him. I hear Astra calling my name as I pin Petrosyan to the wall with my forearm. I lean so close to him, the tips of our noses are touching. He stares back at me, and although his face is darkening as I squeeze the air from him, he smiles at me.

"You may get away with this, but your luck is going to run out. And when it does, I'm going to be there," I spit. "I'm going to make it my life's mission to bring you down, you piece of filth. I'm going to bring your whole world crashing down on you. I swear it."

Astra finally manages to pull me off and Petrosyan stares at me, rubbing his throat and gasping as he tries to catch his wind again. Tinsley looks at me, his expression moving from one of shock at my savagery to one of amusement.

"We will give you that one, SSA Wilder," Tinsley says. "But rest assured, if you ever lay hands on my client again, there will be a reckoning. I will file enough charges that the Bureau will fire you just to be rid of the paperwork."

My eyes are still fixed on Petrosyan, though. "I'm going to get you. I'm going to bring you down if it's the last thing I do. Your days are numbered, you piece of garbage."

"Yeah. Good luck with that," he says.

I watch them walk out and close the door behind them. My rage swirls around me unabated, and with no other outlet, I grab one of the chairs and hurl it at the door. It hits with a thunderous crash and bounces off, hitting the floor with a sharp metallic twang. I take a moment and try to gather myself.

Astra stands to the side, watching me in surprise. "I get it, babe," she says. "But you have to control yourself. The only way to get that prick—and we will get him—is if we're calm, focused, and determined. We can't go off half-cocked like that or it could cost us our creds. And if that happens, he will win."

"I know. I know," I say. "I know you're right. I'm sorry. I just—I lost it."

"You think?" she asks. "But I've never seen you like this before. What is it?"

"Chloe," I sigh. "I promised her things would get better and that she would be in control of her life. But that was when I was certain we had him. What's going to happen to her now that she has to go home with him? I'm terrified for her, Astra."

She steps forward and pulls me into a tight embrace, and I let myself melt into her. And as she holds me, my worry for Chloe overwhelms me. I find myself sobbing.

THIRTY-SEVEN

Wilder Residence; The Emerald Pines Luxury Apartments, Downtown Seattle

Following the debacle with Petrosyan, Rosie suggested I take a couple of weeks off. Well, suggested isn't the right word for it—unofficially ordered is probably more accurate. She told me I needed to get my head on straight, as I'd never before put my hands on a suspect like that, and she was worried about me. I can't say I blame her for benching me. I deserved it. I've never lost my cool like that, and for the first time in my professional life, I voluntarily took some time off. I do need to clear my head.

I realize that I've got a lot of irons in the fire right now. On top of the normal stresses of the job, I've taken on the added burden of worrying about Chloe, not to mention the fact that I have the ever-present threat of being murdered myself by the Thirteen—who have already possibly sent someone to my home. All of that has coalesced into one frightening ball of fear and anger in my head. With all of that churning inside me, it's no wonder I snapped like the way I did.

But it's also the fact that I know Petrosyan killed Ben. Or he at least participated in the killing. I don't think it was a simple as his ordering the hit. He was there. He watched as Ben's body was taken apart piece by piece. And the fact that monsters like that don't just exist in the world but are walking among us because they can pay their men to take the fall for them burns my ass. It enrages me. But there's nothing I can do about it.

As gratifying as I sometimes think it would be to go rogue and carry out vigilante justice sometimes—and I have been sorely tempted to hunt Petrosyan down and put two in the back of his head—I know that would be a betrayal of who I am.

I took this job to hunt killers. Not become one. Which means I need to make peace with losing sometimes. Once in awhile, the bad guy is going to win. My only choice is to do my job to the best of my ability. All I can do is put together a case I think will win the day and bring justice for the victim, but there are a lot of things that are out of my control. It's hard to deal with, but I need to learn to do just that.

I've tried contacting Chloe a few times since that day and haven't heard from her. She's not enrolled at Oakmont and she doesn't return texts. It makes me fear what's happening to her. I worry about what she's doing. How she's feeling. And maybe more than anything, what's being done to her. I have no doubt that her father is trying to turn her into the monster he is, and all I can do is hope it doesn't take. I hope she has the strength to fight it and find a way out. She deserves a life well-lived, not a life of fear.

But none of that is anything I can control. All I can control is what I do. So to that end, I've spent my time switching my obsession from Chloe and her father to trying to unravel this conspiracy. The Thirteen. It's probably just as unhealthy for me to fixate on this as it was to fixate on Chloe, but at least with this obsession I actually do have some modicum of control. I can say how far is far enough.

I stare at the pictures of the replacement Justices I've pinned on the wall in front of me, beneath photos of the dead ones. I've spent a good portion of my time off so far reviewing three years' worth of SCOTUS decisions and the rulings made by each of the new Justices. I haven't found anything overtly nefarious, but what I have found is that in each case the Justices have ruled, those decisions have benefitted the moneyed class.

There have been other cases, of course. But the cases that involve corporations and financial matters stand out to me simply because of something Gina Aoki said to me. She said the Thirteen were all about power and money. That the accumulation of wealth and consolidating their own power were the purposes behind the Thirteen. She said they aren't religious or political ideologues. She said the only thing driving the group is sheer greed.

If that's true, it certainly wouldn't be the most original reason for conspiracy and murder. Granted, murdering a Supreme Court Justice is a new wrinkle on that old story, but it's a motive I can understand, at least. It's one I've seen more times than I can count. The trouble is, I need more information. I need proof. And I need names. And to get those things, I'm going to need Mo's help. She's a wizard when it comes to spotting patterns in finances. If anybody can find out what's really going on behind the scenes, it's going to be her. She'll be able to tell me if this is all smoke or if there's fire there as well.

I worry about asking her, only because I fear that pulling her into this is going to put a target on her back as well. By having her help me, she'll be facing the same dangers I am. And I don't know if I can ask that of her. But to figure this out, I'm going to need somebody with her skills and somebody I can trust. And at the moment, aside from my team, I don't know that there's anybody around I can completely trust.

My doorbell rings, pulling me out of my head and back to the present. I give myself a shake and walk out of the war room, closing the door behind me, then locking it. On my way out to the living room, I feel the adrenaline flowing through my veins like liquid fire. I'm not expecting anybody today. I told Mark I need some time to myself, and I'm pretty sure Astra would have texted me before just stopping by.

I grab my weapon and slip it out of the holster, then quietly approach the door and look at the display screen. I've had one of those doorbell camera units installed just for my own peace of mind. But when I see who's standing at my door, I freeze. I watch as he reaches out and pushes the bell again, then turns to the camera and waves. My fear ebbs and I let out a breath of relief as I unlock the door and hide my weapon behind my back as I open it.

"Fish," I say. "What are you doing here? And in an avocado green lamé suit, no less."

"Good afternoon to you, too, Agent Wilder," he says. "And I'll have you know this suit is at the pinnacle of fashion today."

He holds his jacket open and turns in a circle, the light from the windows at either end of the corridor sparkling off his suit. All I can do is smile at him and shake my head.

"Well, I'll say that nobody can get away with that suit but you," I tell him. "It looks strangely good on you."

"I shall take that as a compliment, then."

"By all means," I say.

"May I come in for a moment?" he asks. "There is something important I want to speak with you about. Something you need to see."

"Of course."

I step aside and let him in. He notices the weapon I've kept hidden behind my back and raises an eyebrow. I shrug.

"I wasn't expecting visitors today," I say.

"Believe me when I say I understand that completely. I have been there myself."

He walks into my apartment and looks around as I tuck my weapon back into its holster and set it back down. Fish pauses in the middle of the living room, a frown on his lips as he continues to look around.

"What is it?" I ask.

"You need color in here, Agent Wilder. It's very cold and sterile," he says. "A little color will not only liven your home up, but it will also have a positive psychological impact on you. Trust me on this. Color, Agent Wilder. Color."

"I'll keep that in mind," I tell him. "Can I ask you something, Fish?"

"Of course."

"How did you know where I live?"

He chuckles. "Really?" he asks. "Do you think there is a scrap of information out there I cannot get my hands on if I wish to have it?"

"No, I suppose not. Silly question."

"I heard about what happened with the Armenian."

"Yeah. Total crapshow," I grumble. "I should have seen it coming."

"I did try to warn you that he is a slippery one."

"Is that why you stopped by? To say I told you so?"

"Of course not. I would never be so gauche as to say something so petty and juvenile."

Aside from the fact that he already said it in a backhanded sort of way, I could believe him. Fish is a lot of things, but petty isn't one of them.

"No, I actually stopped by to hopefully put your mind at ease," he says.

"And how are you going to do that?"

He pulls his phone out of his jacket pocket and opens it up. "Well, you had me looking into the Armenians to see what I could find."

"Right. I remember asking."

He holds the phone out to me, and I take it, looking down at a black screen.

"Just hit play," he instructs.

I do as he says and watch as the video starts to play. The footage is dim and grainy, but I can clearly see Ben Davis standing next to his car. It looks as if he's about to unlock it when he stops and turns, as if somebody had called him. My head snaps up and I look at Fish.

"What is this?" I ask.

"Just keep watching, please."

I lower my gaze and watch as a man enters the screen. He's tall and burly with a dark beard. He makes no effort to hide himself as he approaches Ben, and I recognize him instantly.

"Azad Mushyan," I say.

On the screen, Mushyan raises his arm, and I can clearly see the weapon he's holding. I see the flash of the muzzle and watch as Ben's head snaps backward, a jet of dark liquid spraying out onto the car behind him. Ben's body slumps to the ground and doesn't move. After that, Mushyan throws Ben into the back seat of his car. He then gets in and drives off. Just like that.

"Why are you showing me this?" I ask softly.

"I wanted you to know that you were not duped. That you were not played or did not do your job somehow. Knowing you as I do, I am fairly certain you have spent ample time beating yourself up because Petrosyan wriggled off your hook," he says.

"I wanted you to see this so you know that he is—technically—innocent of killing Ben Davis. He is definitely guilty of a host of other things, but in this particular instance, he did not do the crime."

I replay the video and watch again, disbelief washing through me. "That's fine. Even if Petrosyan didn't pull the trigger, I'm sure he ordered Ben's death."

Fish shrugs. "That's entirely possible. But it also may have happened just as they said—Azad, in a fit of jealousy, killed Ben so that Chloe would not leave."

I hand the phone back to him. "Should I ask where you got this video?"

He waves me off. "Oh, a friend of a friend."

"Of course. Can you send me this?"

"Yes, I will. But I wanted to come by and show you this today so you could stop with the self-flagellation I know you've been engaged in," he says.

"What, do you have cameras in my house?" I say.

"One does not need cameras to recognize a person who cares so much, it is often to her own detriment," he offers. "And it does not take a psychic or a voyeur to know that when that sort of person perceives she failed at something, she does terrible things to herself when she believes nobody is looking."

"I think you're too observant for my own good, Fish."

"Perhaps. But I'm quite fond of you, Agent Wilder. And I do not like to see you torment yourself. You did not fail. You did everything right."

"Then how did I let myself get outmaneuvered?"

"Because people like Petrosyan have spent their lives learning how to do evil and to get away with it. They are professional criminals and know how to navigate the difficult waters in a way that ensures their freedom," he says. "Anyway,

I must be off. Think on what I said, though. You know my advice is always sound."

I chuckle. "Thank you, Fish. I appreciate your trying to cheer me up."

"I don't think it was trying to cheer you up so much as it was to present you with a dose of reality. What you choose to do with that, whether it be cheering up or continuing to mope and flog yourself, is entirely up to you," he tells me with a smile.

"Have a great day, Fish."

"You as well, my dear."

I walk him to the door, then lock it behind him. Fish is an odd duck, that's for sure. But I want to believe he means well. It just strikes me as odd that he would be here defending Petrosyan. And the video, I will reserve judgment on—until I know whether or not it's authentic. I know there are some very convincing deep fakes out there, so when Fish gets it to me, I'll run it through Rick and see if he can authenticate it for me. If it is, we'll waste no time picking up Mushyan. Only then will I be able to rest easy knowing Ben's killer is off the streets. Only then will I allow myself to fully relax.

And only then will I know if I can truly trust Fish or not.

EPILOGUE

Chihuly Garden and Glass; Downtown Seattle

I STAND in front of one of the bright, colorful exhibits in one of Seattle's most unique places. I sometimes enjoy coming to the Chihuly just because it is so quirky and off-beat. The Chihuly is part garden, part museum. All the exhibits are brightly colored glass made by Dale Chihuly. Some of the pieces are abstract. Others resemble giant flowers. One of my favorite pieces resembles spirals of brightly colored leaves of gold, brown, and yellow. It's truly exquisite.

I surreptitiously watch the crowd around me. Between Torres and the Thirteen, I'm jumping at every shadow and loud noise these days. I never know if I'm being watched—and if I am, by whom. The crowd inside the Chihuly is thick, but not oppressively so I can move around without being jostled by anybody. It's also a good place to pick up a tail. With so many twists and turns along the garden footpath, it's easy to spot somebody following you.

It's why I selected the place to meet with Brody. I move on from the spiraling leaves and make my way over to a brightly colored garden of glass. I spot him sitting on a bench, and when he looks up, I give a subtle nod in the direction I want him to follow me. I feel silly for all of this cloak and dagger, but with so many different people who apparently want to kill me, I think exercising a little prudence is probably for the best.

I walk to a secluded little alcove I scouted out earlier. It's between a pair of sculptures and set back far enough that it will afford us some privacy, as well as let me spot anybody coming before he or she sees me. Once Brody is inside, I turn to him.

"I'm sorry for the spy games," I say.

He shrugs. "Hey, in your shoes, I'd probably be even more paranoid. I might not even leave my house ever again."

I laugh softly. "I'm not at that point just yet. But I may be getting there."

"Okay, well, the good news is that I swept your entire place, top to bottom—twice—and there is no electronic surveillance equipment in there," he says.

"Do you think you'd be able to pick up the most cutting-edge equipment out there?"

He chuckles. "I am the most cutting-edge designer out there. Believe me when I say I'm several generations ahead of the government. If I say there are no bugs in your house, you can take that to the bank."

I smile and nod. "That's good enough for me, then."

"Now for the bad news."

"Couldn't we just end on the high note?"

He smiles. "No, I think you're going to want to hear this."

"That's debatable. I'm not sure I want anything of the sort. But I probably need to hear it, anyway," I say.

"Anybody ever tell you that you and Paxton are like mirror images of each other?"

"Not since the last time you told me that."

He grins. "Some points bear reiterating."

"Clearly. So, out with the bad news, then."

I peer out of the alcove and look around. I don't see anybody creeping close or paying any undue attention to us. To me, it appears that the coast is still clear. Brody hands me a thumb drive and points to it.

"Everything I'm about to tell you is on this drive. All of the files and paperwork to back up what I'm saying are there," he explains. "I would only suggest reading that when you're feeling extra masochistic and want to feel extra paranoid."

"Copy that," I say, looking down at the silver drive in my hand.

"Turns out that your boyfriend isn't Mark Walton after all," he says. "Because Mark Walton doesn't exist."

"Excuse me?"

"Well, he exists now. But before ten years ago, your boyfriend didn't exist. Anywhere. He's a ghost."

It feels as if the ground has just fallen out from under me and I'm freefalling into space. My heart has dropped into my stomach and I feel as if I'm going to be sick.

"How is that possible?" I ask.

"Whoever created Mark Walton is good. Really good. But I'm better," he says. "And I found all of the backstopping they put up just in case you did a deep Google search on him. But if you can go to the places in cyberspace that I can, you'll find out that Mark Walton is like one of those Hollywood movie sets where the giant, sturdy castle is being held up by two-by-fours from behind."

I shake my head. "I can't believe this. This can't be real."

Brody frowns. "I'm really sorry, Blake. But this is real," he says. "I'm not sure who he really is, but the man you know as Mark Walton is a fraud. He is employed—legitimately—at the hospital. But his MD license? Fake, although certainly, he has a medical background; otherwise, he couldn't pass as a doctor. College records, driver's license, social security, birth certificate? All fake. As far as I can tell, Doctor Mark either went to a lot of trouble over a long, long time to cover up his past—or he sprang out of thin air."

I don't know how, but I'm managing to stay on my feet despite the fact that my legs are shaking so badly, they're rattling my teeth. I look at Brody and see the compassion in his face. I feel like an idiot. All this time I've let myself be fooled. I let him into my life when all he was doing was watching me. Reporting back on me. I've never felt so utterly stupid and betrayed like this in my life.

"Are you alright, Blake?"

I shake my head. "Not really. I feel like such a moron."

"Don't. He could have fooled anybody."

"He didn't fool you."

Brody shrugs. "Only because I knew what I was looking for. And I only knew where to look because you figured it out and pointed me in the right direction. So, clearly, he didn't fool you, either."

"A little late. But I guess."

I think about how much I've told him. Shared with him. The ramifications of having let him so deep into my life are only just now starting to settle down over me. I want to cry. He knows everything I know—which means the Thirteen know everything I know as well. I have no idea what I'm going to do, and I feel a panic attack starting to come on.

"If you want, Paxton and I can pick this guy up one night and take him for a ride, if you know what I mean," he offers.

"That's really sweet and I appreciate that," I tell him. "But let's hold off on that idea. For now, anyway. I may end up taking you up on that."

"Anytime, Blake. You know Pax has your back. So do I."

I pull Brody into a tight embrace. "Thank you, Brody. You're a good friend."

"Right back at you," he says. "Is there anything else I can do?"

I shake my head. "No, not yet. But thank you. I need to take a minute to figure out what my next steps are going to be."

"Fair enough. And if you need a hand, just give us a call."

"I will. And thank you again."

Brody gives me a small smile and a nod, then walks away. I watch him melt into the crowd as I stand in the alcove, letting my mind play and replay everything he just told me. I know he'd never lie to me, and when it comes to all things tech, I trust him even more than I trust my own tech analyst. If there is something to be found—or not found, as the case may be—it's going to be Brody who uncovers it. And what he's uncovered has shaken me to my core.

How could I be so stupid as to not see what was right in front of me all this time? How could I not see through Mark? How could I not know he was a spy inserted into my life to keep tabs on me—just as Gina Aoki warned me? How could I have not seen this coming? Not only has this revelation shocked me totally, it's making me question everything about myself right now. I'm not used to dealing in self-doubt, but at this moment, I'm awash in it. I'm drowning in it. And I don't know that I'll be able to pull my head above water again.

I need to figure out what my next steps are going to be, but my mind is so full of questions, I don't even know where to start. I'm having trouble even thinking straight. And I know this is the way it will be until I answer the one question that's burning brighter in my mind than any of the others—who in the hell is Mark Walton? Who is he really?

It's the question I most want the answer to. But I have almost no idea how to find that answer. And I fear that the one way I can think of to get the answer is going to cost me my life.

My God, when did my life get so completely complicated? Not to mention ridiculously dangerous?

NOTE FROM ELLE GRAY

I hope you enjoyed *The Chosen Girls*, book 5 in the *Blake Wilder FBI Mystery Thriller series*.
My intention is to give you a thrilling adventure and an entertaining escape with each and every book.
However, I need your help to continue writing and bring you more books!

Being a new indie writer is tough.
I don't have a large budget, huge following, or any of the cutting edge marketing techniques.
So, all I kindly ask is that if you enjoyed this book, please take a moment of your time and leave me a review and maybe recommend the book to a fellow book lover or two.
This way I can continue to write all day and night and bring you more books in the *Blake Wilder* series.
By the way, if you find any typos or want to reach out to me, feel free to email me at egray@ellegraybooks.com

Your writer friend,
Elle Gray

ALSO BY ELLE GRAY

Blake Wilder FBI Mystery Thrillers
Book One - The 7 She Saw
Book Two - A Perfect Wife
Book Three - Her Perfect Crime
Book Four - The Chosen Girls
Book Five - The Secret She Kept

Arrington Mysteries
Free Prequel - Deadly Pursuit
Book One - I See You
Book Two - Her Last Call
Book Three - Woman In The Water